You Matter

Let the stories and time proven strategies show you how to deal with life's challenges and choices

Bill Maynard

ISBN: 1451518919
ISBN-13: 9781451518917
Library of Congress Control Number: 2010903007

BRIEF CONTENTS

YOU MATTER

DETAILED CONTENTS

YOU MATTER

- Traps that prevent change
- How to manage your life transitions

- How to Create Your Future
  - Changing a negative behavior pattern
    - ✓ *Kevin—"I need to change if I'm going to be in a lasting relationship."*

- Creating a Vision for Your Future
  - ✓ *Sasha—"A vision for living my life"*

- Getting Over an Addiction
  - ✓ *Michelle—"I'm making a big change: quitting smoking."*

- You Get to Be In Charge
  - ✓ You create your happiness
  - ✓ The emotional scale
  - ✓ The ending and the new beginning

- Have a Wonderful Journey!

- Key Takeaways from Taking Charge of Your Life

- Important References and Resources

You Matter:

APPENDIX – NAVIGATING THE JOURNEY OF YOUR LIFE

YOUR SELF-SEARCH EXPERIENCES

PREFACE

The purpose of **You Matter** is to provide you with vital knowledge, tools and the ability to deal successfully with the issues that come your way in life. In each chapter you will gain essential insights from the real stories shared by others just like you. See what they faced and what surprising things they learned about themselves as they dealt with the challenges, sometimes tragedies, in their lives. You will learn about yourself through the application of tools, like self-assessments and Self-Search Experiences, and you will increase your ability to interact and contribute in your world. This will all be brought to you through time-proven strategies for creating a great future for yourself and others in your life.

Come On The Journey With Me

You Matter is a result of my own journey, finding my way to a personally fulfilling life, and my desire to share what I've learned with others. For over two decades I have worked in dozens of organizations with managers and executives at all levels of scope and responsibility. Concurrently, over the past fifteen years I have worked with college students in a course called *Leading and Living*, in which we focused on dealing with my students' biggest life issues. I invite you to join me to explore what happiness and success mean to you. One of your discoveries will be that you already have available to you all that you will need in order to achieve your potential in life, including enriching relationships. One of the discoveries on my journey was that what happens in one area of our life absolutely affects every other area. Work issues overflow into our personal lives and what happens in our personal lives affects how we view ourselves and act in our areas of work. This book is about learning how to be successful in all areas of your life.

If I were to boil down everything I have learned thus far from my own life journey, from business people I've worked with and from the students in my classes, it would be this: There will always be challenges (both expected and unexpected), and there will always be choices. People who are happier in life (as they define it) make better choices than those who are not happy and therefore continuously struggle in search of the happiness that eludes them. What you will learn in **You Matter** will help you make those wise choices that will support you in achieving the future you deserve.

You Matter:

Acknowledgments

This book would not have been possible without the help and encouragement of a number of very significant people. I am deeply grateful for their support and hope that I can somehow return their kindness.

First, and of greatest importance, is my wife Nancy. She had the courage to do all of the initial editing and offering valuable feedback and insight. This is not the first marriage for either of us, so between us we have brought five adult children and two spouses together into a new amazingly connected family. The love of my daughters, Michelle and Wendi, has inspired me and at times has sustained me through challenges in my own life. The acceptance and love of Nancy's children, Kate, Scott, Eric (and his wife Katie), have provided me once again with proof that our choices determine so much of our happiness.

I am also deeply grateful to the caring and thoughtful people who have reviewed early drafts, both for their time and for their wonderful suggestions and contributions. Alphabetically they are:

Nancy Buller—a young business woman and friend.

Len Jessup—my friend and the Director of the Center for Entrepreneurial Studies, College of Business, Washington State University, Pullman WA.

Eva Johnson—who didn't know me personally, yet generously volunteered to help me. Eva is Director of Student Involvement/ Leadership, Pacific Lutheran University, Tacoma, WA.

Tony Lael—a former student and friend who is also a very creative and talented business consultant.

Jessica Patterson—my friend and a former student who is now teaching at Highline Community College, Seattle WA.

Jim Traister—my friend who may have ignited this when years ago he asked "what is the meaning of life." Teaching at Tarrant County College South East, Arlington, TX.

I am also deeply grateful to all of the students in the class of January 2010, as they utilized the manuscript as our text. I am especially grateful to Becca DeVere, Serena Schulke, Maggie Baumgarten, Eric Runquist,

Bill Maynard

Jennn Hansen, Andy Wellsandt, Elijah Hewitt, Brandon Harder, Jackie Ferguson, Ali Kisinger, Mariya Mariko, Catherine O'Francia, Laurel Skoff, Carly Starkovich, Jesse Aspuria, Jordan Kisor and John Timberlake for the very helpful feedback and their suggestions.

And finally, a very deep thank you to all of my students, first for having the courage to take the class, and also for the willingness to so deeply explore their lives. I learned so much from you, and as a result, my life is certainly more deeply fulfilled. I hope that your life too, is more enriched as a result of all of us being together.

Who is Bill Maynard?

I have been working as an educator and business consultant, and dealing with people issues my entire adult life. I began in public education and taught junior high science and PE for six years, then went into administration and was appointed principal of a very difficult inner city high school in Seattle, Washington. I loved working with these kids who some referred to as "disadvantaged." I found that most needed an opportunity to believe in themselves. My focus and passion was on how to help them succeed in and outside of school.

Of course in order to do any of this I had to get a college education. I had struggled academically in high school, but had a great time socially! After graduation I couldn't get a job and didn't know what else to do so I enrolled in our local community college. I earned an Associate Degree then went on to a Bachelors Degree in biology and psychology. A few years later I received a Masters Degree in Education Administration and Counseling and several years after that a Doctorate in Education Administration and Business. Wanting to be able to significantly contribute to the development and lives of these kids, and my own need to prove to myself that I was smarter than my high school grades indicated, were the factors that drove me to continue my education through my doctorate degree. Gifts sometimes come in interesting packages!

My career in the school district was rewarding in countless ways. Next I took everything I learned and for two years consulted and did trouble shooting work with individual schools and school districts throughout the U.S. In these varied experiences I learned a lot about dealing with difficult people that was immediately applicable. I began my second career when my partner, Tom Champoux, and I started a consulting and training company called the Effectiveness Institute. We took what we had learned from schools and began working with corporations of all sizes and eventually with many throughout the U.S and a number of countries internationally. This second career lasted 25 years, during which I also started teaching a leadership class at Washington State University. I have since retired from the Effectiveness Institute, but at the request of WSU, have continued to teach the *Leading and Living* class each year.

INTRODUCTION

MAKING LIFE WORK FOR YOU

"When you come to the end of all the light you know,
and it's time to step into the darkness of the unknown,
faith is knowing that one of two things shall happen:
Either you will be given something solid to stand on,
or you will be taught to fly."
Edward Teller

Why You Will Really Want to Read this Book

If you have a desire to learn more about yourself, learn more about others, find new ways of dealing with life issues, or just want to improve your life, then this book is for you. You will read examples of true stories from young men and women just like you. Their names have been changed to protect their identities, but their stories are as they were written. You will be provided with knowledge, tools, and a means for dealing successfully with life stuff that happens to you and to those you know. If you use it, this book can change your life. Regardless of whether you are working on making a serious decision, getting into a new relationship, getting out of a relationship, getting over a breakup, dealing with a difficult parent, facing serious life issues, or learning to find happiness, you will find something here that will help you through the *challenges and the choices.*

For example, after working her way through a relationship issue, here is what **Rebecca** wrote:

"For the longest time I have simply gone along with the flow of life, like being swept along down a river; its path, twists, turns, waterfalls, and rocky areas already decided for me. Because I was never given the opportunity to make my own decisions or take control, but simply because I chose not to take control. Never did I think I would have the strength or courage to get out of that river and take control of my life. Now, I am discovering that strength. I am finally free from myself; from my uncertainty, my perceived shortcomings, my downward spiral of focusing on

the negative things, and my perceived weakness. I can take charge of my life and let my true self and my happiness shine through!"

I have been working with college juniors, seniors and graduate students in a leadership course entitled Leading and Living.[*] These students wanted to learn about themselves, about how to be successful in work, how to make relationships work, how to choose a career, and how to build self-confidence in an effort to discover their potential and to make good choices.

What I discovered was that many of the students were also facing significant life issues, but had been burying their fears and pain. Others recognized their issues but just didn't know what to do about them. They had learned to *not* talk about these things. Being accepted was more important. Most were unaware that their friends and classmates had similar issues: issues dealing with relationship breakups, deaths of family members or friends, parents who were difficult to deal with, friends who betrayed them, depression, issues around sex, alcohol and drugs, and not knowing how to deal with conflicts. Most had no idea that it was okay, even healthy, to talk about the issues and learn how to deal with them.

Their real life stories are shared here so that others in similar situations may understand that they are not alone and that others, too, can learn ways to deal with the "stuff" in their lives. You will learn about creating possibilities and about expanding your potential in areas of your life that may not be working for you. You will also learn insights that are truly life shaping.

Through my consulting work with leaders in organizations, my work with college students, and my own life experiences, I have been able to see that the real key to success in life is finding who you are and who you can become, creating your dream and your purpose, and learning how to get there. These are areas of knowledge and skill that provide the foundation for what people experience as happiness.

---

* *I was co-founder and CEO of The Effectiveness Institute, a national and international consulting and training company based in Redmond, Washington. The course and materials for the course are based on the leadership and team development work we created.*

Happiness is the emotional feeling that results from knowing who you are, having a dream and pursuing it, being with family and friends you love, and finding excitement in your work because you know it will help you in someday reaching your dream. Happiness can also result from knowing that you and your life make a difference. This is what the book is about: taking charge of your life and determining your own destiny.

Let's begin with some brief stories about a variety of **life** experiences. Some of the stories can be difficult to relate to if you have never had such an experience. Some of the stories are quite sad, and others are very inspiring. Look around. You probably know friends who are facing one or more of these same challenges right now. Perhaps it is you.

In Life: You will always have choices.

Nelson came to the realization that many of his choices were made based on what his friends were doing and how he thought they perceived him. He wanted to be one of the guys, but found that he was not doing the things that made him happy. He had lost sight of the person he wanted to be.

Nelson—"I Am Taking Back Control of My Life."

In class we were talking about putting your life together in a way that you can respect yourself for who you are and what you do. To take back control and really enjoy where you're at and where you're going. Personally, I know from firsthand experience that most of the time I don't do what will actually make me happy or be better for me in the long run. My decisions are often based off of other people's perceptions and I don't think enough about things. I have been letting some of my friends influence me.

I just feel like I've lost a lot of the natural drive to be extremely successful. Lately I've started to get that drive back, and I think some of it stems from coming to realize that this is my life and whatever choices are made and things done are done by me and nobody else. I've started to say no to things that normally I would have done at the drop of a hat, and it's actually starting to make me happy again to feel in control.

Sometimes it almost seems like I'll put on a show and completely hide who I am or what I'm thinking depending on who's around. A prime example of putting on a show would be at my fraternity when girls come over for exchanges or parties. My mindset all of a sudden is to get drunk because for some reason I think that's going to get me a girl. I know full well that the better idea would be to just have a couple of drinks and really try talking to them or playing a game of pool with them, but that never happens because I just do what everyone else is doing. Doing what would make me happy and what I want at the moment are two very different things, and the sooner I take control and start doing what I know would make me happy, the better off I, and those around me would be.

There's a restlessness, a yearning emptiness that won't go away. It's as if there is a hole in my soul. I have this emptiness quite often. I used to be able to fill this emptiness through playing video games, sports, school, and hanging out with friends and girls. For the last five years of my life, I've spent my time filling this void with booze, cigarettes, pot, drugs, the strip club, gambling, whatever sounded like fun at the time. Until now, I hadn't been able to find something that would drive me to change my ways.

If we don't realize now that what we do and the decisions we make will impact our lives forever, then when will we ever start making the right decisions? Personally I want to say no to drinking all the time. I want to get up and go to class everyday. I want to work out and eat right. I want to be happy with myself and with the effort I put forth and decisions I make because it's all about me. It feels good to be back on track.

Nelson followed this up with a vision statement for the kind of life he wanted, and how to get there. He wrote, "*If my life were really working, what would I be doing?*" Two months later he had actually regained control of his life. He looked healthy, had lost some weight, and was quite excited about what he had been doing. With a big smile he said, "I've got my life back."

Significant breakthroughs often result from what you learn about yourself after a difficult experience. Annette discovered that she had been in a relationship with a guy who was manipulative and who used her. She came to realize that she had been giving up who she was in an attempt to be loved by him.

Annette—"I am learning that I am loveable."

Never before have I felt so vulnerable or open. I have put off writing this paper for almost a week. I even re-organized my entire room, just so I wouldn't have to start this paper. This made me finally deal with how I felt with him (boyfriend). I always felt the need for his approval and I would bend over backwards to please him. In the end his actions always spoke much louder than his words, and his actions always disappointed me. His words were just a stream of continuous broken promises, another reminder that I was not being true to myself. It is painful for me to look back on my time with him. He hurt me in many ways and stripped me of my innocence. I gave everything I had over to him and he took it all without any consideration of me. I do feel guilt, shame, and humiliation when looking back on my experience with him.

I now intend to be completely honest with myself, because I have not been completely honest with myself or anyone else when it comes to this subject. I lied to my family, I lied to my friends, I even lied to myself so that I wouldn't feel the full force of the pain I was inflicting upon myself. I realize that by coming clean I may face certain criticism and judgments, but this is part of my path and I need to learn from my mistakes. That is why I must be honest about my past mistakes. I have to face them head on so that I can finally let go of them.

Lately, I have been viewing myself differently. I am starting to see how much I sacrifice my time, my interests, and my self for the people in my life. These are painful statements to make but I feel like I am a good person who really cares about other people and I want to make their lives better. Sometimes I do sacrifice my needs to balance the needs of the other people I am surrounded by. I used to think that my love for others was a disadvantage but now I realize it is a part of who I am, and although caring too much can be a weakness, it can also be rewarding when it strengthens a relationship.

I do love myself and I know how many incredible gifts I have. I love the way my mind works, how I crave knowledge and never stop learning. I am a very caring, thoughtful, and loving human being. I am even proud of all my physical attributes and abilities. I would do anything for me. I am on a good path now, and will never go back.

Annette discovered that she had been giving herself away in trying to be loved by a guy she thought was her boyfriend. It had become a pattern in her life and likely would have been repeated had she not come to recognize it. Her breakthrough was the realization that she is a loveable person, and through loving herself she becomes stronger and even more loveable to others. This realization was a life changing experience for Annette. She was able to leave him and move on with her life.

Have you ever given yourself away to be liked or loved? The process that both Nelson and Annette utilized to make their life changes is the process I will walk you through later in the book.

In Life: There is Also the Death of Friends and Relatives We Love.

In a conversation with Karlo, I asked him if there was anything in his life he was struggling with. He said yes, and that he had been struggling with it since he was fourteen years old. He then told me his story, and soon we were both in tears. Mark had been Karlo's best friend since they were nine years old. During the summer when they were fourteen, Karlo, Mark and two other friends were swimming in a lake. They decided to swim to a floating dock. It was much farther than they thought, and when Karlo and another friend reached it, they were both exhausted. Karlo looked back and saw that one friend had given up and gone back to shore. Mark was still trying to get to the raft but was struggling and began sinking into the water. The boys were shouting for help but no one was nearby. Karlo watched helplessly as Mark went under. He knew that if he tried to reach Mark, he too would drown. Mark didn't come back to the surface.

As I sat there with Karlo I learned that he didn't have any help at the time in dealing with his pain and the intense guilt that he felt for not dying with Mark. In fact in all these years since, this was the first time he had talked about it. I told Karlo to find some quiet time and write his story about Mark, then to write Mark a letter and say good-bye. I then suggested that he write himself a letter of forgiveness so he could let go of the pain he had been carrying after watching his friend drown. Here is Karlo's letter to Mark.

Karlo—"I saw Mark, my best friend, sinking into the water."

When I was fourteen, we went swimming in the lake. I watched my best friend drown and have never been able to get over it. I've felt guilty ever since and haven't been able to get over the loss. Last night I wrote him this letter:

"Man, I never got to thank you for giving me my first job when I was twelve, doing the paper route with you. I thought I was rich when you paid me $25 every two weeks. Saying all these thank you's is not enough, but I do want to say I'm sorry. I'm sorry for not telling you that you were like a brother to me. I'm sorry I never got to tell you thank you for everything. I'm sorry I never got to tell you that I did want to jump back into the lake and save you but I couldn't cuz I wasn't a strong swimmer. I'm sorry Mark, I'm sorry for not helping you. I'm sorry for just watching you helplessly die in front of my eyes. I could've tried but I was scared to die too. If I could go back into time I would try to save you. You're not even here to receive this letter. Not one day

passes by that I don't think about that day. Since I never got to say sorry to you, I want to say it now. I never got to tell you I love you as a bro. I want to tell you now. I love you dawg. Thank you for being a part of my life. Saying thank you and sorry is not enough. I know you see me writing this letter and I know you forgave me too. I always carried the burden of being guilty, but now I have to let it go. Writing to you makes me feel really better now. I will never forget you bro, and I hope you haven't forgotten me. I don't believe in goodbyes, so I'll just say I'll see you later. I miss you and I love you bro. See you when I get there. Peace.

Much love and respect,
Karlo

That night Karlo had a very vivid dream of meeting Mark. In the dream they talked and laughed and then hugged and said goodbye. I told Karlo I didn't think it was just a dream; it was much more. Sometimes we do have a visit of spiritual energy "from the other side," and it can come in the form of a dream. Karlo smiled, nodding his head and said to me, "I know it was real."

Actually, for Karlo it was even more than just believing his dream was real. For the first time since Mark's death, Karlo was able to talk about it and experience his emotions. Even more importantly, he was able to realize that it wasn't his fault and that he too would have died if he had tried to help Mark. Karlo was finally able to forgive himself and let go of the deep sense of guilt he had been needlessly carrying for so many years.

Is there any guilt that you might be carrying, and wish you could let go?

In Life: Sometimes Our Parents Divorce, Turning Our World Upside Down.

Divorce touches the lives of many, either directly or indirectly. Invariably the greatest negative impact of a divorce is on the children, and the effect can last many years. Common emotions are anger and bitterness toward one or both parents, and feelings and fears of abandonment. Many who go through this experience bury their feelings and fears and try to go on with their lives. Sometimes, as in the case of Robert, there comes an experience of forgiveness.

Robert—"Our father left us for another woman."

My life has changed significantly over the past three years. Throughout my childhood, both of my parents were very supportive of all of us. I would have to say mom was the backbone of our family. My mom is very outspoken about certain issues and would not let us get away with anything. My dad was the laid back, soft-spoken mentor. My father was an airline pilot and was gone three or four days a week for work, which was very hard on my mother and the family. My mom had to run the home when my dad wasn't there and it didn't always go as she planned. My dad and I were very close before I went off to college. He would always help me with my math homework, played soccer in the yard with us and threw the football around with me.

During my sophomore year in college our family discovered that my father was having an affair with another woman in another state. My dad was still living at home and seeing another woman on the side. My mom had to ask him to leave after he refused to stop seeing the other woman. The strength and courage that my mom displayed in asking the man who meant the most to her to leave the house was unbelievable.

My dad moved to Seattle for about six months before moving in with the other woman down in California. The shock of this news really had an effect on my life. I went through a period of depression, but it wasn't constant. I would think about my dad or something would remind me of him, and I would get very lonely and sad. I wouldn't want to do anything and didn't have the energy to focus on school. I would hide my feelings even from my family and friends who were the closest to me. I tried to solve the problem by calling my dad and telling him what he needed to do and giving my mom advice on how to handle the situation. It has been a long process for me to get to the point where I am at today. During the periods of despair and depression, I was looking to the world to make me happy and solve my problems. This only made them worse.

I have shown tough love towards my dad, but also grace and forgiveness. I know my dad is in a dark period in his life and doesn't even realize the effect that he is having on the family. My dad hasn't spoken with my older brother in over two years. I am saddened by my dad's state, but also disappointed because I know who he really is and who he can be. All I can do now is pray and help keep my dad accountable for his actions. I am the only one in the family who will call and speak to my father. I love him too much to not talk to him. Even though I am constantly disappointed with him, I have learned not to get emotional with him. I can now control my feelings toward him and speak rationally. I know if anything were to happen to him and I hadn't talked to him, I would regret not doing so.

What is so impressive about Robert is how he was able to get through his experience and how he chose to maintain his relationship with his father. Because of the strength of love for his father, Robert was able to forgive his father's weakness. Because of Robert, his father may find the strength to reconnect with his children. There is great power in forgiveness.

Has anyone hurt you, and you still carry the hurt?

In Life: Sometimes Traumatic Experiences Become Gifts.

Lorna's story was one of the most heart-wrenching, but turned into one of the most touching and inspiring because it could have easily ended with her giving up in despair. Instead she not only found herself, but also now gives so much to others who have been through similar family trauma.

Lorna—"I overcame sexual abuse and I now counsel young girls."

When I was three years, old my father left us. With him he took almost all of our furniture and almost all of the money. My mother was forced to raise three children on her own and was bankrupt. My brother, who is twelve years my elder, left soon after to live with my father. My mother worked long hours to support my sister and me. Because of this we spent very little time with her. There was often not enough money to pay for a babysitter. As a result I took on the responsibilities of caring for my sister and the house. This is a tough job for an eight-year-old. I am now convinced that those years shaped me into the responsible woman I am today.

When I was twelve, an older man sexually abused me. I was scared to tell my mom. I went to church with a friend one Sunday and decided I would tell one of the older ladies in the church. She told me that I must have done something really bad for God to have punished me that way. I was mortified. I felt so alone. That same year, I began to drink. I started hanging out with a rough crowd. My grades fell, and I neglected my sister. I also became involved in an abusive relationship with a boy who raped me.

The summer I turned fourteen my mother sent me to France for three months. It was one of the most wonderful experiences of my life. My eyes were opened to life in other parts of the world. I met many beautiful people and learned a lot from them. It was that summer I decided to turn my life around.

When I returned home, my mother re-married. My new stepfather decided my sister and I needed to be raised away from the city, and we moved. I gave up drinking. I made new friends and became active in cheerleading, drama, and studying French. For one of the first times in my life I felt happy.

I have come to understand that sometimes, unfortunate things happen to good people. I am glad that the things happened to me instead of someone who may not have been strong enough to endure the pain. Instead of dwelling on the pain of my past, I chose to create good out of my experiences. I became a counselor for a junior high group, so I could share my story with teenagers who need someone to identify with them or just offer them some direction. I have also counseled friends who have been abused or who suffer from eating disorders.

My life has been so richly blessed by friends and family who love me. I have had many beautiful experiences, and have enjoyed the spotlight more than many will ever experience. I have been blessed by many second chances to improve the life I have been given. I have been set free to realize the joy and fullness life has to offer. Because of the clouds in my life I have been given the ability to recognize bondage and pain in the lives of others. I have developed a heart for helping people to realize the sunshine in their lives. Every circumstance can be overcome with a little effort and a lot of love. I am living proof. I strive to live everyday to see the good in others and somehow inspire them to learn to live in freedom and joy.

Lorna provides a great example of someone who, despite exceptionally difficult childhood experiences, is figuring out how to make life work for her.

Do you know anyone who has carried the burden of an abusive childhood?

In Life: I get to learn how to make life work for me.

Finally a description from Brian of what he was able to learn from his experience with the material in this book.

Brian—"What I have learned."

I learned that everybody has a story. Everybody needs help. You are not alone. I learned that people can be trusted and can be depended upon. I learned to see the signs when somebody needs help and to offer it to them. One person can make a difference. I learned to not be scared of who I am; I should be comfortable being myself in any situation, because if others don't like me for who I am, I don't need them. I learned to speak up for myself. I've wasted too much of my life sitting back and watching others take charge. I always felt like my thoughts were not important enough for everybody to hear, but everybody's thoughts are important. You should never swallow insults or let people put you down. If you don't make your feelings known, they will bottle up inside of you and explode at the worst possible moment. I learned to take nothing for granted. Be grateful for who you are and what you have. Say what you're grateful for every morning. Don't let complaints fill your head, or you will begin a downward spiral into becoming a negative person. Let yourself be loved and don't be afraid to put your heart on the line. You never know what will come out of it. Constantly remind yourself of what makes you happy and what you want out of life. Put your desires out into the universe and believe you will get them. Eventually, you will. Smile. You never know who you're attracting with it or whose day you can brighten. Don't ever tell yourself that you don't deserve to be happy. Love yourself. Don't put yourself down or think negative thoughts when you look in the mirror. Don't compare yourself to other people. Show gratitude to the people who've made a difference in your life and for whom you're grateful. It will brighten their day and make you feel good. You never know when you won't have the chance again. View the world with open eyes. You shape your world—so take it into your hands and start sculpting!

Have you ever lost that positive feeling you have for life, and wished you could get it back?

The Self-Search Experiences.

The information, knowledge and tools contained in this book come from my own research and experience in working with both business and college people, and with life issues. The "Self-Search Experience" tool has been exceptionally successful in focusing on the future and for dealing with a broad range of issues. The applications range from making a career choice to choosing to stay in or get out of a relationship. You will be provided with a variety of Self-Search Experiences for each chapter, and you can choose those you feel will work best for you. In each chapter there are references to the Self-Search Experiences for the chapter topics. The complete description and directions for each of the Self-Search Experiences is provided in the Appendix under the specific chapter heading. In addition, there are a number of stories associated with the Self-Search Experiences in the Appendix that you will not want to miss.

As you move forward, read the chapters that are most relevant to you in whatever order you choose, and do some of the Self-Search Experiences in the Appendix. Then read some of the other material, as these will be about experiences your significant other, your friends, or your relatives might be facing. See what you can learn and how far you can go. You have much to gain and nothing to lose.

Finally, you will want to read this book because there is so much that you will be able to apply to your own life. The following are some of the responses from the question, "What did you learn from this experience?"

> **I've learned -**
> *that sometimes when I'm angry I have the right to be angry, but that doesn't give me the right to be cruel.*
>
> **I've learned -**
> *that true friendship continues to grow, even over the longest distance. Same goes for true love.*
>
> **I've learned -**
> *that just because someone doesn't love you the way you want them to, doesn't mean they don't love you with all they have.*

I've learned -

that maturity has more to do with what types of experiences you've had and what you've learned from them and less to do with how many birthdays you've celebrated.

I've learned -

that you should never tell children their dreams are unlikely or outlandish. Few things are more humiliating, and what a tragedy it would be if they believed it.

I've learned -

that it isn't always enough to be forgiven by others. Sometimes you have to learn to forgive yourself.

I've learned -

that our backgrounds and circumstances may have influenced who we are, but we are responsible for who we become.

I've learned-

that no matter how much I care, some people just don't care back.

I've learned -

that it takes years to build up trust, and only seconds to destroy it.

I've learned -

that it's not what you have in your life but who you have in your life that counts.

I've learned -

that you shouldn't compare yourself to the best others can do.

I've learned -

that you can do something in an instant that will give you heartache for life.

You Matter:

I've learned -
that it's taking me a long time to become the person I want to be.

I've learned -
that you should always leave loved ones with loving words. It may be the last time you see them.

I've learned -
that we are responsible for what we do, no matter how we feel.

I've learned -
that regardless of how hot and steamy a relationship is at first, the passion fades and there had better be something else to take its place.

I've learned -
that just because two people argue, it doesn't mean they don't love each other; and that just because they don't argue, it doesn't mean they do.

I've learned -
that two people can look at the exact same thing and see something totally different.

I've learned -
that even when you think you have no more to give, when a friend cries out to you, you will find the strength to help.

I've learned -
that it's hard to determine where to draw the line between being nice and not hurting people's feelings and standing up for what you believe.

I've learned –
that you cannot make someone love you. All you can do is be someone who can be loved. The rest is up to them.

Key Takeaways: How to Make Life Work for You

- ➤ In life there will always be issues and challenges that often bring new opportunities.

- ➤ A big key to success in life is finding yourself and discovering who you are and who you are capable of becoming.

- ➤ You can learn from and get past even the most difficult situations.

- ➤ You can never change anything from your past, but you can absolutely change the present and the future.

- ➤ There will always be others ready and willing to help you.

- ➤ Don't be afraid to ask for help.

CHAPTER 1

WHO ARE YOU, REALLY?

Whatever you can do, or dream you can, begin it.
Boldness has genius, power, and magic in it.
—Goethe

You can attract what you want in your life, and in the process you can overcome the obstacles that get in the way.

Almost every aspect of your life—your personal happiness, relationships, achievement, personal success, creativity, and even your sex life—revolves around a basic characteristic: the image you carry of who you are. This image is also a reflection of your level of self-esteem and your feelings and opinions of self. You are not alone in this self-image scenario. Almost all of us define who we believe we are and shape our self-worth by taking on beliefs through how others in our world respond to us. This begins with our parents, our siblings, then peers, teachers and even people we work with. Their responses and judgments shape us whether our perception is accurate or not.

Where do the beliefs you hold about yourself come from?

Write your thoughts and feelings in the margin

The image you have of yourself impacts how others see and relate with you. This image drives you through your day-to-day activities and affects everything from your choice of butter on your morning toast, the type of car you drive, what clothes you buy, to what career you follow to the kinds of people you bring into your circle of friends, and even your choice of a spouse.

Do you want to know more about you? Let's begin.

What Is Your Image of You in Your Head?

"The image you hold of yourself controls the range of possibility you can see, and what you will allow in your life." (Joan King, Ph.D., neuroscientist, author, and Tufts University professor and author The Code of Authentic Living, (2009).

Answer the following questions, and let's see where this takes you.

You Matter:

1. Who are you? How would you describe yourself to someone important? What words or phrases define you right now?
2. What do you love about yourself?
3. What do you not like about yourself?
4. What skills would you identify that you possess right now?
5. What talents are you recognizing in yourself that with enough practice will take you to greater heights?
6. What message or information do you KNOW that tells you that you would be successful, given the right support?
7. What kind of training, learning, apprenticeship, money and/or opportunity would help you achieve that success?

What mistaken stories might you be carrying in your head?

Questions like these almost always create awkwardness in the individual trying to give an accurate, honest response. We are just not used to being asked questions like these, nor are these things that many of us have spent much time thinking about. The initial answers are usually pretty superficial. Who are you? "I'm a student. I'm a daughter (or son). What do you mean, who am I? I'm a business major. I'm president of my sorority. I'm working full time and going to school."

We all have fears.

Often people answer the "who are you" question with what they do, rather than who they are. Some feel awkward because they think it's bragging to say something positive. Sometimes they just push back and don't want to answer at all. It's kind of like this: There are lots of roads that will get you to a new city, but if you don't take the time to choose a road to travel, you can't get there. Sometimes you will find that you let someone else choose your road for you.

Answering these questions can help you choose the right road for you. So these questions are very important relative to where you are in your life, where you are going, and what you can achieve, given the right kind of support. Often these thoughts become self-limiting beliefs because of what you don't yet know or have yet to discover about yourself. Know this: The key that opens the door to self-knowledge comes through answering these deeper questions about yourself. This is foundational knowledge you need in order to set up life tools to create a future you *need* and *want* for yourself.

What if you didn't stop at that first question, but answered the whole series? Would you discover who you really are? Here is what Jason wrote.

Jason—"Who am I?"

I am a guy who is in his last year of school and can't wait to get out and start my career. Actually I'm really scared. I've done okay here in my classes and socially, but I wonder how I will do competing with everyone in the workplace.

I just went through a relationship breakup and that was very hard for me. Now I'm not sure how I feel about finding a new one (relationship). I don't like being lonely but I don't want to get hurt again either.

I love that I really care about people and that I like to learn new things. I don't like that I feel so awkward when I meet new women, especially when I think they are really attractive. I also don't like that I'm so unsure of whether I'm going to be good enough to compete when I go to my new job.

I hope I'm capable of becoming a great husband and father someday. This is really important to me. I really don't know what my potential is in my work. I do know that I did a lot better in college than I ever thought I would do. This makes me think that maybe I have a lot more potential than I realized. I think I'm ready to push myself and find out."

Think of it this way: How can you become what you can't even see as a possibility? Those who don't take the time to explore who they are and what their potential really is could go through life narrowing their range of possibilities. They can be blinded by their own tunnel vision. Without a healthy, whole, balanced sense of self as a foundation, you are unable to explore, discover, take risks in order to make choices that lead you on the path to becoming a happy, joyful, and fulfilling human being.

You Matter:

A damaged self-esteem, without support to course-correct can corrode our love lives, careers, and relationships. The more you believe you are able to achieve something, the more likely it is that you will. When old negative thoughts and beliefs get activated, they keep you anchored to the past. Memory is not your friend when you find yourself dwelling on the negatives of the past.

It is in each present moment that you have the power to change. Notice how consciously Shelley explores her inner self and the resulting positive changes she is able to make in her life.

Shelley—"I have always kept my guard up to protect myself."

Throughout my life I have always felt the need to have my guard up when it comes to my feelings. To me this could be due to being hurt and made fun of. For many people, it takes them awhile to get past the sarcasm and the front that I put up. This is one of those things I wish I could change. When people meet me, I sometimes come off as a little on the mean side because I try to find other people's flaws and point them out so people won't really notice mine. Once you break down the wall I have put up it gets better because I know that you are not out to judge me or make assumptions about me. I am not one to put my feelings out on a limb for fear of rejection and being hurt by others

I am the first to make judgments and form opinions about other people. This is not something I am proud of or that I do on purpose. I have just found that it's easier to recognize other people's shortcomings than to deal with my own. What I have begun to realize is that I need to start dealing with my own shortcomings, which is not an easy thing to do. For me, I hate admitting when I am wrong or when I have failed at something. I didn't just get this way overnight, and it didn't just happen to me. It is the result of events that have happened in my life and a process of reactions and interpretations that happened within me.

26

There have been things in my life that have caused me to shut down and hide the person I really am.

In two paragraphs Shelley was able to capture and express things that had been bothering her about herself for a long time. She describes the mistaken story she had been carrying in her head about who she is. Just like so many of us, Shelley had developed a fear of rejection and had learned to defend against it by "guarding" her feelings and using sarcasm to protect herself. Also, like so many of us, she had developed this over such a long period of time that she was no longer aware of her defense mechanism or of how it was keeping her from having people she could trust in a relationship. On the flip side, people who mattered most to Shelley couldn't get through her wall to really know her.

Once she wrote it down, Shelley could see how what she thought was protecting herself from being hurt was really causing more pain and isolation. With this new insight she chose to change her behavior and saw how life around her changed to align with the new Shelley. As you will see, once you are aware of what you are doing that gets in your way, you can learn how to change it.

Contrast the self-image and description that Shelley had been carrying, with that of Kezirah in the next story. In class we had a discussion about the impact of what other people tell us and the positive or negative affect this has on our self-esteem. Shelley had learned to guard herself from others' comments. She had become judgmental. Kezirah, on the other hand, provides an example of overcoming negative comments of other children in her younger life and keeping a healthy self-image in her mind.

Kezirah—"He asked me, 'are you black or are you white?"

You too have much potential.

Growing up, my parents dressed me in African American dress, and my mom braided my hair. It was much different from other black girls' whose hair was 'permed.' Permed doesn't mean curly, because it straightened the hair of African American women. Little girls during this time had their hair permed. My hair was a bit nappy and braided at the time, so I looked different in the eyes of those girls and boys.

I was made fun of about the way I looked and talked. When I entered middle school I was approached by a boy who was in my class. I remember him asking me why I talked the way I did. At first I didn't understand what he meant until he told me that I wasn't the typical black girl. I asked him in what way? Well, he told me, I talked like a white person. I was really offended and upset when I went home that day, and realized that I didn't act in certain ways. I didn't have many African American friends growing up. It was put in my head that I was different from the other students in some way. When high school began, the teasing really hit hard.

One of my male classmates, also an African American, had asked me a question. "Why don't you choose color?" I had no idea what he was asking me. He asked me "Are you black or are you white?" What was I to say at that moment in time, and in front of everyone? I was so upset with the question he had asked me, it made me reevaluate who I was as a person.

The way I talk and the way I dress doesn't change who I am. I was raised in a good home with loving parents, and for the longest time I had lost my identity. One thing I learned from this is that I am an African American black woman who is proud of who she is and of the people I surround myself with. I love all colors and cultures. I don't discriminate, because I love people too much. It has made me a much better person. So, to all the bullies who made fun of me…look at me now!

Can you imagine how difficult it could be for a young African American girl to get hit with critical comments from children both white and other African Americans? Kezirah was able to gain strength as she became clear and comfortable with who she is.

Many of the thoughts and beliefs we hold in our heads about who we are become self-limiting and judgmental. When we judge ourselves in a negative way, we become very judgmental of others as well. The impact becomes twofold; we carry misperceptions about ourselves and misperceptions about others. Then we make up stories to justify our misperception! As you walk through your day notice this pattern playing out with yourself and others in your life.

What stories about yourself are you carrying that might be getting in your way?

People and Experiences Create Stories in Your Head

As you will come to understand, those relationships closest to you (family, friends, and teachers) are the arenas where the *most significant* perception and image of "self" was formed. How teachers or coaches treated you and the feedback they gave you had an impact on you, whether helpful or harmful. Of course your peers had an even stronger impact as you lived through your teenage years. The unfortunate part of these early years of developing your self-image was your likely lack of awareness or the skills to discern the truth about yourself, whether positive or negative. Now you will be able to do this.

Here are some examples of experiences that significantly shaped each person's self-esteem. Can you relate?

Kevin—"My greatest fear is rejection and not being liked."

I am never the person to start a conversation, nor will I ever go up to someone I do not know and ta1k to them. The type of fear this puts in me is unexplainable. People may think that I am just a quiet and shy person, but in reality I am just terrified of the thought of opening up in any way to people. I have this thought in my head that people do not want to meet random people and that everyone is always looking to judge others negatively. I know it is a stupid thought to have, and personally I would love it if people came up randomly and started conversations with me.

Why is this one of my fears? It took me awhile to admit why rejection scares me so much. Admitting that this is

What negative judgments do you make about others?

a fear also means admitting I have been in painful situations. My junior high years were by far the worst I have ever experienced. At this time, puberty is in full effect and everyone is going through awkward phases about how they look and feel. I fit into the group of people who looked more awkward than everyone else did. I was very scrawny, short, wore glasses, had bad skin and bad hair. I was not viewed to be very cool. I would say that this is the time in a kid's life when how you look plays a major role in who your friends are and who you hang out with. All the guys at this point are trying to be cool so that the girls will like them and this means they cannot be seen with people who may not have the cool look.

Two of the more vivid memories I have confirmed these thoughts for me. One was a class project where we were to bring in baby photos of ourselves. One of the popular girls was looking at my photo with me standing right there and she said without any regard for me, "What happened to you?" The second incident was when another person who also was not viewed as being cool and I were standing outside waiting to get into basketball practice. As we were waiting a popular person came up and was waiting with us, when people inside finally opened the door for us. The popular kid's response was, "Why did you make me stand out here with these nerds."

Hearing things like that, and going through many other situations similar, does not make you want to be open and vocal. Instead, it makes you feel very insecure and reclusive. It is a terrible feeling to have a fear like this. I have either ruined or missed opportunities in life due to this fear of rejection. It has made it hard for me to get into relationships with girls, and when I am involved, it is hard for me to open myself up completely because I am scared of getting hurt. If I want to get over this fear, then I have to confront it and go out on dates and be sociable. That does not make me feel secure about this, but it is something I need to do.

Look at the stories Kevin had been carrying in his mind since childhood. "I am quiet and shy and I am terrified to open up to people." "I look like a nerd. People won't like me, and I will be rejected."

He made a statement aloud, "That is not who I am now." Kevin recognized the source of his shyness and uncertainty and was ready to change it. He then set about changing the picture he held of himself and he started on his new path. You will learn more about how to do this later in the chapter.

When someone whom we deem to be a significant or important person tells us something about ourselves, we usually believe it. Once we believe it, we will behave accordingly, regardless of how self-limiting it can be. This is what happened to Sarah.

Sarah—"My teacher said, "I really don't think you will do well in a university."

I can remember a good example from my senior year in high school when I came really close to believing what a teacher told me about myself. It was right about the time I was applying to get into colleges and it was a very confusing, exciting, and intimidating time for me. I was taking a Spanish class just to graduate, and I was struggling quite a bit. I remember the teacher had really been working hard with me so that I could pull at least a C out of it. I was coming in before class and staying late to get help. I have never been the best student anyway, so it was really frustrating to be trying so hard in a class that had a bunch of freshman and to be doing so poorly.

Frankly, I was already feeling pretty stupid. No one had to tell me that I wasn't good at Spanish because I had spent hours almost everyday agonizing about it and crying to my parents. One day the teacher pulled me aside and said, "Honestly, maybe you want to consider going to a two-year college before going to a larger school. I really don't think you will do well in a university."

I can't remember if those were his exact words, but I swear to God, his message was loud and clear. 'You aren't *smart enough, and I don't believe that you will do well.' It made me want to cry. Actually it made me feel really, really stupid. Now I wish I had said "You know what? I could give a RATS ASS about Spanish. The only reason I am taking this GOD AWFUL @#$%ING class is so I can go to a UNIVER-SITY! And if you're so smart, why the hell don't you know that teachers are supposed to encourage their students to aim high and work hard to get an education. What kind of teacher talks their students out of going to college? You are an ASSHOLE for trying to tell me that I am too stupid to get what I want."*

In hindsight, I think it would have been to both our benefits for me to have said this, but of course, I just told him thank you for all the help, and I would look into a two-year school (which I never did). Wow, I didn't even really realize how much that bothered me until I just wrote all of that. Sorry it's a little raw.

What is so amazing about Sarah's experience is that, like all of us she had a choice to believe or not believe her teacher's words. Fortunately Sarah's self-esteem was solid enough to allow her to choose not to buy into the story her teacher was telling her: that she would never succeed in a university. Yet look at the anger she had been carrying for years about this interaction. Expressing her anger in this way was also very healthy for Sarah because she now recognized the strength of her belief in herself and could let the anger go. Look at how limiting her range of possibilities would have been if Sarah had chosen to believe that she was not smart enough or capable of attending a university. Sarah was able to discern the truth of the situation by having a strong and positive self-esteem.

What is your greatest fear?

What is your greatest fear? The deep fears we have reflect insecurities (not good enough, not smart enough, etc.) from beliefs we have carried around in our heads. Until we are able to expose those beliefs as being rooted in our misperceptions about ourselves, it is very difficult to change the habitual thoughts and beliefs in order to change how we navigate through the world. Here is a good example.

Mathew—"My greatest fear is failure."

I have never told this fear to anyone else before in my life. I realized the only thing that could prevent me from being happy in life was if I failed. This is a broad realization but I can now narrow down the word "failure" for me to a few examples: fear of disappointing my family, especially my dad; fear of failing at having a successful career; fear of being single when I need someone the most; and the fear of having money but not being happy. If any of these were to be true, I would have failed at life. The one point I would like to focus on for now is failure when it comes to my father.

What comes to me right off the bat is my experience with baseball, and I am sure this experience has caused this fear of failure. I felt like I failed my dad when I did not get to play in the junior All-Star game. I felt I failed my dad again when I did not make the high school baseball team. I don't remember him saying specifically that he was disappointed in me but I could tell by his voice he was. This single event destroyed my whole self-concept and self-esteem. It put this huge weight on my conscience to never fail again in anything I do. So now I avoid every instance that gives me even a slight chance to fail. This I realize is not the way to live life. I fear I will not take risks in the future out of this fear of failure. I know one of the ways to be happy and successful in life is to take risks. These risks will sometimes be life-changing whether they are for good or bad

By writing these words I feel myself learning how untrue these fears are. I know it's okay to be afraid, but to have it prevent me from succeeding or living is not okay. I've already started dealing with these issues, but there is still work to be done. My goal is to take more risks and try to let people get to know the authentic me. If these people do not like the authentic me, then it was meant to be that way. However, I won't be someone else just for the approval of another individual. I need to learn as much as I can when I fail at something. Worrying what other people will think of me if I fail is a waste of time. If they truly love me and are my friends they will be there to catch me if I fall.

Mathew was so honest with himself when he wrote about his fear of failure. He was finally able to admit it to himself just how much his fear of failing was hindering his life, and where his fear came from. In this experience one of the things that Mathew learned about his father was that his father was doing the best that he knew how at that time and was not intentionally trying to hurt Mathew or diminish his self-esteem. As a result of this, Mathew learned what really mattered and was able to develop a plan through his Self-Search Experience to reduce and ultimately eliminate this issue from his life. He learned the importance of taking calculated risks and trusting himself without having to know the outcome.

In the next story, Michelle carried her fear of being hurt in a relationship from childhood as a form of protection so she would never be hurt like that again. The sad consequence was that she never allowed herself to have a boyfriend or even close friends because her hurt was so deep.

Michelle – "I have difficulty in trusting relationships and had an almost fear of men."

This is something that I have been ignoring for a very long time. But then I really sat down and thought about it. It is not "normal" for an individual my age to still guard myself from hurt in a relationship as fiercely as I do. I am at the point where anything that could possibly lead to more than friendship, I completely bail out. I have never had a serious boyfriend. I've never dated anyone for more than a few weeks. I've never been in love. I've never worked to attract someone's attention. At this very moment I am realizing all of the fun things, and all the potential happiness I have been holding myself back from, just because I was afraid of not being good enough. I am not worth anything more than your friendship, is basically what I have been screaming to the world with my body language and words and actions.

I can relate this feeling back to when my step-dad left us on Father's Day. At that point in time I felt he was my "real" dad, and I was his "real" kid. In my eleven-year-old head "real" and love were synonymous. Then he left us, and he only took his son with him—his biological child, his real child, the one who was obviously so much more important. This made me feel worthless. He didn't go out of his way to take me out on weekends and spend time with me like a real father would have. He didn't call to see how I was doing; he didn't visit. He acted like he'd divorced me too, and it really made me feel unworthy. Unworthy of his love and affection and attention, and this soon snowballed into any male attention. This took years to really happen, but I was so young, and I was guarding myself so thoroughly, that I didn't care that I was closing myself off. Maybe I didn't realize it. I went through my teenage years blaming the boys in my classes for not liking me. It was their fault that none of them wanted to date me. But really the message I was sending to everyone was that I wasn't worthy of anything resembling love. I know that now, but it is six years later, and I can still feel the way he hurt me. I moved on, but I didn't forget.

I am putting these feelings down to rest. They are untrue. They were founded on the basis of a step-father who had no idea what he wanted in his life. He was leaving my mother, not me. He was pushed by sons who wanted him for themselves. He eventually came back to us, and he still keeps in constant contact with me. Why I never let this simple fact register is a mystery. There must be something there that is loveable for a man who has no obligation to be connected with me any longer, to actively work to stay in my life. This is huge. I don't know anyone else whose ex-step-father would push so hard to be there for them. It's amazing to me how one person can affect your life in so many ways.

Where did your fear come from?

35

You Matter:

> *My feelings about myself now that I finally understand: I am worthy of being with someone. I am loveable. I am fun. I am a wonderful person. Who cares if I'm not perfect, I don't want to be perfect. I like myself now, more than I ever have before. I am funny, and it has taken some really good friends to show me just how funny I am. I am a good person, and as a good person I deserve to be happy. Instead of dwelling on something that happened twelve years ago, I'm going to dwell on the here and now. I am now back in my life and happier than I've been in a very long time. I am almost done with school, a feat which I had almost talked myself into giving up. I am about to embark on the rest of my life, and I am genuinely excited to figure out where it will take me.*

What are the common challenges in these last four stories? What threads of fears, not-good-enough, and/or insecurities can you relate to? If you've named some of your own insecurities you're not alone. What fears are you ready to deal with? If you are beginning to shift your beliefs through discerning the truth of who you are and who you could be, then you are on your way to changing your self-esteem.

In the Appendix on Page 217 you will find the first **Self-Search Experience: Who Am I?** This is a process for your own self-development. As you complete this process it will provide you with *what you need to know, where you want to go*, and *what you will want to do* to get there. The notes that you have made in the margins will be a great help as you do each Self-Search Experience.

How is your behavior determined by your beliefs?

A variety of **Self-Search Experiences** are provided for you to try throughout this book. Each will have a little different style, or a different application. Give each a try and, if it works for you, follow it through. If it doesn't feel right or is not of interest, don't complete it. There is no one-way of doing this kind of work. Instead, you get to discover and choose which best fits you.

Right now it would be best if you complete the *Self-Search Experience: Who Am I?* on Page 217, and then come back to read further.

Your Fixed Beliefs Establish the Limits of Who You Can Become

Here are some effective ways to strengthen your self-esteem. It is true that your thoughts and beliefs about *who you are* and *who you are not*, are the "colored lens" that you look through to interpret your view of you and your world. Do you avoid trying new things because you might fail? Are you willing to try anything regardless of the outcome? Are you confident going into new relationships? Are you skeptical, timid, or fearful? Your level of self-esteem is based on what you think and believe about yourself. Life is a course in recognizing your insecurities and how they affect your abilities, your relationships, the opportunities you seize or not, and the choices you make in dealing with the challenges.

Why You Do What You Do

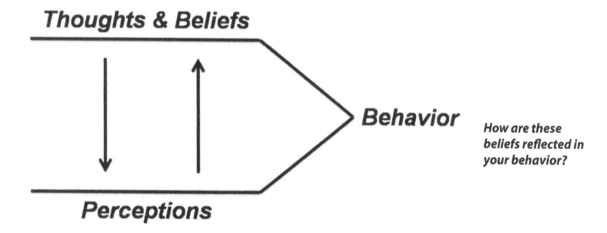

This model shows how your behavior will consistently reflect your thoughts and beliefs. Those thoughts and beliefs are then reflected in your life in: how capable you are, how loveable you feel you are, how successful you are, whether or not others easily accept you, and whether or not you are good enough.

Your **perceptions** are the information you gather about yourself, about others and about the world you live in. Perceptions are the filtered lens you look through to interpret yourself and your world. As defined in the dictionary, a belief is the "acceptance by the mind that something is true or real, often underpinned by an <u>emotional</u> or <u>spiri-</u>

tual sense of certainty. "Emotional" and "spiritual" are underlined to emphasize how deeply held our beliefs about good or bad, right or wrong can become.

Do you have negative thoughts or beliefs about another race? Political group? Religious group?

For example, if you believe you are overweight, then no matter how many people tell you that you look great, your conditioned mind will not accept what they say as true. Do you know someone like this? Habits and patterns that do not serve you are rooted in your conditioned mind, and wait to be dissolved by your willingness to look them "square in the face." If you see yourself as *not good enough, unattractive,* or a *failure,* then any information you see as confirming those beliefs will pass through your perceptual screens and filters, and any other information that is contrary to these beliefs will get screened out. Even though the contrary information is telling you that *you are* okay, *you are normal, you are wonderful*, the messages cannot make it past your own personal filters! In other words, we collect evidence to support our beliefs *whether healthy and true, or not*.

As you have seen by the testimonies and stories of others in this book, when you are willing to look at those ideas and misperceptions that cripple you, then you create a possibility to overcome and conquer those habitual and conditioned thoughts and beliefs about yourself. Every thought is just that, a thought and thoughts can be changed.

What are your thoughts and fixed beliefs that you hold to be *absolutely true* about such things as interracial marriage, about gay or lesbian marriage, about abortion, and/or fundamental religion? What do you believe about Democrats? About Republicans? About our President? How do those beliefs guide your choices and how are they reflected in your thoughts and in your behavior. Have you ever tried to change somebody's fixed beliefs? Have you had others try to change yours?

Only you can change you. As true as this statement is for you, it is true for others as well. You can only cultivate your own awareness about how your thoughts and beliefs may not be serving your highest path of self-discovery in this life.

Self-Limiting Thought Patterns

Our thoughts become our beliefs, which become our habits and patterns. When these habits and patterns become deeply rooted in your conditioned mind, you begin to navigate through your life on *autopilot*. You are no longer in the present moment with a given situation, but now are operating in memory (the thoughts and beliefs deeply rooted in your conditioned mind). You then stay stuck in patterns that can greatly limit who you are capable of being and what you are capable of doing.

What characteristics of yourself do you find yourself comparing to others?

Here are four common self-limiting thought patterns. Do you have any of these patterns? If you do, this is an important place to immediately begin making change.

1.   Comparing yourself to others.

What are you going to stop doing?

2.   Negative "Self-Talk" and/or listening to negative "Other's Talk."

3.   Not focusing on the person you want to be.

4.   Being too hard on and/or critical of yourself.

Self Limiting Belief #1 – Comparing yourself to others.

This can be the source of a great deal of negative information that we pour through our perception screens, proving that we are not as good or as capable, or as attractive, or anything else we think is important. Here is the problem. When you find yourself doing a comparison in an area in which you feel less adequate or inferior, what usually happens is, you will compare yourself with someone who you see as one of the best in this category. For instance, if you feel unattractive you will see all those who look great, and then look at yourself and go "yuk." You can pick anything that you don't like about yourself and you can find all kinds of people who are wonderful in those categories, thus totally reinforcing your negative self-beliefs. Because you will evaluate yourself against only their best, you will never know anything about the insecurities of the other individuals. The message in your head becomes: *I'm not as good as you.* Which often ends up with: *and I don't like you.* Or your belief might be *I am not as good as you,* so you put that person on an unreachable pedestal.

You Matter:

Stop comparing yourself to others and focus on learning what makes you happy just as you are. If you catch yourself in those conditioned mind thoughts, just gently remind yourself by saying, "oops" or something that strikes you funny, and then change your thought to what is uplifting about yourself. You will immediately feel better.

Here is another example of a defeating thought of comparison with another: "I hate him! He always looks so good. He can talk to anybody. I can never … oops! I'm comparing myself again. Maybe I'm never going to look just like him, but I'm definitely a good guy." Then let it go. I thought this poem by another student was perfect in capturing this self-limiting habit. What do you think?

The Personality Mask
by Matt

Every morning I look into the mirror
And wonder if this is really me?
To myself have I been dear,
Or have I become what others want me to be?
Have I fallen into a trend
Of trying to be another,
Thinking I'll find that perfect friend,
Who will love me like no other?
So what has this shown?
Why is it this I do?
Perhaps I'm afraid to be alone,
Or perhaps just to impress you.
I know I'm not pleased with who I've been,
I've done all just to fit in,
Wearing this 'Personality Mask.'

Self Limiting Belief #2 – I often think negative thoughts about myself, and/or I believe the negative talk of others.

The thoughts and beliefs you have about yourself, good or bad, come from your conditioned mind, which stores your imaginations, fears, self-esteem, and self-worth. You add to this what others tell you about yourself, which you then perceive to be true. These thoughts and beliefs become grounded as habits and behavior patterns that you hear over and over in your mind. This self-talk is what you are telling yourself about who you are. I screwed up again. I look so fat. Why can't I do it like he does it? I just don't get it. I'll never get statistics. I'm a failure. I'll never be able to be happy. No one will ever love me. And so on.

Can you see how this kind of self-talk could negatively impact your life and can limit your potential? In earlier examples, both Kelly and Kevin had developed long-term habits of negative self-talk. For Kelly it became a belief about being rejected and hurt in relationships. For Kevin it was his fear of failure. Once they became aware of the negative messages they were conditioning their mind to accept as real, they began to realize that change in their self-image was possible through dissolving those thoughts, ideas, and beliefs.

When have you worn a personality mask?

Take a moment to sit quietly and think about yourself and your life right now. Are there any thoughts that immediately float into your awareness? If so, write down any significant negative self-talk patterns that come to your mind.

Try to capture the exact words you are using. They are often around failure, not being good enough, not looking good enough, not being liked, or not feeling worthy. Save these for your Self-Search Part 2 in the Appendix, Page 218.

Others'-Talk

What **others** say to you and you then believe can become another contributor to negative self-esteem. This is Others'-Talk. The more credibility the other person has, the more impact their words will have, positive or negative. The words of parents and older siblings can have a huge impact. "You're so clumsy!" "Why aren't you good at that like your sister?" OR "You are so beautiful (or handsome)." "You are so talented." "You are going to be so successful." And, you are fun, delightful, loveable. Particularly with parents, it was not just their verbal but also their non-verbal communication that sent you messages. Did they

Can you find examples of when you screen out information that is contrary to your current beliefs?

hold you and hug you, or not? Did they smile and nod affirmatively? Did they make eye contact, listen to you, pay attention, or not?

What were your perceptions and beliefs about yourself as you were growing up? People will put others down in an attempt to bolster their own shaky self-esteem. Wisdom is knowing the difference between those who care about you and are giving you feedback with the intent of helping you, and those who are trying to make themselves feel better but it comes at your expense.

Most of the time the others are just making a judgment based on their beliefs. Have you ever had a teacher, a professor, or someone of stature tell you that you would never succeed, like Sarah experienced in the earlier example? I remember even today when I was in the fourth grade and the class was singing songs. My teacher came over and whispered in my ear, "Billy, I think it would be better if you would just mouth the words." Sadly for me (probably not sadly for others) it took a couple decades before I would ever sing aloud again.

What significant others say to us and how we are treated also can have a huge positive or negative impact on how we see ourselves and on our lives. The following is an example from Martin, who describes his father's negative impact first, but ending in a positive surprise.

Martin—"What I usually got was 'you did this wrong,' 'you could have done that better."

My earliest recollection was when I was about eight years old. I was playing soccer and could have been considered a fairly decent player. The game finished, and we won by a single goal, a goal that I happened to score. It was my second goal of the game, and we won 3-2. I was pretty proud of myself until I got into the car to go home with my parents. I did not receive a "good job," or an "I'm proud of you son" from my dad. What I did get was "you did this wrong" and "you could have done that better." I began to cry as I always did, and my mom comforted me by forcefully speaking with my dad about his behavior.

Without gloating, I suppose you could say that I was a fairly decent athlete. I was a three-sport athlete in high

What kind of person do you want to be?

42

school and received many honors in both football and baseball. During my senior year, my peers elected me captain of the baseball team and co-captain of the football team. I received first team honors in both sports, and at the end of the year sports banquet, I was awarded the male sports athlete of the year honors. None of these awards mattered to me because I did not think they mattered to my dad. This all changed at the final ceremonies of the last baseball game of my career.

My final game was a playoff game in which we lost by one run. At the end, we were gathering as a team in order for all of the parents to take one last picture before we could finally call it quits. I remember so clearly that my dad came down onto the field and gave me one of the biggest hugs that I have ever received. Right then, I knew that my dad really had cared about my accomplishments and that he was very proud of me. As we embraced, I heard him crying and then I began to cry. We hugged and cried for almost thirty seconds before we parted in order for the pictures to be taken. This was the happiest day of my life. I finally felt that everything I had done was not a disappointment to my dad and that he had acknowledged me for who I was. I will cherish this moment always.

How do you want to live your life?

Think of it. Martin spent the years from age eight to eighteen trying to prove himself to his dad and never feeling that he was good enough. Think of how it could have been for Martin if his father had praised him at eight years old, and then supported him along the way. What do you think Martin might have been able to do if he had really believed in himself during that period of time, plus having the knowledge that his dad was proud of him? Can Martin still change his beliefs about himself? Of course he can!

There is one more source of Others'-Talk: your friends, roommates, acquaintances, men or women you meet socially, your enemies, someone who makes negative comments to you or about you. You hear them and then you start believing what they have said, especially if they are validating a fear that you have or something you have been thinking. Most people pay way more attention to critical remarks than we do to compliments! Are you paying more attention to people who are supportive, or are you listening to those who are critical and condescending?

Here are some of the most important takeaways of this section. STOP LISTENING to negative Others'-Talk. STOP comparing yourself to others and then putting yourself down. STOP giving up who you are or who you can be in order to try to please others. Because this is an old habit, it will not be easy. Becoming aware is the first step, and if you work on it for twenty-eight days, it is likely to no longer be an issue.

Self Limiting Belief #3 – I rarely (if ever) think about the kind of person I want to be.

You have the ability to create your own YOU. In fact, you can create a design for the kind of person you want to be and for how you want your life to be. Yes, there will be things that happen that can throw you off track and derail you at times. However, once you have a clear picture in your mind of the person you want to become, the challenges will be much less than what you have experienced in the past. You will know where you are going, and you will be able to align your choices with what will help you get there. You can apply what you have been learning here and it can change your life. Here is an example from Stephanie taken from her Self-Search Experience.

Stephanie—"I finally have come to love that I am me."

Remember, you become what you believe and what you think and talk about.

"I am someone who is a product of a very loving home. This has shaped me into someone who truly cares about others. I know that sometimes I allow myself to care too much about others and do not focus on myself enough. I am someone who has grown up with many self-esteem issues and has had difficulty expressing my emotions and myself. But I know now that I am beautiful, I am smart, I am caring, I am a wonderful listener, and I am someone who can succeed in life.

I love that I am me! There is no one else in this world who is exactly the same as me. I love that I am able to get along with so many people even those who are very different from me. By surrounding myself with people just like me I am not allowing myself to grow or change. I love that I have an easy-going personality. I love that I am a good listener. I love to serve others, and this allows me to do just that in my own way. I love my sense of humor. I love that I have embraced my purposeful awkwardness. I love that I have learned I can love myself."

Give this Self-Search Experience a try. You have nothing to lose.

Self-Limiting Belief #4 – I am pretty hard on myself; I am my own worst critic.

Be gentle with yourself. Many people are so hard on themselves; so self-critical. Be gentle. Treat yourself as you would treat a loving little two-year-old. Treat yourself as you would your best friend. If you offend someone, apologize. Get your ego out of it. Do the same for YOU. If you tend to be self-critical, stop trying to prove yourself, to yourself. You can't. You will always find something wrong. Focus on your strengths and get stronger. There is a common saying: "Wherever you focus, your attention grows." Focus on what you want in your life. When you make a mistake or don't do as well as you wanted, be gentle, forgiving, and encouraging. You will go much farther much faster than you would have imagined.

Do you ever find that you are trying to prove yourself to someone and to no avail? To whom, and why?

Catch yourself in just one of these habits (or more if you wish), and turn the negative thought into a positive one, and see what happens. It's hard at first because habits are deeply ingrained beliefs and patterns. But it will get easier and easier each time, and you will be VERY HAPPY with the results.

In the Appendix you will find **Self-Search Experience: Who Am I? Part 2** on Page 218. This will help you get very clear on where you are now and where you want to be, and will help you identify any habits you will wish to change. It will also show you how to change them.

You Matter:

Key Takeaways from Who Are You, Really?

Statements from students:

> You cannot make someone love you. All you can do is be someone who can be loved; the rest is up to them.

> No matter how much I care, some people just can't care back.

> Don't compare yourself to the best others can do.

> No one should ever tell children their dreams are unlikely or outlandish. What a tragedy it would be if they believed it.

> Our background and circumstances may have influenced who we are, but we are responsible for who we become.

> Sometimes it's hard to draw the line between being kind and not hurting people's feelings, and yet standing up for what you believe.

> Be open and ready for change.

Please also include:

> Your beliefs establish the limits of what you can achieve.

> Labels are frequently intended by the labeler to be harmful, to put someone down.

> Your behavior will consistently reflect your beliefs.

> Notice negative "Self-Talk" and "Others'-Talk" and CHOOSE to stop it.

> You can plan and create your own YOU.

> Positive change will happen more quickly if you are gentle with yourself.

> Focus on what you want in your life.

> When an old limiting story comes into your mind, say "I'm done with that."

> Stop giving up who you are or who you can be in order to try to please others.

> If things are going badly, be willing to seek and accept help.

A final thought: You must be willing to illuminate and dissolve those ideas and misperceptions that keep you in a perpetual negative cycle. When you act on this willingly, then you will know that a truer knowledge has taken hold of you. How will you know this? Your world opens up; you feel on track and lighter inside; you notice life holds all kinds of possibilities that begin to unfold and that you've yet to discover. You are ready to journey forward. You sense a peacefulness and a quietness in your thoughts. You become more aware of and comfortable with who you really are. You find your passion for purpose, which invigorates your life and you re-engage fully in following your dreams.

Important References and Resources:

Feel The Fear…and Do It Anyway, by Susan Jeffers, PhD, Ballantine Books, (December, 2006).

Healing Your Emotional Self: A Powerful Program to Help You Raise Your Self-Esteem, Quiet Your Inner Critic, and Overcome Your Shame, by Beverly Engel, Wiley, John & Sons, (June, 2007).

The Everything Self-Esteem Book: Boost Your Confidence, Achieve inner Strength and Learn to Love Yourself, by Robert Sherfield, PhD, (November, 2003).

CHAPTER 2

INSIGHTS THAT CAN SHAPE YOUR LIFE

"And it is true what you said,
That I live like a hermit in my own head."
Death Cab for Cutie

You Don't Have to Learn Everything Through Your Own Personal Experience

Life is definitely a series of learning experiences. The good news for you is that there is an opportunity for you to learn much from the experience of others and be able to apply it to your own life.

In the following pages, you will find five insights into life that come from a variety of exceptionally reliable sources. Some are from research and some are from the experience of people who have been successful in growing from each challenge. Take a look at these insights and see how they apply to you, and how you can use them to make your life work most successfully for you.

Insight #1 – There is meaning and a purpose for your life.

I believe the very purpose of our life is to seek
happiness. That is clear. We are all seeking
something better in life. So I think the very motion of
our life is towards happiness.
The Dalai Lama

I'm kind of embarrassed to say that I spent the majority of my life not thinking about whether my life had meaning or a purpose. I just didn't give my purpose much thought, that is until two events happened that jolted me into focusing on my life's purpose. The first event occurred during a racquetball game. I had been invited as a guest speaker in the College of Business at Washington State University on several occasions. After one of my presentations, I met a young man, Jim, who was about to graduate and move to Seattle. When in Seattle, we met again a number of times and became friends. He had been an athlete, very bright and very serious about his career. We both loved

Jot your thoughts and feelings in the margin.

racquetball and played almost every week. I was more than twenty years older and I felt good if I could win one game out of three! Over dinner following our games we talked about life, work, dating (we were both single at the time), and pretty much anything.

Make changes in any one of these five insights and watch your life change in rich and wonderful ways.

One evening Jim called and he was upset. The woman he had been dating for some time had broken up with him and he didn't understand why. Jim had thought they were doing well and that maybe she was *the one*. After expressing his pain and confusion he suddenly said to me, "Bill, I just don't get it. What is the purpose of our life anyway? You're older. You must have thought about it. Why are we here?

I was stunned, not by his question, but that I didn't have an answer. I think I was too embarrassed to tell him that I hadn't thought much about it and I didn't know what the meaning of life is. We were scheduled to play racquetball the next evening, so I told him that we could talk about it at dinner, thinking this would buy me some time. But the next day I still didn't know what to tell him.

What do you think is the meaning and purpose of your life?

Jim was so competitive that, if he lost a game, he would get upset and lose his concentration. I figured if I could beat him two games out of three, he would forget about the meaning of life and I would be off the hook. I did win two, but my plan didn't work because at dinner he asked me again, what did I believe is the meaning and purpose of life?

Out of my mouth came a statement that I not only hadn't thought about before this moment, I hadn't heard about it from anyone else either. I found myself saying that I believe the meaning of life is **to learn how to love, to learn how to *be* loved, and to make a positive difference**. This proved to be a life shaping experience for me and, as Jim expressed later, it did for him as well. I learned that this statement was true for me and it was how I wanted to live my life going forward.

What do you think is the meaning and purpose of your life?

A second experience happened, equally unexpected and profound, that also showed me my life has meaning and purpose. I had visited my family on Christmas day and left to drive home the day after. The weather was lightly snowing and a bit slushy on I-5 and traffic was heavy with many semi trucks. I was driving a Nissan 350 Z sports car, not a good car in the snow, but I intended to pull off if the snow got worse. Traffic started backing up so I began to move from the middle lane to the left passing lane, as it was moving a little faster. Just as I started to change lanes I heard a voice say, "Don't go there." I was totally startled. I knew it wasn't really a voice, but it was so real in my head that I obeyed and didn't change lanes.

A few miles later I had forgotten the voice and again started to move into the left passing lane, and again I heard the voice inside my head, "Don't' go there!" I didn't. I couldn't figure this out. I had never consciously heard voices or messages so clearly before. Forty-five minutes later I had again forgotten about the voice and I had moved into the passing lane. Traffic and many semi trucks filled the right two lanes. The highway was slushy, but I felt pretty safe because I had left a lot of distance between, me and the car ahead of me. Since I was getting close to my exit, I started to ease over three lanes to the right. All of a sudden my car started into a 360 degree spin across the three lanes of the freeway! Knowing that there were semi trucks everywhere, I was just waiting to feel the crash and death. In rapid succession I saw one car coming toward me but miraculously missed it by inches, and then saw that I was headed for a concrete bridge abutment. Suddenly my car abruptly stopped. I was so shaken that I hadn't put the clutch in and my engine died. Quickly restarting the car I looked all around for the cars and semi trucks I was certain must be headed toward me. To my complete surprise there were none. Where had they gone? Why hadn't I died?

Even though I made it home in the middle of the afternoon I still went straight to bed, emotionally and physically drained, and just lay there, trying to sort it all out. I thought about the voice, "Don't go there!" and of course realized that I had gone into that lane despite the urgent warning. I lay there for some time asking myself why? Why did I not die? How did I not hurt anyone else? Then the same voice or thought came to me just as clearly. *You are not done here. You have more to do.* Have you ever had such an experience?

It took several days before I could begin to unravel what had happened. Two totally unrelated events were actually very related. From

Jim I got the meaning of my life: to learn to love, to learn to be loved, and to make a difference. From the spinout I learned that I had a purpose to fulfill. The work I was doing was helping to make positive changes in organizations and in people's lives. I had much more of this work to do. (I also learned that I had better pay attention when I get information from strange sources, although I have never heard the voice since.)

Your life has meaning and purpose. Every life does. Interestingly, each year I find that more people are asking about the meaning of life. The intent here is just to get you thinking about meaning and purpose, if you're ready for it. Thinking about it can be simple, not complex. However *achieving* meaning and purpose can get pretty complex. I invite you to try on the meaning of life that came to me: that you are here to learn to love, to learn to be loved, and to make a positive difference. Of course you will tweak this to reflect your own insights as you live your unique life. Some would say the meaning of life is to find happiness. Yet happiness is not a state of being, instead it is a result of your actions, behaviors, and experiences. Would you be happy if you loved yourself and had love for others? and others loved you? and you found some way to make a positive difference through something you do?

What do you think is the meaning of your life?

Your *life purpose* is different. You can separate your purpose into two categories: one that you can begin thinking and working on now, and the second, which may not come to you for a long time. The first category of your purpose represents the bigger picture for what you want to do in this world. It is the process of finding the kind of work that you love, the people you want to work with and the organization where you best fit. As you evolve, these choices may change. Here is an example from one of the students who wrote:

> *"As soon as I found myself in this situation, something inside me clicked. I knew, for the first time in my life, I was doing what I was meant to do.*
>
> *Best of all, I couldn't believe I was getting paid to do it."*

This *purpose* also includes the choices you make about finding a person you love and want to spend your life with, the kind of parent you become (should you choose to), and the close friends you attract and are attracted to. Beginning with where you are now, and as you move along, ask yourself these three questions:

- Am I doing something worthwhile for me?
- Am I doing something worthwhile for others?
- Am I doing something worthwhile for my community, my country, or my world?

If you can answer these "sometimes," or even better, "often," then you are likely on your *life purpose* path.

The second category of your *purpose* is much deeper. It is about reaching a point in your life when you know that you are here to make a significant positive difference in some way. It might be through writing or through artistic creation. It could be through contributing in a business venture, or creating and building your own business and taking good care of your employees. Or it could be through volunteering time to work with the homeless or with disadvantaged children, or through coaching children, or even through raising money for charities that help those in greatest need. The possibilities are endless and will be based on the multitude of choices you make throughout your life. Many don't find their deeper *Purpose* until later in life. Many others are not even aware that there is one, so they never look. The intent of this paragraph is simply to plant the thought in your mind. Whether or not you ever think about it is completely up to you.

Do you believe that what you do and how you live your life makes any difference? If this matters to you, then it's worth exploring further. You don't have to go into depth about meaning and purpose to receive great benefits from the process. Just take a look inside yourself. Here is a way to get a good start. (This is best done in your journal, but the left margin is also available for your notes.)

1.   Write down your thoughts on the question: "Is there meaning to your life? What are your beliefs? What matters is what you think and what you are open to considering. This is all you need

to do for now. Let it sit for a while and see how it feels and see what you think.

2.   What is your purpose? What matters to you most? What do you stand for?

3.   If you were told you had one year to live and money were no object, what would you do with your life?

Just writing down your thoughts about these questions will give you a big jump start in sorting out your meaning and purpose, and will provide you considerable direction in many of the choices you make going forward.

Insight #2 – There are few coincidences; things happen for a reason.

We call it synchronicity when things come together and connect in an unexplainable way. The dictionary definition of synchronicity is "the coincidence of events that seem related, but are not obviously caused one by the other." These are events that could never have been predicted, are seemingly unrelated at the time, and yet they guide us along our path as we continuously make choices. Synchronicity also means that we live in a world of possibilities, and that there will be many paths available to you for finding your way to what you want in your life.

I am going to share with you two stories of synchronicity in my life that had dramatic impact on my opportunities and the choices I made. The first was about the choice to pursue a college degree, because I wasn't going to. The second launched me on a career path that I would never have imagined. In both situations I had no idea what was happening and didn't realize the significance until much later. I now am able to look for connections and opportunities in my life.

In high school I was a pretty popular guy but not extraordinary. I was student body vice-president and lettered two years in football. Even though I only had a 2.2 cumulative grade point average when I graduated, this didn't bother me much because in my brain at that time I didn't see myself going to college anyway. I did think about going to the local community college so I could play two more years of football, but I had no clue how rapidly my life was going to change.

In my next to last high school football game and on the last play, I got a concussion and severely separated my shoulder. It wasn't "okay" to be hurt, so I didn't tell anyone. I played the last game and two weeks after this, I experienced my first of many severe shoulder dislocations. My football career was over. Since I couldn't use my right arm, I couldn't work either, so I did enroll in the local community college. In my second month there I had shoulder surgery and, though I didn't know it at the time, an alcoholic surgeon performed what a specialist surgeon two years later told me, was the worst surgery he had ever seen. It had actually compounded my problem. I had my right arm taped to my side for the first four months of my college career, and I am right handed. For the first time in my life I was faced with choices I had never had to make before. All of these events and experiences provided new possibilities I was yet to see.

I couldn't do anything else so I had to learn how to study. Lesson one: I discovered that I was smarter than I had come to believe. Because of my injured shoulder I wasn't able to take my required PE courses and without PE credits I would not have been able to get my Associate Degree and thus would not have been able to transfer to a four year university. The synchronicity continued. It turned out that the teacher who was the head of physical education at my community college had been my teacher when I was in the seventh grade, and one whom I had liked. He took a personal interest in me and bent the rules regarding my PE credits. For three school quarters he put me in a swimming pool with a small group of nine-year-olds who were severely mentally disabled. I received all of my PE credits and I also discovered that I loved working with kids. I worked hard in school, and at the end of two years, my grade point average was 3.8, not bad considering my high school 2.2 GPA I decided to major in education and was accepted at the University of Washington in Seattle. This time I went there with the new belief that I could be successful.

There is no doubt in my mind that if I had not been injured I would not have gone to college. I did not believe that I had the ability. I now believe there is a purpose, and opportunities can and will be presented, and often in unexpected ways.

Here is my second example, a story I heard my mother tell many times during my pre-teen years that also illustrates synchronicity in action. When I was six months old, my mother had placed me on a bed to change my diaper. She turned away to get a fresh diaper, and when she turned back towards me, she saw me putting an open safety pin into my mouth, and I swallowed it. She was in shock. If the pin stuck in my throat I would choke to death. If it went down and punctured pretty much anything, I could have died. She was helpless to do anything. My father wasn't home and there was no car. Panicked, she ran next door for our neighbor. He took us to the local small town hospital, but they had no equipment to deal with this situation, so they sent us to Children's Hospital in Seattle. At that time it was a five-hour drive. My good neighbor drove us there.

According to my mother's story, at the hospital they whisked me into the emergency room and, because I was still alive and surprisingly in a good mood, they were preparing to do whatever was necessary, including surgery. They opened my diaper and, lo and behold there was an open safety pin in the diaper. Somehow it had passed through my system. I survived and had the opportunity to go on with my life. Many years later I found out that the name of my neighbor was Joe May, though I never met him. As you will see, things do happen for a reason.

Here is the second part of this event. While at the University of Washington, I wasn't able to do my student teaching until the last quarter of my senior year and, I was seriously questioning whether I wanted to be a teacher. I had also run out of money and just wanted to get out of school. For my student teaching experience I was sent to a junior high school where the enrollment was approximately eighty percent minority students. I had no experience with people of color and was totally intimidated, wondering how I could possibly have been sent there. On my first day I found that I was one of five young white male student teachers, and we were escorted to a room where a faculty meeting was being held. The five of us sat at a table together feeling very out of place and scared. The principal came to our table and introduced himself. He seemed gruff and intimidating, which didn't help. He asked each of us questions: our names, where we were from, our major, our interests. I was last, and twice he asked me my name and where I was from. I couldn't understand why. Then he started the meeting and began by introducing each of us, telling the faculty everything he had heard each of us say. This time he was playful and funny. It was quite impressive. When he got to me he said, "And this is Bill Maynard. He grew up in Aberdeen (WA). I'm going to tell you a story about Bill." I was totally stunned. How did he know me? "When he was six months old," he said, "Billy swallowed an open safety pin. I was his neighbor and I took him and his mother to Children's Hospital in Seattle." The principal's name was Joe May. Yes, the same Joe May who was my neighbor twenty-one years earlier. Joe got me hired as a teacher in his school, even though the District was not hiring new teachers that year.

I had to ask, how could this have been possible? How could I end up in his school? How could I, who hadn't enjoyed the academic side of school, end up becoming a teacher?

What are you focusing on that you do want?

This launched me on an amazing career. Over the next eleven years I was a junior high science teacher, a junior high vice principal, a high school vice principal and, at the age of thirty-three, became the principal of an incredibly wonderful inner city high school.

So why do I tell you this? I am still humbled by it all. It took me many years to discover the pattern of events, all connected, that led me to this place. There are no coincidences. Just as in my life, things happen for a reason in your life as well.

"Synchronicity"

"Some who are called to adventure choose to go. Others may wrestle for years with fearfulness and denial before they are able to transcend that fear. We tend to deny our destiny because of our insecurity, our dread of ostracism, our anxiety, and our lack of courage to risk what we have. Down deep we know that to cooperate with fate brings great personal power and responsibility. If we engage our destiny, we are yielding to the design of the

Can you identify synchronistic events in your life?

universe, which is speaking through the design of our own person. In the face of refusal, we continue our restlessness, and then, as if from nowhere, comes the guide: something or someone to help us toward the threshold of adventure. This may take the form of voices within or people who guide us to see the way."
—Joseph Jaworski, *Synchronicity: The Inner Path of Leadership*

Look for synchronicity in your life. In the Appendix, Page 219, is located the **Self-Search Experience: Synchronicity in Your Life.** It will be both enlightening and insightful for you; perhaps even shocking as it was for me.

Insight #3 – Focus on what you want in your life, not on what you don't want.

How many times in 24 hours do you complain? What do you complain about?

Whatever you focus your thoughts and energy on is what you will attract. Focus on where you are going, not on where you have been; on the windshield, not the rear view mirror. Focus on what you want to achieve, not on what has failed. Focus on what makes you happy, not on the reasons you are not happy. What you think about is a reflection of what you are focusing on. You move towards and become a part of that which you focus your thoughts and energy on, positive or negative.

Most people think about what they don't want, what they don't like, on what gets in their way, and then they are wondering why this is what shows up over and over again. Complaining is a deeply ingrained thought habit. It keeps you focused on what is wrong, not on what is right, on who is annoying, or why you don't like someone or a certain group of people. Then you complain about all of these things. Not necessarily aloud, but often in your thoughts. Complaining keeps you focused on the negative. Ironically, as you will see, it almost always gets you more of what you don't want.

What do you find yourself focusing on that you don't want?

Hal Urban, a teacher at the University of San Francisco, asks every class, "How many times a day do you complain?" Then he gives the students an assignment to go the next twenty-four hours without complaining about anything, valid or invalid. He also asks them to carry pen and paper and record each time they complain and what they complain about. (This usually results in some groans and complaints about the assignment.) The following day he conducts a debrief session asking how many students out of thirty were able to go twenty-four hours without complaining. The answer is usually zero. They then talk about the number of complaints and what they are about. The outcomes included, "I complain aloud or in my mind a whole lot;" "I learned that I don't really have much to complain about;" and "What I complain about is stupid."

The continuous complaints are a result of what you focus on and the thoughts that result. If you look for what is wrong, you will find it. You will find it in your surroundings, in people around you, and even in those you care most about. Once you start focusing on the negative and then complaining, you set up a pattern that is very difficult to break. You are focusing your energy on what you don't want, and it has a negative affect on how you see and interact with your world and it drains your energy. Negativity begets negativity.

There is a powerful and scientifically supported reason why focusing on what you want is so important. It is directly related to the Law of Attraction which says:

"I attract to my life whatever I give my attention, energy, and focus to, whether positive or negative."
—Michael Losier, Law of Attraction

According to Losier, the Law of Attraction responds to your thoughts, which put out signals to the universe in the form of energy. "If you're complaining, the Law of Attraction will powerfully bring into your life more situations for you to complain about. If you're listening to someone else complain and focusing on that, sympathizing with them, agreeing with them, in that moment you are attracting more situations to your self to complain about."

Your thoughts result in feelings and together these are the sources of both the energy that you produce and the behaviors that result. You have the power to change anything because you are the one who chooses your thoughts and you are the one who feels your feelings.

You Matter:

Your life truly is in your hands. Whatever is happening in your life, you can begin to consciously choose your thoughts, which directly affect your feelings, and you can change your life. You can choose to believe this or you can choose to not believe it. Either choice will determine an outcome for you. When you are feeling down, you can turn it around in an instant by simply standing straight, shoulders and back and smiling. Try it. You can read something fun, put on great music, call someone you care about and thank them. Do something that will change the emotion for you and at this point you will also begin attracting more of the positive energy that you are thinking and feeling. You really do get to choose how you are going to live your life. It is about your thoughts and your feelings and how you react to what happens.

Quantum physics research has shown that our brain cells produce an extraordinarily high frequency of measurable vibrations. Positive thoughts and feelings create a higher frequency of vibrations and negative thoughts and feelings a lower frequency. These vibrations are emitted from each of us into the universe and, following the laws of quantum physics, attract matching vibrations to you, thus the Law of Attraction. (More references are included at the end of the chapter.)

I have a friend named Carl who was a student in my high school when I was principal. He was an outstanding athlete and a very popular kid. I knew him then, but not well. Ten years after he had graduated, I ran into him at a community event. Seeing former students was not unusual for me, and I always enjoyed the connection; and then we would both go our own way. This time, however, it turned into an experience of synchronicity. Over the next several years, Carl and I became very close friends in spite of our age difference, and have continued our friendship over many years now. When I first ran into Carl at a community event he was limping, and I asked about it. He told me he had sprained his ankle playing basketball, but I found later he had just been diagnosed with Multiple Sclerosis, a tragically debilitating disease.

Slowly through the years, Carl has gone from walking with a cane to an electric wheelchair. Now Carl is confined to a bed and is totally immobile except for a little movement of his head. He uses a voice command cell phone and voice command television remote, and he listens to books on CD. When I visited with him recently, I realized that this moment was the best his life will ever be, and the same will be true for him tomorrow and the next day. How does the Law of Attraction and focusing on what you want apply to Carl?

Carl did not attract MS because of negative thoughts and feelings. In fact, even today, Carl is one of the most positive people I have ever met. In life bad things can happen to good people. At first he was in denial. Then he made a choice to get some help from an incredible and wonderful therapist. From this point on Carl made the choice to make the best of his life, knowing that it was going to get increasingly difficult, and he likely would not live a full life. He continuously focused on what he wanted in his life. He has chosen to live the best he can while he is here. He has a bright mind, a big heart, a great sense of humor, and still wants to learn and grow. Carl inspires all of us who "walk" out of his room to question ourselves: Could I be this courageous if I were in that bed?

Carl uses the Law of Attraction by choosing to live his life to the fullest possible in a very difficult situation. Every day and throughout the day he chooses what he thinks about and how he feels.

Here are some things you can do **right now**.

1. Get clear in your mind what you want in your life.
2. Catch yourself complaining or judging, and stop.
3. Focus your energy, thoughts and feelings on what you want. Look for what is good in your life. Collect the evidence.
4. Make a list of things you are grateful for and express your gratitude.
5. Grateful is a great way to live a rich life!

Insight #4 – Expressing appreciation and gratitude can change your life.

Remember the University of San Francisco teacher who gave the assignment on complaining? After discovering the prevalence and effects of all the complaining, there was a second part to the experience. He had them make a list of all the people and things for which they were thankful. He then had them read their list four times in the next twenty-four hours; after lunch, before dinner, before going to bed, and before going to school or work the next morning.

He reported that the students were different when they come in the next day. He said that there were more smiles, bigger smiles, their eyes were open wider and their body language was livelier. "When we focus on what is right instead of what is wrong, life improves considerably."

We all have much for which to be thankful. Expressing gratitude stimulates the Law of Attraction to bring us even more. Gratitude positively changes our lives. It changes the way we feel about ourselves, the way we feel about life, and the way we feel about others. What we focus on not only impacts us personally, positively or negatively, it also impacts the workplace environment. Can you see what a profound impact you can have?

I recently conducted a workshop with a group of hospital professionals who were unhappy with each other. They were a mix of a number of people who had been there for many years and those who were fresh out of college. There is a shift occurring in this particular field from predominantly men to predominantly women. In the past, seniority determined who worked what shifts, vacation times and who received many of the informal benefits. In addition, there had been significant changes in the leadership of the department. A great deal of tension had developed with the advent of these changes and had resulted in polarization and the formation of cliques. People in one group won't talk to those in another group. Certain people eat lunch together and talk about the other people. The newest people do not feel welcomed. You can imagine, much of the talk within each group is rumor, gossip, and hurtful comments about others. They are very committed to the quality of patient care, but it really isn't a very pleasant place to work. One of the newer employees described it as being as uncomfortable as a transfer student to a new high school. I knew it would only be a matter of time before a lot of their best people would start leaving. An unhealthy organization doesn't attract and retain the best talent.

The intent of the workshop was to help them turn this situation around. These were good people who had allowed a bad situation to develop. It was caused by just a few who were able to influence others through negative talk, criticism, and a focus on anything that was wrong. At one point in the workshop participants were asked to write down all of the things they were proud of in the department, things they were grateful for, and anything or anyone they appreciated. Then in groups of five, they put all of their collective responses on flip charts. As they sorted through their long lists the discussion that followed began to take a positive tone.

These two columns of three words were written on two flipcharts:

Gossip	Appreciation
Sarcasm	Gratitude
Hurtful comments	Admiration

They then had a discussion of the impact of these two sets of behavior on both the workplace culture and on individuals within the workplace. It is obvious that gossip, sarcasm, and hurtful comments have a very negative impact on the recipients and on the workplace itself. *It is also true* that this behavior has an even greater negative physiological and emotional impact on those who are thinking and speaking these thoughts. On the other hand, people who frequently engage in the expression of their appreciation, gratitude, and admiration tend to be more energized, happier and more productive.

The same dynamics exist in your personal relationships and your interactions with others. The impact of gossip, sarcasm, and hurtful comments, versus those of appreciation, gratitude and admiration will either bind you or break the relationships.

It continues to amaze me how much of the appreciation we express comes back to us. This week while writing about gratitude and appreciation, I received a wonderful e-mail from Jim (my "what is the purpose of life" friend), an e-mail and a phone call from two former students who had been in the high school where I was principal many years ago, a card from a young lady who was in my Washington State University class ten years ago, and an e-mail from another. It is difficult to express how good all of this can make you feel. Is this the Law of Attraction at work?

Your expressions of gratitude have a binding power. They pull us together. They connect our hearts. On the deepest level they are expressions of love. Recently, Maria talked about her relationship with her mother. She described how their relationship had been difficult throughout high school, but how much it had improved since. The class had been talking about appreciation and gratitude and Maria said she was going to write a letter to her mother that weekend. The following Monday Maria read her letter to the class.

Dear Mom,

In class one day the subject of telling people "I love you" was brought up. I was proud to think that you and I have been telling each other "I love you." However, then the question was asked, "Do you tell them why?" and I realized I don't think I have ever told you why I love you.

I love you because you always made us a priority, even when you were too busy with work and school. You were always there to yell at our teachers if they were doing something wrong. I love you because despite the millions of baby-sitters I made you hire and fire, you never put us in daycare. All my life you have held a full-time job, worked so hard at your marriage (everyone knows men are impossible), and have been a full-time mother. I never felt like I was neglected or ignored because you were at work.

I love you because you were always supportive of all our activities. You or Dad always made it to one of my games. You had no idea what any of the rules were in soccer or basketball, but you learned because you wanted to share it with me. I will always remember you screaming in the bleachers. I always knew you cared.

I love you because you care so much about this family and everyone you come into contact with. You understand my faults but you love me unconditionally. In those couple of years when I was flunking out of school, you still stood by me when Dad and I couldn't even have a civil conversation. You have always tried to sympathize with me and see it from my perspective.

I love you because of all the sacrifices you made for the boys and me to get us where we are today. I love you because you still fix dinner after working a long day. I love you because you always asked us how our day was even if you were too tired to stand. I love you because you would drive out in the snow at three in the morning to get me cold medicine, even though you had to work the next day. I love you because you still send me cold medicine.

Over the last couple of years, you and I have grown into a new relationship… best friends. I know that I can call you when I am having a problem, or just a bad day. This new relationship is priceless to me.

You are the heart and soul of this family and I wouldn't be half the person I am without your love and support over my lifetime. I love you so much because you love me so much.

Love, Maria

After Maria read her letter, there were very few dry eyes in the room. Even the guys were coughing and hemming and hawing. Every one of us felt uplifted and energized. Maria later said her mother called her, saying the letter was the most wonderful gift she had ever received, other than the birth of her children.

Expressing gratitude is an extraordinary and powerful experience for both parties. You will find the **Self-Search Experience** and process in the **Appendix o**n Page 220. Maybe there is a letter you could send someone. Try it and see what happens for you.

Who are you grateful to and what are you thankful for?

Insight #5 – Forgiveness is a liberating experience.

The act of forgiveness is one of the most powerful tools you have to keep your life on the path that is right for you. Forgiving yourself frees you from carrying the guilt that can come from events, relationships, conversations, or actions in the past that went badly. This can be true whether you were "the cause," or whether you felt like "the victim." Not forgiving tends to keep a part of you stuck in the past, continuing to carry around the memory of all that went wrong, beating yourself up with guilt or blaming others. All of the energy it takes to carry this weight could be freed through forgiveness and would then be available to use positively in your life. Freedom comes from forgiveness, and the most important of all is self-forgiveness.

FORGIVENESS:
Free at last

For example, if someone else caused you hurt or pain, your "victim" thoughts tend to be like these: "If she just hadn't …,""Why would he do something like that?""If it weren't for my stupid parents…""My boss is such a jerk…""Why does this always happen to me?""How could this have happened to me?"

Another scenario would be if you caused your own situation. The thoughts then tend to be like these: "Sometimes I am so stupid…""If I had just stopped having more to drink…""I didn't study and I blew it." "If I were as pretty as she is …" or, "I made a big mistake now what do I do?"

In the first situation you tend to place blame on another and avoid exploring what your role might have been, what you might do in the future so you can learn and grow. In the second scenario you tend to blame yourself and beat yourself up. Again, the focus could be so much more productive, as in: How can I learn from this and grow? Try being gentle with yourself and saying, "I'm truly sorry and I forgive myself no matter whose fault it might appear to have been. I'm moving on and I won't make the same mistake."

Both of these situations are fruitless ways of thinking that become patterns of reoccurring negative thoughts and focus resulting in the sense of being the "victim." Underlying "victim" is a feeling of helplessness either created by others, by happenstance, or created by you. Forgiving yourself not only frees you as a victim, it also allows you to take back your personal power and resume your path.

In a situation where you have wronged someone else, there is a tendency to make yourself right by justifying, blaming, and denial. In this case the thoughts might be, "He should never have done that," or "Look what she did; she asked for it." Or, "It's not my fault!" When it is something that you caused, the first step of forgiveness is accepting responsibility for what you did, remedying what happened if you can, and then forgiving yourself.

Remember this: you cannot change anything that happened in the past and you can't change others. They must choose to change. You can only change yourself and what you do from this moment forward.

Forgiveness is about freeing yourself from being a slave to your own fears, guilt, anger, hatred, and even your possible need for revenge. Do you remember reading in the Introduction about Karlo who carried so much guilt after having watched his best friend drown? As big as the breakthrough was for him after writing about and telling his story, the greatest change occurred when he accepted that he too would have drowned had he tried to help Mark. Karlo finally was able to forgive himself, and let go of the guilt and move on with his life.

When your thoughts are of what is wrong with you or what you should or shouldn't have done, or thoughts about your pain, anger, or hatred for someone else, then these thoughts become weights that can prevent you from moving forward. Forgiving yourself will free you up so you can move on and live your best life.

If you have repressed the experience or if feelings of anger, rage, helplessness, or victim remain, one of the best choices you can make is to see a counselor.

Here are important points to know about forgiveness.

- Forgiveness is not about forgetting what happened.
- Forgiveness is not about excusing what somebody did.
- Forgiveness is not necessarily about reconciling.
- Forgiveness is not intended to set others free.

You Matter:

Forgiveness is about freeing yourself from packing through life a load of anger and/or pain.

You will find the **Self-Search Experience** and process for **Forgiveness** in the **Appendix**, Page 221.

Key Takeaways from Insights That Can Shape Your Life

➤ It's not only what you *have* in your life, but also who you *are* that counts.

➤ There is meaning to your life and you will find your life purpose, if you look.

➤ It is no coincidence that you are here doing what you are doing.

➤ The appreciation and gratitude you express will come back to you in wonderfully surprising ways.

➤ Forgiveness means setting yourself free.

Important References and Resources:

Find Your Purpose, Change Your Life: Getting to the Heart of Your Life's Mission, by Carol Adrienne, HarperCollins (March 2001).

Forgive to Live: How Forgiveness Can Save Your Life, by Dr. Dick Tibbits, Thomas Nelson Publishers (2006).

Forgiveness Is A Choice: A Step-By-Step Process For Resolving Anger And Restoring Hope, by Robert Enright, American Psychological Association; (January, 2001).

Focus on the Good Stuff: The Power of Appreciation, by Mike Robbins and Richard Carlson, John Wiley and Sons, (August 2007).

Synchronicity: The Inner Path of Leadership, Joseph Jaworski, Barrett-Koehler, 1996.

The Law of Attraction: The Science of Attracting More of What You

Want and Less of What You Don't, by Michael Losier, Wellness Central, (June, 2007).

The Purpose of Your Life: Finding Your Place in The World Using Synchronicity, Intuition, and Uncommon Sense, by Carol Adrienne and James Redfield, Eagle Brook; (March 1999).

Further resources can be found for the meaning and purpose of life on the website www.themeaningoflife.org.

CHAPTER 3

RAISING YOUR PARENTS

"It's not only children who grow. Parents do too.
As much as we watch to see what our children do with their
lives,
they are watching us to see what we do with ours.
I can't tell my children to reach for the sun.
All I can do is reach for it, myself.
~Joyce Maynard

Understand how your parents influenced who you are, and choose who you want to be in relationship to your parents going forward.

Did you ever think you could help in "raising your parents?" Well that's not likely to happen. However, at this point in your life there is a great deal you can do to enrich a good relationship or to improve a not-so-good relationship with your parents. The information in this chapter will be helpful to you in understanding the place you are now with your parents and where you can go.

First, there are no great step-by-step, how-to manuals for parents and very few opportunities for them to learn when and how to start letting go of their responsible role as your parent and begin moving to a different kind of relationship. Some parents are never able to let go and will continue to treat you as a child, unless *you* choose to bring about a change. Others will let go too soon and expect you to figure everything out on your own, sink or swim, and seem happy that you are moving on. There are still others who are proud and confident and supportive, and believe in you. In a healthy relationship parents will continue to be there for you and may be looking for clues from you about how to change the relationship, how to transition from the "parent-child" relationship to one that is more adult-adult. Some may even find that the relationship evolves into a long-lasting friendship.

Here is another important understanding, and it's about the role of a parent at this stage of your life. As you are growing up, healthy parents see their responsibility as that of helping you to become independent of them, to learn to live on your own. This is critical for you in becoming a healthy adult. Some parents know this; perhaps many don't. You, of course, are an equally important part of this process. At this point in your life, regardless of the role your parents are currently playing, it is important for you to be in the process of learning to live as an independent adult.

Stages of Parent Relationships

Here is a continuum of Stages of Parent Relationships. Each stage is described so that you can determine where you are with one or both of your parents. It is not unusual to be in a different place with different parents, especially in a divorce situation. As you read through the description of each stage jot down your thoughts regarding where you are with each of your parents.

STAGES OF PARENT RELATIONSHIPS

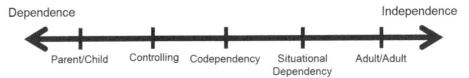

Parent-Child Relationship

This is when the parental mindset is: "I am the parent and you are the child. You do what I say." The parent makes all the decisions, knows all the answers, and continues to try to enforce all of his or her rules. This is a parent who continues to treat you as a child and reinforces your childlike behavior and your dependency on the parent. Often the parent exhibits childish needs of his/her own and is unable to let you go. This is not a healthy relationship for either of you and, ultimately it cannot survive, since a primary goal for any child is to mature into an independent, healthy adult.

Overly Controlling Parent

This is a parent who is authoritative and demands that everything be done his or her way. If you fight, you will lose. Unfortunately such parents are rarely willing to change. This also is an unhealthy relationship.

Jennifer's dad is an example of a controlling parent. She wrote:

> *Everything was a fight between us. On family outings to the beach, I wanted to go play in the water and jump off the dock, while my dad wanted to make it a competition. How far could I swim? How long? Could I perfect my diving? I was constantly being challenged. I could never swim long enough or far enough, and my dive was never perfect. He always made my life harder. I couldn't seem to do anything to please him. Even when I would come home with a 98%, I would be questioned on why it was not 100%. I felt inadequate and unimportant.*

Co-Dependency

Co-dependent behavior tends to be a family pattern and is learned by watching and imitating other family members who display this type of behavior. It takes two people to create a co-dependent relationship. Here is a common example. You are older, out of the house and no longer in a parent-child relationship, yet your mother wants to talk with you a lot. Sometimes she calls several times a day. She expresses her love by telling you everything, problems and all. She wants your attention, your understanding and your sympathy. Sometimes she may want to know your problems, too, so she can connect even more, but most of the time, it is about her. She wants you to be as dependent on her as she is dependent on you. The co-dependent will do anything to hold on to a relationship and avoid the feeling of abandonment. There is usually a lot of manipulation on one or both sides. As an example, if you find yourself text messaging a parent numerous times everyday, this is probably a co-dependent pattern on your part feeding the co-dependent need of the parent. If you are unable or unwilling to set boundaries, the result is that each will feed the co-dependency patterns. *In all three of these stages, it is common that nobody talks about the problems.*

Situational Dependency

This is where it becomes more about you and what you do. For example, you have been on your own for a while and have established your independence, at least in those areas where you want independence: the decisions and choices you make, where you go, who you are with. You may call every few weeks, but less than you used to. You also may tell your parents very little about what's going on. But then you want something—like money, a car, a vacation—or you need something—like a major car repair or new clothes. This time when you call, you have lots to talk about: your classes, your grades, dating someone new. Maybe it takes two or three calls before you ask for what you want. Of course different parents respond in different ways, but the result of this pattern is to move you back toward dependency. To them, most of the time you are independent and then suddenly you are acting dependent. This can be very confusing to a parent.

Adult-Adult Relationship

This is what can result when you and one or both of your parents reach a place where there is mutual respect and trust. You have learned to talk openly and honestly with each other, how to respect differences, and how to avoid arguments and fights. You are able to express that you care about each other and are even able to express your love. They believe in you and are supportive. (This doesn't mean that you need to tell them everything!) This relationship is achieved more as a result of the level of maturity of each of them and of you, than it is related to age.

It is at this stage that the relationship can also begin to evolve into a friendship. This is a very special level of relationship and results in a desire to see each other, to talk with each other and, when necessary, to help each other. There can be much sharing of thoughts, feelings, and stories. There can also be much laughter and, sometimes, moments of shared sadness. It can also be a place of deep love and gratitude. If for whatever reason you are not able to achieve this level with your parents, then you can, through desire and learning, someday achieve this kind of healthy relationship with your children.

Here are some questions to stimulate your thinking about where you are in your relationship with your parents:

- What is the current "stage" of your relationship with each of your parents right now?

- At this point in your life, what do you think your parents' role should be, if any, in helping you to find your way to your independence?

- What do you need to be doing for yourself? What changes in beliefs, in thinking, and/or in how you relate with your parents are important now or will be in the near future?

You are in this life for many good reasons, most of which you will discover along your path. There are many ways you will be able to help yourself in the process of living, and one is in understanding your past and current relationship with your parents, and what you can learn from this. In the process, your new understanding and growth as a human being may even help your parents to a new level of understanding and a new relationship with you.

The Positive and Negative Impact of a Parent

Whatever your relationship was with your parents as you were growing up, positive or negative, it affects you today. How you were raised impacts how you view yourself, what you believe you are capable of, or incapable of, how you relate with others, and even the kind of person you are attracted to or repelled by. Here are a couple of real examples, one negative and one positive.

Eric—"My father was very verbally abusive and had a direct effect on my self-confidence."

Along with the strengths my dad gave me, there are some glaring weaknesses that stick out. He was very verbally abusive, and that had a direct effect on my confidence, especially when I was younger. The verbal abuse dealt mostly with negative thoughts or feelings. My dad typically found a way to bring out the worst situation possible and to implant these negative thoughts in my head. Consequently, years and years of negativity eroded my confidence until recent years. The ability to trust someone is a characteristic that eludes my dad. There are many instances which show his lack of trust for people he doesn't know. For example, he will not let any company change the oil in his car unless he personally talks to or knows the mechanic. Honestly, sometimes I believe that he does not even trust me. He will not let me touch anything of great value to him because he thinks I will break it. I do not think he trusts me with a lot of things even though I feel I have a proven track record in regard to trust. My dad is also a firm believer in playing safe. The result is that I have had a difficult time taking life-changing risks.

These are characteristics I got from my father and are what I have had to deal with since I was born. It is a constant battle in my head not to show or demonstrate these same weaknesses.

We often learn certain behaviors that our parents model for us; good or bad. In this case, as soon as Eric wrote these words down, he realized the source of some things about himself that he wanted to change. Awareness is the first step! Without being aware, you cannot change.

Here is an example of an adult-adult healthy relationship with both parents.

Renasha—"If someone asked me who I most admire in this world, it would be my parents."

To this day I have not met a stronger woman than my mom. When she was a few years old, she was adopted from India by a family in Malaysia, and to this day she does not know who her biological mother and father are. She was not treated well by her adopted family and had to go through many hardships, which I think made her the woman she is today. When she was twenty-one, she went to Sweden to help her stepbrother look after his kids, and there she met my dad. After she married him, they moved to Sri Lanka. She did not know the language or the culture, but she managed to handle living there even though she was not used to it. She told me that many times she was tempted to go back to Sweden, but she wanted my brother and I to grow up knowing our culture, so she was deter-mined to stay on in Sri Lanka. My mom has sacrificed so much for my father, brother and me. We owe a lot to her.

My mom and I are the best of friends. I can tell her any-thing, and I know that she does not judge me. She gives me the encouragement I need to do what I do and advises me on what she thinks is right and wrong. Even though she does this, she never expects me to do what she tells me. She always gives me the freedom to do what I think is right. I think this is a very special quality as a lot of my friends' parents expect them to do what they tell them to.

My dad is my role model. He has been through so much that sometimes it is even hard for me to understand how he has gotten to where he is today. My grandfather died when my dad was three months old, and then my grandmother remarried. When my dad was about nine he was put into a boarding school, even though his home was five minutes away from the school. When he was sixteen, he dropped out of school and started working in a garage washing cars. He collected money, and when he was about twenty went to Malaysia and paid his way through college. He got a degree in mechanical engineering. Later on he went on to Sweden and worked as a mechanic. It amazes me to see what he has accomplished. I am so proud to be his daugh-ter, and I am his biggest fan.

One of the most remarkable things about Renasha's story is not just that she has a solid relationship with her parents, but also how much she knows about the history of each parent. Often parents don't communicate feelings and personal stories with their kids, which is unfortunate, because communicating at a deeper level helps bring us together and gives us a feeling of belonging.

Some Parents Do Weird Things

So why do parents do some of the things they do—things that are hard to understand, and/or are embarrassing, confusing and hurtful? Growing up you probably sometimes wondered why they did what they did. Here are some examples of parent behavior that had a lasting impact on their kids. Some are pretty funny, and some are not.

Shauna—"My greatest fear from grade five to grade twelve was hearing my parents have sex in the room next door."

This may sound silly. Now, I look back and am grateful that my parents share a loving and nurturing relationship and that after thirty+ years they are still passionately in love with each other. However, in the fifth grade when over-hearing your parents having sex in the room next door for the first time, it was a) scary b) yucky and c) bothersome, because you can't sleep and you are afraid your mother is getting hurt. After hearing them a few times, I became agitated, nervous, and too scared to sleep. I never knew when I would hear the yucky sounds especially because I did not know what I was hearing. My parents never talked to me about sex then and they don't talk to me about it now.

I started to develop coping mechanisms. I slept with the radio on always loud. I would put pillows over my ears. I would fall asleep "accidentally" on the couch in front of the TV downstairs. I would start off in my bed and then creep downstairs in the middle of the night, trying to make it upstairs again before my parents awoke. I even slept in the corner of the laundry room on a linoleum floor once or twice. These mechanisms did not calm the anxiety I felt, but they provided a buffer from the sounds. In fifth through eighth grade, this really messed with my school-work because I was always tired and falling asleep in class. How could I explain to my teachers why I was falling asleep in class?

The one time I talked to my mom about the fear I felt and the frustration with overhearing them, she responded the next day by placing earplugs near my radio. Needless to say that response was not what I was looking for or needed.

In the future, I can use my panic and fears as a child to motivate me to talk with my children about relationships and sex to ensure that we have open communication to discuss topics of emotional and seemingly scary significance. I want to sit down with my kids at an early age and tell them the technical aspects of sex, but also explain the emotional significance. I don't want to scare my kids with my relations with my husband. I want to set an example of a healthy relationship.

Bryan—"Growing up, my dad would never say he was proud of me or that he loved me."

He still can't. Deep down I know he does, but he just can't say it. The reason I know this is true is because I am the same way as my dad. I have not been very good at telling people just what they mean to me. I have gotten into a bad habit of letting them know when they have done wrong, but never the opposite.

It took me a long time to tell anyone in my family I love them, and it still is awkward for me at times. It is especially awkward to say it to my father. In fact, I don't think I ever have and, since I can remember, he has never told me he loves me.

I don't want to be so unemotional with my kids like my dad has been with me. He has been a great father and a super role model. I want to have the family values he has exemplified and I want to open up some of my emotions. I think my starting place has to be my father. I don't want to make it too awkward right away, so I thought I would send him a letter to let him know how much he means to me and that I love him.

Bryan wrote a letter to his dad and the result was really interesting. The letter and the response is presented on Page 78.

In the following example, Jennifer's situation was different from Bryan's, but one that happens all too often. Her father was very controlling, and nothing she did was ever good enough to him.

What have your parents done that continues to have an impact on you?

You Matter:

Jennifer —"I feel like everything is a competition with my dad and his authority."

When I was growing up, I remember having to work for everything that I wanted. Even the smallest, most simple things would become a challenge when I had to ask permission from my dad. When I was in the sixth grade, I wanted nothing more than to have my ears pierced, but my dad would not let me. No matter how good I was, what chores I did, he would not let me get them pierced. He would say that he would consider it if I did jobs for him. I had to look up in the encyclopedia the reasons that tribes would pierce their bodies so that I fully understood what it was that I wanted to do. After months of trying to convince him, he still would not let me get them pierced. The next summer while I was in Michigan visiting my family, my aunt took me to get my ears pierced without my mom or dad knowing. I was so excited to have finally gotten my ears pierced. My father made me write up a document saying that I will never get anything else on my body pierced and I will never get a tattoo. That document was typed signed and dated, and is still in a file at home.

Nothing was easy. Everything was a fight between us. On family outings to the beach I wanted to go play in the water and jump off the dock while my dad wanted to make it a competition. How far could I swim? How long? Could I perfect my diving? I was constantly being challenged. I could never swim long enough or far enough, and my dive was never perfect. I just wanted to have fun, splash around, like every kid does.

There are so many of these types of memories that are engraved in my head. Looking back on my childhood, I was most happy when my dad wasn't around. He always made my life harder. It was a competition of who could outdo whom. I never felt smart enough in school. He never congratulated me on a job well done. I wanted recognition from him, in any way, shape, or form. I worked hard to get good grades in high school, but no matter how well I did, it was not good enough. I felt an immense amount of pressure from him to be better. I couldn't seem to do anything to please him. Even when I would come home with a 98% I would be questioned on why it was not 100%. I felt inadequate and unimportant.

Can you hear how much frustration and pain Jennifer has held in for so long as a result of her father's behavior? Why would a parent be so controlling? Why is it that nothing she did was ever good enough? It is quite possible that one or both of his father's parents was also controlling, and/or that he believed he was helping her to be stronger. However, even knowing this would not make it any easier or better for Jennifer. Fortunately, Jennifer gained some emotional distance from her father by going away to school. As she looked back on this relationship and its impact on her, she gained more clarity and was able to begin looking at her new choices. It was really important for her to come to the realization that his behavior and actions were not in any way her fault. This gave her a new beginning.

It isn't just dads who do weird things. There are moms who do so as well.

James—"My mom pushed me to be my very best in anything I ever did."

From homework, to sports, to playing the piano, she wanted me to excel, even if I didn't like doing it—like playing the piano. My mom wanted me to have at least one year of playing a musical instrument and said after one year I could quit. According to my teacher, I was the best and fastest advancing student she had ever taught. That's all my mom needed to hear, and I was pushed even harder. If I didn't get through two new songs a week, she thought I was failing. Even with all this praise from my teacher, once that year was up, I quit.

This was also instilled in me through my homework and sports. My mom gave me a grade point to achieve, or I would be grounded until I brought it up. Now some people say that it is good to set a grade point and try to distill a value in your kids, but the grade point I needed to get was straight As.

She brought her "enthusiasm" to soccer game days also. At times other parents wouldn't stand next to her because of it. So, the way I saw it, if I didn't want to be yelled at, I better be absolutely perfect. The thing that happened, though, was that she instilled this fear of failure in me. I can still hear her in my head telling me what to do and the disappointment in her voice. Now I am my own worst critic. I think I finally really realize how hard I am on myself and I'm ready to change it.

Is there something you would like to change in your relationship with a parent?

These are some of the difficult experiences stemming from parent behavior. The important point is that you likely will take on many of the beliefs and behaviors of your parents, both good and bad, and you will tend to carry many of these beliefs and behaviors into your relationships with others. Should you become a parent, you are also likely to carry some of the behaviors into how you parent your child, unless you decide to change the pattern.

What are some of your positive characteristics, behaviors, and beliefs that came from one or both of your parents? Are there any behaviors that you would like to change? (We will look more closely at these in a Self-Search Experience, Appendix, Page 225.)

Most Parents Did the Best They Could with What They Knew

It is important to know that the majority of parents did the best parenting they knew how to do, given their experience, situation and capabilities. This doesn't change the impact on you; however, it can provide you with some awareness and understanding that can sometimes eliminate a negative judgment of your parent.

One thing we know for sure about life is that it is constantly changing. This is certainly true for your parents in their lives as much as it is for you in yours. It is also important to know that dealing with young adult children can be very challenging for many parents, just as it can be challenging for you dealing with one or both parents. Here's an interesting insight: If you have read even this far in the book and have completed even a few of the Self-Search Experiences, then you already know more about life skills and relationships than your parents were exposed to while raising you! This is part of the problem for parents. Most of their parenting knowledge and skills were learned from their experiences with their parents.

Many parents have read a book or taken a class on how to raise a baby or small child. Fewer have read about raising a teenager (certainly a challenging time of life), and very few have any real knowledge about transitioning from a parent-child relationship to one that is adult to adult.

Moving Forward to a New Relationship

Now that you know the current stage of your relationship with each of your parents (Page 72) and have thought about how you would like the relationship with a parent to be, you have a starting point for moving forward. Change requires a desire on your part, and change could be immediate or might be a process developing over several years; or the relationship may never change, regardless of what you do. If you have the desire, the result of achieving a healthy relationship with your parents is worth the effort for them and for you. A solid and healthy relationship with your parents can be greatly beneficial, but is definitely not the only gateway to an independent and fulfilling life. However, you can only change your part of the relationship. Your parents are in control of what they do, and if they are not willing, no change will occur. If what you do doesn't work it's important for you to move ahead with your first responsibility, which is to fully develop yourself as an independent, healthy, happy person.

If you have a parent who is unable to let go (parent-child), or a controlling parent, or are in a co-dependent relationship with a parent, chances are you have experienced some heavy emotional impact of which you may not even be aware. One of the best and smartest things you can do in this situation is to let a trained and experienced counselor help you through this. Many counselors and therapists have a great deal of experience with these issues, and the good news is that it doesn't have to take a long time to resolve issues and move on. The important point is that you do not have to live your life with heavy emotional baggage weighing you down. It is unfortunate that some people avoid counseling because they think there is a stigma of some kind attached to seeking help. The truth is, seeking counseling is a healthy choice made by one who sees a better way to be in the world and wants to live a healthy life. In actuality, it does not mean that you are flawed, and there is no stigma to seeking the help and support of a professional counselor. We all will run into things in life that a little help can get us through.

Here are some good examples from those who were able to move forward. Jennifer (with the controlling father) began with journaling the situation as her Self-Search Experience. She then generated a list; "How I am now feeling," which was originally two pages long. As you read some of her feelings, can you see how she got to her core, genuine hurt and needs? Jennifer was able to boil down a big, confusing set of feelings and interactions and come to a clarity that was quite helpful and profound for her.

My Father

I need to see and feel love to know it's there.
I feel like I can't talk to him.
He walks away when I tell him how I feel.
He tells me that he is ignoring me.
He tells me that he will forget and I have to remind him
to be considerate of my feelings.
He will not respond.
He never congratulated me, never said I love you.
I feel rejected, unimportant, unwanted.

When Jennifer completed the process, she realized that she would have to be the one in charge of the relationship, because she would not be able to change her father's behavior. She knew that she wanted to get past the hurt and the feeling that something was wrong with her, so she decided to work with a counselor and took her writing to the first counseling session. With the relief of letting go of what wasn't going to be in the relationship with her father, and with some new knowledge and skills, she started a whole new and healthy path in her life. It remained to be seen whether her father would someday change (which is not likely). She on the other hand, was able to move on without him and leave the pain behind.

Remember Bryan (Page 79), who discovered that he had become just like his father and was unable to express his emotions or feelings? He loved his dad and wanted a closer relationship with him, and he wanted to change his own negative pattern in order to have a better relationship with his girlfriend (who is now his wife). For his Self-Search Experience he wrote this letter to his dad and followed it with a telephone conversation. Bryan then wrote about the outcome of this conversation.

> *Dear Dad,*
>
> *For my project, I decided to extend thanks to those who have had a significant impact in my life. I have not been good at letting people know that I appreciate them. You are the first person I thought of who I need to thank. There are many things you have done throughout my life that I am grateful for. You have been a great role model for a true family man. It meant a lot to me that you were at almost every sporting event or other extracurricular activity I participated in. I was grateful to see your excitement for my achievements in athletics, but I was even more appreciative of your support when my athletic career came to an end. There are dads we both know who push hard for their children to continue doing things they don't want to do, but not my dad. You supported my decision all the way, and that made it feel so much easier. Thank you for that. It is these types of acts that make me appreciate having you as a role model and father. I hope that one day my children will have a dad like you.*
>
> *I can't imagine what it would be like right now to be without a father, especially a father who I love very much. I am glad that I will hopefully have many years to spend in your company. I just wanted to let you know that I love you and appreciate the many wonderful things that you have*

done for our family. They have had a significant impact on my life. I love you.

Bryan

Did you notice that Bryan only expressed gratitude and love and did not express criticism in his letter? Here is what Bryan wrote about the outcome of his experience. Then you will get to see why this process works so well.

My personal project was amazing to me. The first thing I did was to write my dad a letter. I was really nervous about mailing it, but I did. After mailing it, I felt really good. I know I was not supposed to have any expectations, but sometimes you just can't help it. The days went on and I heard nothing. I kept thinking my dad would call or something when he got it. One day, I called my sister to check in on her, and she told me my dad called her when he got my letter. He called her to say that she was demoted from number one to number two. My dad likes to hide his emotions behind humor, so I think this was a way for him to avoid his feelings. It was not until about a week later that I heard from my parents. My dad said "thanks for the letter, it was nice" in a tone of voice that felt really uncomfortable to him. When the conversation on the phone ended, there was an extremely long pause. I could hear through the silence he wanted to say he loved me, but he just couldn't. I was going to just say it to him, but I waited a little too long, so he said, "all right talk to you later."

When I went home, my dad and I talked about the letter and he told me how much it affected him. When we were done, he hugged me and told me he loved me. It was a great day.

Why the Process Works

Expressing yourself in writing is a very powerful means for beginning to resolve issues and for improving a relationship. Several things happen. As in the example of Jennifer, it helps you to get clear about what is really going on and narrow it down so it becomes manageable. Writing a letter specifically to a parent is also very powerful. First, it is almost always a new and surprising experience for the parent and really gets their attention. Sometimes it's a shock and they think something serious is wrong, like you're seriously ill or dropping out of school. Then they will read it again and think about what you are saying. They will be able to process their thoughts, which will make it much easier for them when you are ready to have a conversation. The preparation you do prior to writing the letter is really important, and is spelled out in the Appendix, Self-Search Experience: Changing A Difficult Relationship With A Parent (Page 225). This process works exceptionally well in dealing with issues and for improving the relationship with parents.

Overcoming The Negative Impact of a Negative Parent

Abuse comes in many unfortunate forms: physical or emotional abuse, demeaning comments, anger, manipulation, being emotionally unavailable, abandonment, an alcoholic or drug addicted parent, always making you wrong and/or making you feel dumb, making you feel like you are never going to be good enough, overly controlling, caustic, sarcastic, and more. Any of these behaviors can shatter your self-esteem and can have a long lasting negative affect on you. However, it doesn't have to be this way. As is the message of this book, you can change how things are for you and you can have a healthy life.

Unfortunately, many child victims of the abusive behavior of a parent try to repress, forget, ignore, or pretend it didn't happen. You can hide the pain for a while, even years, but it doesn't go away and will likely surface in some unhealthy form. So what can you do?

First of all, it is vitally important that you know **it was not your fault!** You are responsible for *your* behavior, but you are not responsible for the parent's behavior. This was your parent's behavior, even though they likely blamed someone else, including you.

How often have you heard, "I will never be like my parent in this way!" Most parents did not become a husband/wife or parent with the intention of being abusive. Many, perhaps the majority, are behaving in the same way they were treated as children by one or both of their parents. A child who was frequently physically hit is far more likely to become a parent who hits his or her child. A child with alcoholic parents has a higher probability of becoming an alcoholic. This is another good reason why it is important to break the pattern and get on a path that is healthy for you.

Second, don't try to change your parent's negative behavior, because you can't. Your parent could change the behavior with professional help, but only if the desire is sincere, and, sadly, in many cases the parent is not capable of doing any better.

Third—and this is so important—get professional help. There are many counselors and therapists available who are really good at this. It is an act of courage on your part, not a weakness. It takes far less time and effort to turn your life around and onto a positive path than it took for you to reach this point.

There is one more thing you can do in the meantime and a way to get started. In Chapter 2 there is a piece about "Forgiveness" (Page 66). **No**, this is not about forgiving your parent. You may want to someday, but that is your choice and remains to be seen. This is about you! If you feel any guilt, shame, remorse, have been hiding, pretending or repressing pain or hurt, or have felt that you are obligated to your parent, then you could benefit significantly by doing a *self-forgiveness*. In the Appendix there is A Self-Search Experience: Forgiveness of Self (Page 230).

Dealing With An Abusive Parent

Being in a relationship with a parent who is either physically or emotionally abusive is a harmful, frightening experience for a child. Obviously in younger years it is hardly possible for the child to exert any control or have the ability to change the parent but must, rather, learn to adapt and try to avoid the parent. Unfortunately for many, the behavior of the parent continues into young adulthood and even later in life. It can be a very difficult pattern to break because it becomes so deeply ingrained in the relationship that it begins to feel normal. Demoralizing and humiliating as these experiences can be, they can continue as long as the parent is alive, unless *you* decide to stop it. The best thing for you to do at this point is to separate yourself from the parent, to avoid contact and to get professional help.

How the Relationship Could Be

Regardless of what happened to your relationship with your parents when you were in middle school or high school (the time when the relationship is usually most strained), many find the relationship greatly improves from mid-college life on. You see things differently, they see you differently, and there is often a mutual desire for a healthy relationship. Here are examples of how some were able to move in this direction.

Liz began with her "desired state" of her relationship with her father as a foundation and then wrote him a letter. Later she and her father got together and talked about their relationship. He was deeply moved by the letter and they have since made great strides in becoming good friends.

Liz—" I want to be best friends with my dad."

Desired State of my dad and my relationship:

- *I want us to talk without me feeling awkward.*
- *I want us to hang out, go to lunch or dinner, just me and him.*
- *I want to connect with him on a deeper level.*
- *I want him to know I am proud of him, and I hope my future husband has many of his qualities.*
- *I want us to laugh together.*
- *I want to be one of the things in his life he is most proud of.*

Dear Dad,

First of all, I want you to know I love you. There is nothing I want more in my life than to make you and mom proud. I feel so blessed to have been given such amazing parents;

you have raised three bright, intelligent children. Ever since I was little I can remember just adoring the time we spent together. Some of my favorite childhood memories are of us lying on my bed while you read me stories. I loved watching your lips move as you would read me stories and how you would talk to me about what lesson the fable was teaching me. All I wanted to do when I was little was be with you.

I know when I was in high school we didn't always see eye to eye. I know I was mad at you a lot of the time. I now understand that this was a difficult time for you, too. I have always wanted us to have a better relationship. One where we could hang out more and plan dates, just for us two. I know that I seem to never be around, even when I am at home, but I want you to know that I want us to have a deeper connection. Things still haven't changed since I was little; I still love being with you.

I love you. I have never wanted anything more than to be the one thing in your life you are most proud of. You are an amazing person and I am so blessed to have you as my dad. You are loyal, you are strong, you are hard-working, and you are giving. I am proud to be your daughter and the older I get, the more of you I see in me. You have given me so much more than I could have ever asked for. You are one of my greatest role models, and you have shown me the right way to live my life. Most of all dad, I want you to know that I would be very, very blessed to have a husband who has all the qualities and values you do. You really are an extraordinary man. Thank you for being one of the greatest blessings in my life. You mean more to me than I could ever tell you, and I love you with all my heart.

Love, Liz

What Would You Like to Say to One or Both of Your Parents?

By now you have likely noticed how many times letters have come into play in different situations where someone wanted to work out an issue with a parent. They actually have an almost magical impact on people, far more personal and appreciated than an email. It takes time and thought, and the process of writing it out, putting into an envelope and mailing it. The recipient holds it in his or her hand, opens it, and is often totally and emotionally surprised by the heartfelt message inside. The effort it takes to write a letter lets the reader know he or she is worth it. The psychological impact of this kind of letter can be transformative and those who have done this have been very happy with the outcome.

Kenneth provides us with a good example. He has a father who he really cares about but who has always been emotionally unavailable. He decided he wanted to change his relationship with his dad.

Kenneth—"I now want my dad and I to be close forever."

Growing up, everything was always my dad's way and on his terms. I'm not saying that is a bad thing. I don't think I turned out that bad. There have only been two times in my life where I have seen the soft side of him. There are a lot of things I have never told him, and I never thought I would. We just never had the type of relationship that warranted emotional subjects. He has been the most important person in my life and I want us to be close forever. Here is my letter to my dad.

Dear Dad,

I know that you will find it odd, me sending you a letter from out of the blue. There are just some things that can't be said through an email or over the phone. The past month has been a real changing time for me. It has been a time where I have found out a lot about myself, and my relationships with other people. From this, I have discovered many things that I have always wished to tell you but never had the nerve or opportunity to. This is the reason for this letter.

First of all I would like to thank you for everything that you've ever done for me. It is hard to express in words how

What are your good memories of growing up? What are you grateful for?

much all of this means to me. Dad, I just want you to know that it means a lot.

Secondly, there are a couple of events that happened in the past that we never really talked about. I need to tell you that these two events made me realize just how much you really do care about me. Remember when you and I drove up to WSU? It was the first time that I had ever left home for an extended amount of time. I remember you helping me move all of my stuff in and you even made my bed because mom told you to make sure my bed was made before you left. The last thing that happened before you left took place right before you drove home. With tears swelling in my eyes you told me, "Now you know why I coached all your teams, and spent as much time with you as I could. I'm very proud of you." It is now Dad, over three years later that I realize just what those words meant.

The second event wasn't such a pleasant experience but I think we grew a lot closer because of it. Remember the last real fight we had, the one where we almost threw punches at each other? I don't really even remember what sparked the fight. I do remember what happened the next day when I was about to go back to WSU. Right before I left, you came up to me, gave me a big hug, and said, "I'm sorry about what happened last night, that won't happen again. I love you and I am very proud of you." That hasn't happened again Dad, and it never will. After that experience I felt like we truly understood each other and we have gotten along awesomely ever since.

When I walk down that aisle, diploma in hand, I will be looking for you. I just hope that at the end of all this, you will be as proud of me as I am of you. I can't wait to see you in a few weeks. I love you, Dad.

Kenneth

Several days later, Kenneth wrote about his follow up experience with his dad.

> *My dad got his letter two days ago. It was a very positive response to say the least. I'm glad that I got some of that off my chest. My dad is fairly old, and I'm glad that I said what I said while I still had the chance. I have enclosed what my dad wrote back to me.*
>
> ***E-mail from my dad:***
>
> *Kenneth:*
>
> *I got your letter today. I'm e-mailing you because I couldn't talk about it without getting all choked up. The day I left you in Pullman was the hardest thing I have ever had to do. It was necessary, but it was a bitch. All the way home, I thought about all the practices and all the ballgames, all the duck hunts, and all the track meets. I didn't remember one mile of the trip home. Thanks for the letter. It was the best letter I ever received. I love you, Dad*

The examples of letters included here all had very positive outcomes for the writers. It is important for you to know that it isn't always like this. There is the possibility (the risk) that you get a negative response or none at all. These are rare because most who would send such a letter to a parent are pretty aware of their parents' abilities and readiness to hear, and wouldn't send it if they thought it would be a negative result. If this should happen to you, it is *really* important that you:

- Don't make up stories in your mind as to why there was no response, or a negative response, such as "Oh, no," "What if …" "She probably didn't have time…" etc.

- Don't blame yourself, such as: "I must have said it wrong."

- Know that it is not about you; it is your parent's "stuff."

- Be gentle with yourself relative to whatever thoughts and emotions you may have.

- Accept what is. Move on, and don't look back.

You Matter:

The process of moving toward your independence is healthy and normal. Through this process you may have an opportunity to develop a stronger, healthy relationship with one or both parents. Here is one great way to move forward. Write them a letter and express your *gratitude*.

Focus on the good memories and how you want the relationship to be. Avoid the tendency to focus on unpleasant experiences. This can be a most beneficial, rewarding and loving experience, both for them and for you. I want to close the chapter with a letter Karla wrote to her mother. Like many of us, their relationship was strained at times in her earlier school years, and now Karla wanted to take the relationship into a new direction.

Karla—"Dear mom, you are truly my best friend"

Dear Mom,

I am writing this letter to let you know how much you mean to me, and the reason that I love and care about you so much. There are so many ways that you have helped me grow and mature as a woman. You have instilled many wonderful qualities in me. So, for every time I told you that I didn't want to be like you when I grew up, I have said twice as many times how much I want to be the same kind of parent you are.

The time and energy you put into my life as a child to make sure that I had everything that I needed and could ever want is something that I have never thanked you for. Without your determination to raise me as a truly genuine human being, I wouldn't be half the person I am today. You showed me how to love and what it takes to have a wonderful relationship with other people. You always made sure I was a strong person always standing up for what I know is right.

You were always there to support me when I needed it and in some way always knew when to let me learn from my own failures. You have supported me in everything I have done, even though you didn't always agree with the way I think. You have taught me to forgive and forget, and move past the imperfections that we find in people because everyone has something good to offer. You are always willing to put other people before yourself. This one thing I will always admire about you.

I love the freedom you have given me in life, to let me grow and develop my own sense of individuality. You never told me that I was doing something completely wrong. You have always just suggested an alternate way of doing it. I can never thank you enough for letting me be myself in every sense of the word. You never tried to change me.

The one thing that I love about you most is letting me make my own decisions even if they weren't the ones you would have made for me. In closing, I want you to know that even though I may not show it, you are truly my best friend and always will be. No one could ever replace the friendship that we have formed over the last 21 years, through all the ups and downs. I never could have asked for a better mother and best friend.

Forever and Always, Karla

It is possible to develop a healthy relationship with one or both parents. Expressing your gratitude is a great way to start. In the Appendix is the **Self-Search Experience for Building a Good Relationship with Your Parents** (Page 230).

Key Takeaways from Raising Your Parents

> ➤ Most parents did the best they knew how at the time.

> ➤ Your relationship with your parents impacts how you relate with others.

> ➤ You can overcome the impact of negative parent behavior.

> ➤ It is true that we tend to unconsciously adopt some of their negative behaviors even when we say, "I will never be like my parent!"

- Getting professional help in addressing serious issues is a very smart thing to do.

- You can choose to change your way of seeing and doing things.

- You cannot change your parents, but you can show them the way.

- Becoming friends with one or both of your parents can be a wonderful life experience. However it may take time and, sadly, sometimes it doesn't happen.

- Your responsibility to yourself is to become an emotionally healthy, independent adult.

Important References and Resources:

A book for your parents:

Don't Bite Your Tongue: How to Foster Rewarding Relationships with your Adult Children, Ruth Nemzoff and Rosalind Chait Banett, 2008, New York: Palgrave Macmillan.

Books for you:

How to Manage Your Mother: Understanding the Most Difficult, Complicated, and Fascinating Relationship in Your Life, Alyce Faye Clees and Brian Bates, 2000, New York: ReganBooks.

Embracing Your Father: How to Build the Relationship You Always Wanted with Your Dad, Linda Nielson, 2004, New York: McGraw-Hill.

Websites on emotional abuse:

http://www.wikihow.com/Deal-With-Emotional-Abuse-from-Your-Parents

CHAPTER 4

BEING IN LOVE AND BREAKING UP

"I was never one to patiently pick up broken
fragments and glue them together again and tell
myself that the mended whole was as good as new.
What is broken is broken—and I'd rather
remember it as it was at its best than mend it
and see the broken places as long as I lived.
Margaret Mitchell

What causes breakups? How do you predict a breakup? How to do you survive a breakup, and even possibly end it with empathy?

Why All The Breakups?

The single most discussed topic in our class was that of being in a relationship and the breakup that often followed. Almost everyone had experienced one or more breakups, and agreed that the emotional impact and pain of breaking up are significant. It is obvious that men and women see and do things differently, and the same is true in breakups. We each experience the pain of a breakup in our own unique way. How you deal with that pain can have a significant impact on how you view relationships going forward. Do you risk falling in love again? Have you learned from the breakup so you enter a new relationship with less emotional baggage? Do you keep picking the wrong person? Did you learn enough to create a healthier relationship the next time?

Jot your thoughts and feelings in the margin.

As you look at what others have written about their experiences, be sure to notice what the opposite sex is telling you. For example, guys tend to understand how guys experience a breakup and women tend to understand how women experience a breakup. If you're a guy, read about what the women are writing as it will help you to learn a great deal more about being with a woman. And the same for women: read what the guys are saying and see what you can learn from them. How much can you relate to what they experienced? What can you learn from these experiences that will help you avoid another breakup.

Are Breakups Predictable?

Believe it or not, most breakups are predictable. I'm not talking about casual dating where you're just wanting to have a good time. I'm referring to a relationship, where one or both think, "this might be the person I'll spend my life with." There is the rush of feelings and the physical/sexual/emotional attraction. Talking for hours. Wanting to spend every moment together. Wanting these feelings to last forever. As good as this is, these are also the relationships in which breakups can be predictable. John Gottman, author of *The Seven Principles For Making A Marriage Work*, states that, in his research, after a five-minute interview with a couple, his researchers can predict with over ninety percent accuracy whether the marriage will fail.

The good news is, if breakups are predictable, then there must be signs that, if recognized, make the situation preventable.

Signs That Something Is Broken

How many of these "signs" were there in your relationship?

So what are the signs that it's not going to work? Think of a serious relationship as a committed partnership. Each partner is responsible to himself/herself and responsible to her/his partner for what happens in the relationship. Think of it as a three-legged stool; you, your partner, and the relationship. Each partner contributes to the success or lack of success of the relationship.

The following is a list of signs or indicators of problems ahead for the relationship. It will not usually be only one of these factors that indicate the likelihood of a breakup, but rather a combination of two or more.

Here are the signs that something is significantly wrong:

Has someone you thought was "the one" broken up with you? What was that like?

1. The relationship started off wonderfully, but now your thoughts are about being out of the relationship, or you are thinking of someone else.

2. She/he went through a breakup within three to six months of getting into a relationship with you.

3. He wants to talk about the future and you do not, or you try to postpone or avoid this conversation. (or the other way around)

4. The two of you have significantly different values around religion, money, sex, marriage, or having a family, and are not addressing these differences.

5. You have chosen a partner who is very similar to others in your past relationships. You may not see this pattern until now.

6. One or both of you have been unfaithful in one or more past relationships.

7. There are trust issues that have not been addressed.

8. You have different views on what commitment means.

9. You find yourself giving up being you in order to be loved by your partner.

10. You've been together for quite a while but still don't know who your partner really is.

11. You seem to argue and fight all the time.

12. It's a long-distance relationship. They are difficult to sustain.

13. Your partner insists that almost everything be done her/his way.

14. If your parents are divorced, the probability of you going through a breakup or divorce increases.

If you find yourself in any of these circumstances, don't panic. Also, don't ignore them or pretend it isn't happening. Don't go into denial and convince yourself that it's not true. If there are serious issues and you both want the relationship to work, then both of you must focus on the challenges and begin working them through. Your focus is not on who is right or wrong. The focus is on the relationship. With the relationship as the focus, you will learn a great deal about your partner and what it will take to make the relationship successful. If you get stuck, or don't know what to do, get professional help. Getting help does not mean that there is something wrong with either of you. It is absolutely the wise thing to do. Trying to deal with serious issues by yourself hinders you because you miss out on the perspectives of others and the choices that emerge from a broader view.

Predicable Patterns of Behavior

Patterns of behavior are also a very good predictor of a relationship break up. A behavior pattern is a combination of thoughts, or of behaviors that keep getting repeated. For example, "He is *sooo* cute AND athletic. I think he could be the one." Then three dates later you are bored with him, just like the others. This may be a pattern for you. Or, "I find myself staring at her all the time. My heart starts pounding and I get sweaty. I want to talk to her, but I just can't. Why does this keep happening?" Or, "Why does she keep picking guys who are dating someone else?" Here is one more example. "In every serious relationship I've been in, after a while we end up fighting; and I know that I'm the one who usually starts them."

The above dialogues show you that the type of person you are attracted to can become a pattern. Ask yourself, who do I find myself attracted to? Is it someone who is physically attractive? Someone who has status on campus (or in sorority or fraternity)? Someone I think is popular or who is an athlete? Some are even attracted to another who is emotionally unavailable. Sometimes it is consistently a sexual attraction that keeps drawing you. Sometimes it is someone who you think you don't deserve. There are myriad reasons and patterns of repetitive behavior.

The reality is that if you have been in several relationship breakups, it is quite possible that you are dealing with a pattern. We often pick up negative patterns from our parents, which make them even more difficult to recognize. Frequently, close friends see the patterns but often are afraid to say anything. If you are not *aware* of the pattern you won't be able to change it, and unless you address the pattern you will likely do it again and again.

The good news is, once you see a pattern, you can choose to change it. The Self-Search Experiences in the Appendix will also help you discover whether or not you have a pattern that would be important to look at in order to avoid repeating your same experience in a new relationship.

Four Signs to Get Out Now!

An abusive relationship is terminal! It doesn't matter whether the abuse is physical, emotional, or the use of abusive or demeaning language. It is all harmful and deeply hurtful. In an abusive relationship, it is the intent of one person to control the other, usually through destroying the self-esteem of the other. This is not the behavior of a true partner. Abusers and manipulators usually get very good at it, and can have you feeling confused and even make you think everything is your fault. In the following "signs" I have used "he" as there is far more evidence of males abusing females, but abuse can happen in either gender.

If any of these experiences happen in your relationship, then GET OUT NOW! He will make excuses. You will make excuses for him. You will convince yourself that he's going to change. You may even get to the point where you think the behavior is normal. It isn't. Both of you must get professional help, and if he is not willing, then get out and get help.

- There has been **even one** act of physical abuse; slapping, hitting, pushing, shaking, or even threatening to do any of these.
- He has become verbally and emotionally abusive through the use of sarcasm, demeaning comments, shouting, and he might start doing this in front of his friends.
- He slowly isolates you from your friends, your family, and social situations, and becomes domineering and controlling.
- He wants to know where you are all the time and frequently calls and checks.

If any of these happen to you, even once, get out! Get help from a trusted friend, a parent, or a counselor. Do not try to deal with this by yourself. An abusive person is not your friend. He will try to convince you that he is your friend, that he didn't mean it, that it won't happen again, that he is sorry, and so on. If he is truly sorry and he can see he has an anger problem, then he will be willing to see a counselor. If he really does want to make the relationship succeed, he will have the courage to accept help working through his underlying issues. If he is willing to do this, then there can be hope for the relationship, otherwise all of his promises are just an attempt to further manipulate you and keep you under his thumb.

Breakup Experiences: Anyone You Know?

Heidi—"I clung to him to boost my self-esteem."

Reflecting back on my first and only real relationship, I think of so many things that were truly wonderful about it. I honestly loved this person with all my heart and soul and would probably have given up anything just to be with him, and in many ways I did. It is hard for me to believe that all the good feelings I once felt will return with another person at another time, but I trust that I will find that love again. My current obstacle though, is to let go of all the pain and anger that I seem to be holding onto so that I can move forward in life. After nearly two years, the very thought of my ex-boyfriend still makes my stomach turn upside down.

What were the early signs?

He and I dated for over three years on and off. I fell in love with him because I felt he really saw and understood the "real" me. There was chemistry between us that I can't describe and I put all my faith into following my heart. Looking back I now realize that in the beginning of our relationship, I clung to him to boost my self-esteem and expected him to meet all my needs. This pushed him away and he broke up with me. This devastated me beyond belief, and I became depressed. I realized that I had deserted all my friends for him and, in return, was abandoned when I really needed a friend. He immediately began dating other girls and "exploring his options," which thrust me into an even deeper depression where I couldn't eat and I cried myself to sleep night after night. Throughout our break-up, he continued calling me to tell me how much he loved me. We eventually got back together, but he had broken my trust, and I promised myself that I would not lose sight of my friends or myself from this point on.

Our rocky relationship continued, and, in the last year or so, I began having doubts about his faithfulness. We were at different colleges and, whenever I spoke to him or visited him, I had an awful gut feeling that something wasn't right. My mind was screaming that he was cheating on me, but my heart couldn't let go. He had become such a large part of my life. I wasn't quite sure who I would be without him. I began searching for any proof of infidelity. I needed something solid that would push me to completely let go and end the relationship, and I eventually found it.

Ending that relationship was the best thing I could have done for myself, and I regret not ending it the first time we broke up. However, I am proud that I was able to walk away when I did.

Moving forward will be my biggest challenge. I've decided that there are a few things I need to do whenever I am reminded of him. The first is to try to not speak or think badly of him because the more I do, the more I am bound to spend time dwelling on the past instead of focusing on the present. The second is to truly accept that the relationship I had with him is completely over. There will be other relationships if I open up my heart. If I continue looking at every guy as another him then I will be unable to move on. The third is to allow myself to own my feelings. Instead of holding my feelings in, I will commit myself to express those feelings when they start to bother me. By letting those emotions out, I will be setting them free. The fourth is to trust again. Every relationship involves risk, but I can't allow a bad experience to keep me from living my life to the fullest.

I already feel as though I've lifted a heavy weight off myself that I have been unconsciously hanging onto. Sitting down and writing out my feelings allowed me to recognize lingering pain and anger. I've grown extremely tired of carrying that load around with me. I am happy with myself and who I have become over these past few years. I have accomplished many things on my own two feet with no one holding my hand, and because of this I should be thankful for the lessons my relationship taught me.

Heidi's experience is actually quite common. Do you recognize some of the following: "hanging onto pain and anger," "I clung to him to boost my self-esteem," "I expected him to meet all my needs." Here is a big sign that something is wrong. "Throughout the breakup he continued calling me to tell me how much he loved me, even though he was known to be seeing others." Notice that even though he was seeing others, he was simultaneously trying to hang onto Heidi. This is very manipulative and controlling behavior on his part.

Heidi then began doing all the right things. "I am proud that I was able to walk away when I did." She faced the challenge of moving forward with her life. In her own words, "first, try not to speak badly of him (it would keep her stuck), second, truly accepting that the relationship is over, and third, allow myself to own my feelings." If you were to re-read the last two paragraphs and then the first two, you can see the huge shift Heidi made in how she views herself and the positive energy she has in focusing on her future.

Ken—"I trusted her and she cheated on me."

From July until the beginning of September, I lived with her and her mother at their house. Her mother was not a good influence on our relationship and, whenever she was around, I was afraid to even hold her hand. Needless to say, we fought a lot, and we both said some things that we regret. It wasn't good, I admit that, but it wasn't anything that I thought was relationship threatening.

What could Ken have done differently?

In September she left for her job in Phoenix, and the day she left I felt that everything was fine. We both cried, told each other we loved each other, and she left. From my perspective that was the last time I saw the girl I fell in love with. As soon as she got down there she started hanging out with people she'd met, and with a particular guy that she knew from high school. I trusted her, I trusted her like no other girl. However, out of the blue she said that things weren't working. So we broke up about four weeks ago. I had a feeling it was because of this guy but she would not say. So for the past four weeks I had always felt that we were going to get back together. Finally, two days ago she told me the rest of the story; that she's been with this guy for several weeks, and that we were never going to get back together. I was hurt, and I'm still hurting.

From my perspective she has lied to me to save my feelings, but at the same time she's held onto me for a long time for basically no reason, and I guess that's why I'm really pissed. I told her that we couldn't be friends. I can't be friends with someone I don't trust, and I don't think I'll ever be able to trust her again. Is that wrong of me? Should I be able to just forget everything that she's put me through and grin and bear it? I don't know, man; this whole situation is messed up. I moved to Phoenix for that girl. I took the job I did for that girl so I could be close to her. I did everything I knew how in order to somehow make it work for the long run. In the end my best wasn't good enough. How can that just disappear? And where do I go from here? I'm putting my heart and soul into my job, but there is a void in my heart that I don't know how to fill.

In talking it through with Ken, and exploring different perspectives, he was able to see what happened and why. He thought he was in love, but in reality, he didn't really know her. She saw him as fun, exciting, and a possible long-term relationship, until she ran into an old boyfriend and her feelings for him were stirred up again.

Here are a couple things to remember:

-What one thinks and believes about the relationship is not necessarily what the other thinks and believes.
-You need to discover and talk about the your differences in beliefs.

You Matter:

(You will find much more about this in **Chapter 7, Making Your Relationship Work.**)

Mathew—"We did the long-distance thing, not knowing where we were going."

I decided I would like to write about what happened to me this weekend. On Saturday night, my girlfriend of eight months and I decided to break up. I always told myself that I would never do a long-distance relationship, but I couldn't let go after this past summer. I lived in San Diego this summer and had the time of my life. I had an awesome internship and an awesome girl to spend the days with. We started dating, not knowing what we were going to do when I had to return to school in August. We just never talked about what we were going to do and didn't want to spend time worrying about it. I believe that is where our problems started.

So, for the past five months, we did the long-distance thing. We would talk on the phone every day like three times. Right before Christmas she called me at home and told me she got drunk and kissed some dude in Mexico the night before. I was mad at first but then realized I had kissed at least six other girls throughout the semester, so I really had no place to be mad. We both concluded that we didn't have it out of our systems yet to be totally faithful to each other, but we decided to still be together. Well that didn't work, because I got jealous when she'd go out and be mad if she didn't call me. I called her on Saturday to tell her I was upset that she wasn't calling me until 3am every morning. She cried and said this whole relationship is just too hard for her. This kind of angers me because she said it like it wasn't hard for me, and I feel like she just gave up.

I'm going to miss her, and we're still going to be good friends. Unfortunately, I have taken the wrong path to deal with this. For the past two nights after the breakup, I've just been getting very, very, drunk. I haven't allowed myself to come to terms with what has happened. It also doesn't help when I feel physically horrible all day until I'm drunk again the next night. Starting today, though, I'm not going to drink for once and take a breather. I'm not sure if it's going to help me at all, but at least I'll be able to make it through class tomorrow. Another thing I'm not too sure about is what I'm going to do with the non-refundable plane tickets I have to San Diego for spring break. I asked her and she still wants to see me, but I'm not sure if that's very healthy emotionally. I have other friends that will be there as well, but I'm still not quite sure what I'm going to do yet. I guess that's how my life is going to be for a while.

You are probably seeing the clues now, aren't you? As soon as Mathew read over what he had written, he began to realize what had gone wrong: "We started dating, not knowing what we were going to do when I had to return to school. We never talked about what we were going to do and didn't want to spend time worrying about it." They had just wanted to spend their time having fun together and so set the reality of their lives aside. This insight surfaced: "We both concluded that we didn't have it out of our systems yet to be totally faithful to each other." I asked Mathew if "partially faithful" would have worked and, of course, he said no.

What were the signs to "get out now?"

One of the biggest insights for Mathew came when he realized that the path he had chosen for dealing with the breakup was really messing him up. "I've been getting very, very drunk. I haven't allowed myself to come to terms with what has happened." He made the choice to stop the "sorrow drinking" and focus on what he could learn from this experience.

Annette—"He manipulated me to think I was a bad person."

Let me explain why there is a void in my life. My last boyfriend, named Lowell, lowered my self-worth as much as it could be lowered by manipulating me to think I was a bad person and that I was not as great as he was. He told me that "my personal stock has risen because I was dating him," meaning that I am seen as better-looking and more popular because I was dating him. He broke me down more than I have ever seen happen to any of my friends in their dramatic relationships. After breaking up, I have found out that he cheated on me about ten different times with numerous different people. So my love was growing for him while he was spreading his love all over campus. It has been almost eight months now, and, to this day, I still struggle with standing proud and being the true me. When I get sad I relieve my feelings by writing out all of my feelings in a journal. I call it the "love journal." I have always put my emotions down on paper but this situation is taking up too much paper. I have this void still, and, due to this void, I have lost my authentic self and my self-worth, for that matter. It is hard to get back on track when you have so much weighing you down, and all you're doing is trying to un-bury yourself to find that true authentic self.

He told me I was less than him all the time. It is still hard for me to see that I am better than him. He depleted my self-worth by at least half. He made me feel undesirable, not valuable, and not worthy of any guy who comes into my life. Therefore, I know now that I need to come in touch with my esteem and know that I was the best thing that he will ever have, and that he only made me feel smaller because of his insecurities about himself and about him losing me. I have a void that I know I need to fix. I have the inner strength to do it, but I just need to let go of him so that this can be done and I can focus on my life with my friends and family.

I hold onto people so much, and maybe that is why they have the capability of hurting me so much. I rely on people and am dependent on them for my self-worth. Ideally, I would like to be taken care of, never left, and be secure with someone who will think I'm just amazing. This may also be how my ex-boyfriend had the capability of hurting me even after we broke up. I relied on him so much to be the security I was looking for. I need to stop being so dependent on others and actually explore being independent so I can stop being hurt or taken advantage of.

Ask yourself this question, "Am I giving up me to be loved by him or by her? This is what happened to Annette, and it is more common than you might think. Annette let her boyfriend manipulate and control her, and strip her of her self-esteem. He, in the meantime, maintained his freedom to pursue other women whenever he wished.

For Annette, writing this out was a turning point. She took responsibility for her role in letting herself become the victim in the relationship. "I hold onto people so much; I am dependent on them for my self-worth." The turning point for her began with the expression, "I truly feel I am extremely emotionally strong," and "It is a vigorous battle that can be won if your heart, your soul, and your mind work together to get through it. I strongly believe it can be done."

Annette took back control of her life. She continued working her experience through and came to the realization that much of her dependency needs came from her childhood and the divorce of her parents. It only took a few sessions with a wonderful counselor on campus, and Annette was able to totally turn her life around.

We finish this section about breakups with a poem written by Darren.

A Poem To My Ex

*She taught me so much—I have
Taken it for granted—she took
Me for granted too—I swore I would
Never do it. That it would never get to me.
But the pain and hate have consumed me—consumed
Me to the point of madness—the insanity
Of letting go of the first person you ever really loved.
Only to find out that she never really loved you—
Or did she? The only one who knows is her,
And perhaps she doesn't even know—the heart
Which beats with such a passion for her every
Time the wind whispered her name, now
Blackened and burns with the very thought*

What are the signs that it's time?

You Matter:

Of her. But why? What has she done that could
Not have been done by another? Why must
What once brought me so much joy suddenly
Consume me with hatred? This answer lies not
With her but with me—the passing of love,
Like that of a death, must somehow be dealt
With inside my own soul. Not with hatred
And anger, but with understanding.
And understanding that the road I once
Traveled with a companion I now travel
Alone—alone to make my own choices—
Alone to make my own mistakes—
Alone with the ability to find someone new.
The road to the future goes far past the horizon—
No need to speculate on what the road will bring,
Just stick out your thumb, hitch another ride
And hope it is better than your last.

You certainly get the idea that it takes a lot of work, as a couple, to make a successful relationship, and it is totally worth the effort. The level of happiness you can achieve is even greater than you have imagined. Chapter 7, Making Your Relationship Work, offers insights and tools for building a great relationship.

Breaking Up Is Hard To Do

Almost everyone has broken up with someone or had someone break up with him or her. It can be a very painful experience. The more "in love" you think you are, the more painful the breakup. I have broken off a number of relationships and, on two occasions, was absolutely shocked when it felt like without any notice, they broke up with me. Though years apart, I totally believed both relationships were the real thing. From my own experiences, and those of many others who have shared theirs, I have learned three things for sure: 1) there is no easy way to break up; 2) HOW you breakup with someone really does matter, both to the other person and to you; and 3) what you learn about yourself and life in the process helps you make better choices for yourself in the future.

How To Break Up With Someone You Once Cared For

Except when someone has been abusive, everyone should be treated with respect and decency. It is a matter of giving a person that you have cared about a way out with dignity, and also the way you conduct yourself is a reflection of who you are. Keep in mind that there will always be hurt and emotional pain when you break up with someone. The more the person cares about you and the longer you have been in the relationship, the greater the emotional impact. Once the decision is made, out of respect for yourself and the other, it is best to be addressed sooner rather than wait. Tensions and emotions can build up rapidly and result in a far worse ending.

Here are some of the meanest and most cowardly breakups I have come across.

- He just disappeared.
- She sent an email.
- He got drunk and called.
- She asked a friend to tell him.

The following is a process that can help both of you. Even though the breakup will still hurt and you likely will be met with anger and/or sadness, the process will help to bring closure so that your partner too, will at some time be able to move on. **Number One: treat your about-to-become-ex-partner with respect.**

Are you certain you want to break up?

Once you tell your partner you are ending the relationship, you can't take it back. Be sure you think it through and are clear as to why the relationship is not working for you. Your partner is going to ask you why, and you need to be prepared with an answer. "It's really not you. It's me," is not a good answer. If there is a possibility that issues could be resolved through counseling, then bring this up and state your willingness to work together with your partner and a counselor. You will both benefit, no matter what the outcome. If your partner is reluctant or refuses to go, this too is a response. You then know that can move forward.

You Matter:

1. *Plan a place and time.*

You need to be there in person. If it's a long-distance relationship, this can be a challenge, but to be there as a person is still best, if you can do it. If you don't live together, break the news in your partner's home or in a neutral place, and in private. This is a safer place for dealing with emotions. It would be horrible to have someone break up with you in a public place or where family or friends were present. Making him or her leave your place would be awful as well. If you are at your partner's home, you can leave after you have finished your conversation.

If you live together, it is going to be even more difficult and stressful. You will need a place to stay and, in preparation, pack some of the things you will need for a couple days with the intention of coming back and getting the rest of your belongings when things have calmed down or no one is home.

2. *Be calm and be clear.*

Sit down and let your partner know that you have decided to end the relationship, and why you have made this decision. Be clear with your intentions. "I just need some time off," doesn't cut it and will leave your partner confused and probably hopeful that you will get back together. Presenting a long list of complaints and things done in the past will likely lead to arguing and anger. Keep it brief, genuine, respectful and to the point.

Expect any of these common reactions:

Questioning – Your partner wants and needs to know why, and whether he or she could have done anything to prevent it. He/she will also want to know if you are seeing someone else.

Crying – Your partner is going to be upset and/or may hope that crying will cause you to change your mind.

Arguing – Your partner may dispute any one thing you said, or dispute everything you said, and try to make you wrong. Don't get sucked in, and don't start explaining. Let your partner know that arguing is not going to change your decision.

Bargaining or Begging – Your partner may promise to change or do anything you want in order to keep the relationship going. If there has been no change before, then it's not likely there will be change going forward. If you become uncertain and consider giving it one more chance, then insist on couples counseling as an absolute condition for staying in the relationship.

Lashing Out – This is an expression of intense hurt and anger and needs to be taken seriously. Stay calm and leave quickly. If you are frightened, then tell someone you trust about it. Use good judgment to protect yourself. If you feel your safety is actually at risk report it to the police.

3. *Make the conversation relatively short.*

Don't make the breakup conversation last any longer than it needs to. This can actually lead to more misunderstanding, arguing, and bad feelings. Say what you have to say, listen to your partner's feelings, comfort if you can, and then say something like "I'm really sorry that things turned out this way. I have to leave now," and go.

4. *Don't expect your ex-partner to want to be friend.*

It will take some time before a person who just experienced a breakup will want to be friends. It can and does happen, but it takes time.

Here are three big **don'ts**:

- Don't drink alcohol before or during your conversation. This is one of the dumbest things you can do.

- Don't break up in the heat of the moment. Do it when you are both calm and you will have the best chance to treat each other respectfully and come to closure.

- Don't threaten that you will break up with your partner. This makes the relationship worse.

Breaking up is hard, but remember this, staying in a bad relationship is ten times more painful and the pain lasts for a much longer period of time the longer you delay. Every day that you stay in a relationship that isn't working is a day that could be spent attracting a relationship that is right for you!

How To Survive A Breakup

Breaking up can leave you depressed and unable to concentrate, can shake your sense of self-worth, and can make you feel like you'll never find someone special. Sometimes you just can't stop thinking about him or her and feel like the hurt will never end.

Getting Over Him – Getting Over Her

Because getting over someone after a breakup is usually painful and difficult to do, most of the time we just want to forget it. We just want it over. We just want to stop hurting. If we don't learn and heal, though, the probability is that we will repeat the pattern we have established and experience a similarly disappointing outcome in future relationships. Running away or jumping too quickly into a new relationship can both become harmful patterns. Another common pattern is to blame the other person, and to think about and remember all the awful things that person did to screw up your relationship. When you hold on to this mindset you avoid looking at yourself and what you contributed to the breakup of the relationship. You don't examine your role and what you might do differently, and therefore you remain stuck.

Survival Tips

1. Stop Blaming

    Whose fault is it? It doesn't matter anymore. It's over, and it's a waste of energy to focus on the past and all the negative stuff. Guilt or blaming will keep you stuck in the past.

2. Alcohol will not help you get better faster.

3. Get back into your life as quickly as you can.

4. Go to work. Attend your classes. Get back together with your friends. Staying home alone only contributes to feelings of

depression. Whatever your feelings and experiences, you need to get back into your life quickly.

5.   Talking about it to your friends can really help.

6.   This also reconnects you with people you are comfortable with and know. They will be supportive and you get to clear your system of all the pain and anger. Dump it and move on.

7.   Get back into exercising.

This is one of the best things you can do for yourself. Not only will you feel better and look good, it also causes the release of endorphins, which will help you feel good.

Your Self-Search Experiences

In the Appendix, Page 235 you will find three Self-Search Experiences. The first is designed to help you discover any patterns of behavior that may be getting in your way. The second is a process for discovery after a breakup. What do you need to learn, and what will you do differently going forward?

Key Takeaways from Being In Love and Breaking Up

➢   Most realize that ending the relationship was the best thing they could do, and then regret not ending it sooner.

➢   To speak badly about him or her just keeps you stuck in the past.

➢   Alcohol doesn't help things get better.

➢   You must not give up who you are in order to be loved by someone else.

➢   The reasons you were attracted to each other will not be enough to keep you together.

➢   Some men and women, are manipulators, users, and are very controlling.

You Matter:

- ➤ It is easy to get into dysfunctional patterns. Be aware and then you can change them.

- ➤ Mutual trust and respect are the critical foundation pieces for a successful relationship.

- ➤ When you are not sure what to do, ask for help.

- ➤ Forgive yourself and move on.

- ➤ Give yourself time to heal and let go before getting into another relationship.

Important References and Resources:

We Love Each Other, but…: Simple Secrets to Strengthen Your Relationship and Make Love Last, Dr. Ellen Wachtel, 2000, New York: St. Martin's Griffin

Love Is a Choice: The Definitive Book on Letting Go of Unhealthy Relationships, Dr. Robert Hemfelt, Dr. Frank Minirth and Paul Meier M.D, 2003, Nashville: Thomas Nelson Publishers

Act Like a Lady, Think Like a Man: What Men Really Think About Love, Relationships Intimacy and Commitment, Steve Harvey, 2009, New York: Amistad

http://www.amazon.com/Love-Choice-Definitive-Unhealthy-Relationships/dp/0785263756/ref=sr_1_7?ie=UTF8&s=books&qid=12474 26960&sr=1-7

Extreme Breakup Recovery, Jeanette Castelli, 2004. : Urbantex Publishing, Miami, Florida

It's Called a Breakup Because It's Broken: The Smart Girl's Break-Up Buddy, by Greg Behrendt and Amira Ruotola-Behrendt, 2006, New York: Broadway Books

I Used To Miss Him … But My Aim Is Improving: Not Your Ordinary Breakup Survival Guide, Alison James, 2004, Cincinnati: Adams Media

CHAPTER 5

MAKING YOUR RELATIONSHIP WORK

*The search for contentment is, therefore,
not merely a self-preserving and self-benefiting act, but
also a generous gift to the world. You cease being an obstacle,
not only to yourself, but to anyone else. Only then are
you free to serve any and enjoy all people.
Eat, Pray Love by Elizabeth Gilbert*

Assess the state of your relationship and determine what it will take to make it healthy and long lasting.

Finding the Right Partner

Are you in a serious relationship, or do you want to be in one some day? This chapter is for those who want to meet the "right one" and make the relationship work. The intent here is to provide you with some very experiential and effective processes and tools for assessing your relationship and identifying those areas most important to address. These experiences work very well for couples of any age and any level of relationship experience. The discovery processes you will find here are very enlightening and quite helpful.

I tend to be attracted to someone who... (list)

Is there just one "right" person out there waiting for you? Or are there many who might fit exactly the kind of person you will want to be with in a life-long relationship? As with most things, whatever you choose to believe greatly impacts what will come true for you. There will be a wide variety of relationship possibilities for you in this lifetime. However, even when you find the right one, the partner who really feels like the right one, it will take a willingness to continually grow and change together from both of you to make the relationship successful. One of the biggest mistakes we make (yes, I include myself) is to meet someone and "fall in love" too quickly. The chemistry is wonderful, and you find you can't think of anything or anyone else during the day. The excitement when you are together is electric. You keep telling yourself, "I think he's the one!" Or "I know she's the one I've been looking for!" The endorphins and excitement of a new relationship can last for quite a while, thus convincing you that your perception is accurate. Well, sometimes it is right. Unfortunately, many other times it is wrong. How can you avoid going through another breakup like we discussed in the last chapter? This chapter is about what you can do to greatly increase the probability that you will attract and connect with someone who very well might become the right one.

Here are some questions to get you started. What kind of person do you tend to be attracted to? Did you find any patterns of your behavior in Chapter 4? What do you think causes you to be attracted to someone? Are you one of those who just runs around chasing anyone who looks good, hoping to find someone they like? Now let's turn this pattern around. How might you attract the person who you want in your life? Instead of chasing after others, how might you attract the right person to you?

As I wrote in Chapter 2, my research and life experience have made me a believer in the "law of attraction." As you recall, whatever we focus on and think about, *positive or negative*, is what we tend to attract. Simply stated, what we focus on grows. People who focus on what is wrong about themselves and about others, frequently attract into their lives those with the same or similar negative characteristics. Others focus on and think about the characteristics they desire in a potential partner. They then find, seemingly by "coincidence," that they begin meeting people who have these desired characteristics.

Applying the Law of Attraction

You can put the law of attraction to work in your desire to find the right one. "I want someone I love, who loves me, and who I can grow and change with." Even if you are skeptical about this, why not give it a try. After all, you have nothing to lose. First though, here are some key points to know about the law of attraction.

- The law of attraction is a law of nature. It is as important as the law of gravity.

- Whatever you focus your thoughts and attention on, positive or negative, expands.

- Your thoughts about things that are important to you result in emotions and feelings, positive or negative.

- Along with this, it is impossible to feel bad and at the same time have good thoughts.

- When you feel bad you will tend to attract more negative things. When you feel good, you will attract more positive things.

- Pleasant memories, nature, or your favorite music can change your feelings and shift your frequency in an instant.

Here is how you can apply the law of attraction.

Step 1 – Get clear on what you do want in your relationship. Only focus on what you want. Give this some deep thought. Narrow it down to what matters the most to you. This becomes your program for a loving, intimate relationship. Here is an example.

- I want someone I can love and who can love me in return.

- I want someone I like, with whom I can grow and change.

- I want someone I'm attracted to and who is attracted to me.

- I want someone whose philosophy of living is similar to mine.

- I want to recognize this person when I see her/him.

- Thank you.

Step 2 – Write your program up and place it where you can easily see it. You can type it with large font or have fun handwriting in colors, or whatever works for you. You can tape it to your mirror or place it in front of a notebook that you carry. Look at it every day, visually seeing experience feeling the end result you want.

Step 3– Believe, and be patient. The "program" works. Don't put a timeframe on it, as you can't force things to happen. Just know that you will begin meeting new people who have the characteristics on which you are focusing. Experience the emotions of gratitude and happiness in everything you can. Be patient and just let things happen. Impatience will only turn into negative thoughts and will therefore defeat your purpose. Your strongest position is to believe the right person is coming your way.

If you find you have a hard time believing in this process, then of course it won't work for you. If this is the case, return to Step 2, because no matter what, it is really important that you get clear on the qualities and characteristics of the kind of person you want to find. How else will you recognize the one who will bring out the best in you?

Making Your Relationship Work

If you learn nothing else, know this, it will take both of you working together to make your relationship successful. There are no shortcuts. It is common for people to go into a relationship thinking that their partner has the same beliefs and expectations, wants and desires, and dismiss the importance of even talking about these things. You might think, "It would be awkward to bring this stuff up. Who would do that? It would ruin the moment, right? Besides, I can tell by how she/he is when we're together that we are right for each other." In other words, most people just let things happen and hope that all is going to turn out the way they want, rather than taking charge and working together to create what they want to happen.

How Are We Alike and How Are We Different?

This is a discovery process for you and your partner, and it is meant to be insightful and enjoyable. Who is he/she? There is nothing good or bad in the responses here. Having lots of similarities doesn't mean the relationship will be great, nor does having some big differences mean it will fail. In fact, your similarities and differences can strengthen the relationship. The most important thing to know about significant differences is that they can be the source of confusion and even irritation until they are unpacked and explored. It is so easy to make the assumption that your partner has beliefs and values similar to yours in many life areas. People do this all the time and then are surprised when they discover how different their partner can be. The most important thing is to get to know each other, to understand each other without judgment, so you can be there to enjoy, love, and support each other.

The following are two areas where couples frequently differ and that can affect your relationship. The first relates to the importance of your values, which are primary drivers of your thoughts and behavior. The second relates to the differences in how you express your love to each other. So, read the following then ask yourselves, how well do you know each other?

My Values – Your Values: Do We Have Similar Values?

The following are sixteen common values, presented in alphabetical order, that affect your decisions, your choices, and your behavior. Identify *your* most important top five values and write them in the order of priority of importance to you. Then identify *your* least important bottom five values and also write them in order of priority. When you finish your values lists, identify what *you think your partners* top five and bottom five are. Have your partner do the same for him-/herself and then for you.

- Career (personal accomplishment, career advancement)
- Competition (winning, being the best)
- Cooperation (helpfulness, working together)
- Courageous (standing up for your beliefs)
- Creativity (using imagination, being innovative)
- Excitement (adventure, challenge)
- Having children (becoming parents)
- Honesty (sincere, truthful, integrity)
- Independent (self-reliant, self-sufficient)
- Loyalty (faithfulness, trustworthiness)
- Money (having it, financial security)
- Recognition (respect, admiration from others)
- Responsibility (feeling that others can depend on you)
- Devotional practices (actively practicing beliefs)
- Self-Confidence (self-esteem, faith in your talents and abilities)
- Sex (a satisfying sexual relationship)

You Matter:

My Top Five Values Are (priority order):	I Think My Partner's Top Five Values Are (priority order):
1. _____	1. _____
2. _____	2. _____
3. _____	3. _____
4. _____	4. _____
5. _____	5. _____

My Bottom Five Values Are (priority order):	I Think My Partner's Bottom Five Values Are (priority order):
1._____	1._____
2._____	2._____
3._____	3._____
4._____	4._____
5._____	5._____

Now you have an opportunity for a great discussion. Remember, it is not about who is right or who is wrong, or whose values are more important. It is about learning and understanding each other. Some of your questions might be, "How are we alike and how are we different? Why is this one so important to you? Why is this one of least importance to you? How do similarities and differences show up when we are together?

Which ones sometimes get in the way? How can we use what we have learned to make our relationship stronger?" Ask whatever questions come to mind. You may find that, as a result of your discussion, one or both of you may change some of your top or bottom values priorities. Let the last questions be, "What have we learned from this experience together, and will our values get in our way as a couple or help us strengthen our relationship?"

Love Languages: Is the way I show I love you the way you experience being loved?

What are your love languages? What are your partner's?

Have you ever asked another, "Do you love me?" How would you know if your partner loves you? What is your evidence? Is it what he says? Is it what she does? You of course, will express your love in your way, the way that you understand being loved. You may also make the assumption that your partner will understand your way and will express love to you in the same way. Let's say that you express your love through little gifts that show you are thinking of him. To you, this is definitely an act of love. If "gifts" is not one of his "love languages," then he likely will not experience it as an act of love for him, but rather as just something nice that you did. So he says, "Oh, thank you," and goes on with a different conversation, and you end up hurt because he didn't notice how much you care. Here is another example. He loves doing things for you, and you never have to ask. He takes the garbage out, washes the dishes, takes your car in for servicing, and so many other things. For him, "acts of service" is a predominant language of love. You, on the other hand, just love spending time alone with him. You love it most when it is the two of you doing things together. This is your predominant language of love. It is very confusing to you when he wants to spend a lot of time with his friends, though he often wants you to be there too. Understanding each other's predominant love languages can greatly enhance the feelings of intimacy in the relationship.

Gary Chapman wrote a book titled *The Heart of the Five Love Languages*, and he distinguishes the different ways of expressing heartfelt feelings of love. (This is an excellent book for couples.) Most of us have only one or two languages of love that we understand and use. If we are unable to recognize the other languages as expressions of love, we might totally miss our partner's intent. Which of these are your most predominant languages of love?

Words of Affirmation – you feel loved when your partner tells you that he or she values you as a person and appreciates your special way with the most ordinary tasks. This includes words of praise and compliments for how you look or something you did.

Quality Time – you feel closest to your partner when the two of you are alone together, doing things together and are focused on each other without distraction.

Receiving Gifts – gifts are expressions of love and provide assurance that your partner is always thinking of you and cares enough to show it.

What we have learned from this (write your thoughts in the margin)

Acts of Service – you feel most loved when your partner helps you with things, and offers to help without being asked.

Physical Touch – you feel most loved when you are making physical contact with your partner. You enjoy being embraced and being touched.

Which of these five experiences makes you feel most especially loved? Which have little meaning to you relative to feeling especially loved? For example, it is absolutely clear to me that my two are Quality Time and Physical Touch. In my past, I have been guilty of entering relationships assuming the same was true for the other in my life, only to discover that *receiving gifts* was her main language of love, but is one of my least important languages.

Before you share your choices with your partner, see if you can identify what you think his/her primary love languages are, and which are totally not. Have your partner do the same for you. Have a great time sharing your choices with each other. When you finish, ask each other, "What can I do that will help you feel most loved?"

What Is Our Purpose in this Relationship?

What is the purpose of a significant relationship? What makes a relationship meaningful to both partners? What does it take for a relationship and a marriage to happily endure? No one that I know has gone from a significant and meaningful relationship into a marriage with the thought that the marriage would end in divorce. Yet sadly, nearly half of the marriages in the United States do end this way. So what are some things you can do that will help the relationship grow and deepen over the years?

One purpose of your relationship can be that of self-discovery. In a truly loving relationship, each of you has an opportunity—actually, a responsibility—to contribute to your partner's growth and development, in addition to your own. You can create your own relationship purpose that reflects who each is and how the two of you want to live your life together.

Our Relationship Purpose

Here is a great way to get started in designing the relationship you desire.

1. Each of you write your response to the statement: "What I want our relationship to be is…" Here are some questions to get you started.
   - What is the purpose of our relationship?
   - Why are we together?
   - What do I want from this relationship?
   - What is meaningful about our being together?
   - Why are we better off being together than not being together?

2. When you have finished, read to each other what you have written.

3. Together, combine your statements into one; "We want our relationship to be …" (finish the statement).

4. When you both have a clear picture, what commitments would you make to each other to support this new vision of your

unique relationship? "I am committed to…(each write down your thoughts, and then share them).

Focus On What Is Good

In a love relationship, the experience is usually one of a sense of belonging, of being loved, feeling safe, and joy in being together. Everything is wonderful, fun, funny, and you see what you want to see. All of the qualities that you love, you see in your partner. It isn't that you stop seeing these as time goes on, but quite often your focus changes. You start settling into a routine. Your old habit patterns emerge. You likely see things that you don't like as much, like she is always late. He doesn't talk when he gets home. He never talks about his feelings; she then talks even more. He seems only interested in sports. … Do any of these sound familiar?

A shift in focus from all that is good to what is not so good can sneak into place, often without much conscious awareness on the part of either partner. Your focus on the negative intensifies with more stress—for example: not having enough money, work, carrying a full load of classes, or not having enough time together. It doesn't take long before seeing what is not good, turns into complaints about the partner stemming from these stresses and other life challenges. Think of the Law of Attraction, whatever we focus on, look for, think about, talk about, positive or negative expands.

Remember the teacher in Chapter 2 who had everyone record how many times a day they complained? Mathew Kelly pointed out that we all complain too much, and that our complaints are mostly insignificant. "Whom do we complain *to* the most? The people we supposedly love the most. Whom do we complain *about* the most (either out loud or to ourselves)? The people we supposedly love the most. Our complaints are poisoning our relationships."

The flip side of complaining is the expression of gratitude. This, of course, requires focusing on what is good. Focusing on and expressing what is right, rather than what is wrong, has a wonderful effect on the body, on the mind, and on the emotions. It also has a positive effect on the chemistry between two people, especially when they are in love.

So the powerful question is: Where is your focus in your relationship? In the Appendix, Page 243, you will find a very powerful Self-Search Experience on Becoming a Very Healthy Couple.

How Is Our Relationship Doing?

If you are in a committed relationship, this would be a great time to check in with each other and see how well you are doing as a couple. If you've gotten this far into the book, you are likely in a pretty good place, or at least can see clearly where you might focus next. On the other hand, if you are not in a good place, this next part will help you figure out why, and what you can do to get the relationship on the track you both desire.

Check Your Level of Trust and Respect

In addition to having a shared purpose for your relationship, the level of trust and the level of respect you have for each other are essential to your happiness and to the health of the relationship. Let's take a look at each.

The Trust Continuum

Trust is the foundation of any healthy relationship. We tend to trust people more if we know that we can count on them, that they will always do what they say they will do, and that they mean what they say. We trust more when we experience a person as genuine. You are trusted more when you act consistently, as the same person, and do not change behavior from one person or group to another, not trying to impress others, always being authentic. Trust is linked with integrity. Your experience is that he is honest and tells the truth. If he doesn't know, he says so rather than fabricating something to try to impress or convince you, or to deceive you. You trust more when the person in your relationship genuinely cares about you; about what you're doing, how you are feeling, how things are going. Someone who cares about you would not be deliberately hurtful, and if he is unconsciously hurtful, he wants to understand this so he can change to become loving and supportive.

You Matter:

Some people have the perception that you either trust or distrust and there is no in between. This is not really the case. Actually, trust is on a continuum, with "distrust" at one end and "trustworthy" at the other. The trust continuum looks like this.

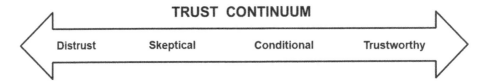

TRUST CONTINUUM

Distrust · Skeptical · Conditional · Trustworthy

Where is the level of trust in your relationship?

Once your trust in someone has been seriously betrayed, it can be very hard to repair. One act of unfaithfulness can destroy trust. However, if both parties really want to address the causal issues, it is possible to regain the trust between you. Often a third party "coach" or counselor is the key to helping regain each other's trust and a healthy commitment to the relationship.

"Distrust" and "Skeptical" are difficult levels within which to make a relationship work. To move beyond these states requires considerable effort. Both parties need to comprehend the underlying causes and to know what it would take to move up to a level of "Conditional" trust. One of the reasons for going with someone over a period of time before moving into a serious relationship is that it enables you to get a sense of the level of trust, and of respect, you can have with this person. Those who are needy or hungry to be in a relationship may think that a new relationship is really serious before even considering how the other person is viewing the relationship, or whether there can be a high level of trust. They often jump into it, get hurt, and then later do it again with someone else, until they take time to understand where they got off track in the first place. Unfortunately for some, this pattern continues through several marriages and divorces. If you find yourself in a relationship with someone you distrust, or are skeptical about whether he or she can be trusted, then you need to proceed very cautiously or not at all. At least not until the underlying trust issues are understood and resolved.

Conditional trust is common. Most people put conditions around their trust, especially in a potential love relationship. "I trust you, but don't be seeing someone else." "I trust you, but not when you look through my stuff." "I have a hard time trusting you when …" Problems often occur when you don't let your partner know about these conditions. Sometimes you avoid telling him because you worry that it will lead to a conflict. At other times, you don't say anything because you don't want her to think you are insecure. To move to a deeper level of trust, it is essential that you talk to each other about the conditions that are important to you, and come to an agreement about what you can expect from each other.

If you want a lasting relationship, then the level of trust you will want to achieve is that of "Trustworthy;" meaning you are worthy of my trust, you have earned my total trust. This also can mean different things to different people, so it is really important to talk about, share your thoughts, and get clear on what this level of trust means to each of you.

Do not make assumptions that your partner thinks as you do. As previously stated, trust is the foundation of any healthy relationship. It is a must-have if you want the relationship to be healthy and lasting.

The Respect Continuum

The level of respect that one has for another is reflected in how you treat each other on a day-to-day basis. It matters when you are alone together, when you are in bed, when you are with his friends and her friends. If the behavior of one partner is disrespectful in some situations, then there *will be* problems in the relationship, because disrespect also erodes trust. Couples can disagree and even argue, but still be respectful. This doesn't mean that one or the other won't make a mistake. If you do, then apologizing sooner rather than later can help reestablish the respect.

Where is the level of respect in your relationship?

Respect is reflected in your actions. This includes the words you choose, your tone of voice, and your body language. Some who become experts at manipulation can fake words, tone, and body language, but their actions will eventually be inconsistent with respect. Respect is pretty hard to fake over time. You have a right to be treated respectfully and a responsibility to treat your partner the same. If one partner does not respect the other, it will show up in their behavior. When respect is displayed on a continuum it looks like this.

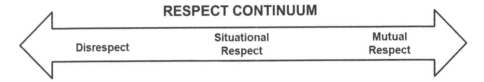

RESPECT CONTINUUM

Disrespect — Situational Respect — Mutual Respect

If one of you is respectful of your partner in one situation—for example, with your partner's friends—but is not respectful when with a different group, this is situational respect. If either of you frequently behaves disrespectfully toward the other—painful sarcasm or demeaning or hurtful comments—then you are only a step away from finding yourself in an emotionally abusive relationship. If either of you is at the "situational respect" level, then unless you address the underlying issues, whatever they are, you are going to have a difficult time maintaining a healthy relationship. If you find yourself in an abusive situation, the best course of action is to *get out*.

In the Appendix there are two We Search Experiences for couples (Pages 242 and 243). Each of these can greatly enhance your relationship.

If you do work through any of the approaches provided in this chapter, you will greatly improve the probability of having a successful relationship. Don't be like some people who take a relationship for granted or just cruise from day-to-day, oblivious to issues that may arise and hinder their relationship. Perhaps the most important point of all of this is to continuously express your gratitude to each other for all that is good. Write a note to the one you love, send a card, a quick e-mail or a letter. Everything about being grateful and having gratitude matters and helps you stay focused on all that is right in your lives. Catch your partner doing something right!

Thinking about Living Together? Thinking about Marriage?

Obviously, making a decision about marriage is a big deal. A decision about living together is a big step as well. There is no nice little structured process that will lead you to the right decision for either situation. Take the time to work these decisions through and to avoid making an impulsive, but-we're-in-love decision.

The following is a process that has worked well for others. The first example comes from Tonya's self-search experience. She began with a list of characteristics for a life-mate that are really important to her—a vision statement—then examined her fears and concerns about living with her boyfriend, and the reasons why she wanted to live with him. She also took some time to reflect on each of the steps before making her decision.

Tonya – "My personal dilemma: Should I or should I not live with my boyfriend?"

Characteristics I Want in My Husband:

- *Loving, kind, caring*
- *Trustworthy*
- *Willing to try new things*
- *Sexy!*
- *Makes me laugh*
- *Strong, but also sensitive and willing to show his emotions*
- *Helps me be the best person I can be*
- *Values women and supports me having a career*
- *Good listener*
- *Optimistic, positive, and always smiling*
- *Loves me for me, even with all of my faults*
- *Doesn't run away from problems*
- *Open-minded*
- *I want my future husband and me to have an undying love for each other that can last a life-time.*

She then focused on whether or not to live together prior to the marriage she envisioned. First she began with the identification of her fears—reasons to *not* live together—then followed this with a list of the reasons *for* living together.

I will break it down and figure out all of the reasons that I am scared to live with him:

1. *I don't want our living together to ruin our relationship.*

2. *We have been in a long-distance relationship for the past two years, only seeing each other about once or twice a month. Would going from long distance to living together be too big of a step?*
3. *Will we be able to deal with the little things that might bother us about our living styles/habits?*
4. *Will I be missing out on other opportunities both career-wise and with my friends?*
5. *I am a little scared about telling my parents and family, but I will still do what makes me happy, and I have learned a valuable lesson: that I shouldn't run my life according to what other people think.*
6. *I have always said that I don't believe in 'pre-marital cohabitation,' and I never thought that I would live with my significant other until we were married; but after I met him, my view on this topic has changed a lot, and I do want to live with him. Should I stick to my original values or is it okay to change them?*

I'm glad to see that my list of fears isn't too long. Now for the better part. Here are the reasons why I do want to move in with him:

1. *He is the love of my life, and it is so hard for me to spend even one day without him.*
2. *Our relationship will be able to grow and get stronger.*
3. *We will learn even more things about each other and probably ourselves as well that we didn't already know.*
4. *We will be able to experience so much more together and face many obstacles as a couple, as one unit working together to solve problems.*
5. *We will be working toward our future and marriage.*
6. *We can get a better understanding of what our lives will be like when we are married.*
7. *It makes sense financially, to both live in one apartment if we are in the same city, rather than each paying for an apartment.*
8. *We really are a highly compatible couple, and I know that we could get through any adversity because we would each do anything for the other.*

9. *I want to spend the rest of my life with him, so why not start now?*

Writing things down really does help a lot! After writing my pro & con lists, I feel even better about the possibility of living with him. I know that no matter what, it will be a worthwhile experience, and I know that we can make it work.

Fast-forward one month:

It has been just over a month since I originally wrote these feelings about moving in with him. I am even more confident now about this subject. I have no worries either way. If I do live with him, or if I don't live with him, I know that whatever happens will work out how it is supposed to, and my mind is at ease. I believe that we can be strong as a couple living together, but I also believe that if I get sent somewhere other than Portland and he can't move there with me right away, then we will still make our relationship work and last. The good thing is that now it doesn't seem so much like a dilemma. I am excited for what is to come with my career and the love of my life. I have no worries!

This is *a helpful decisi*on making process:

Jot your thoughts down as you go along.

1. What do you want in your situation?
2. What are your fears, concerns,; the negatives?
3. What are the reasons for doing this, the positives, and what are the alternatives?

Then let it sit for a bit. Do some reflecting, talk things over with each other or with someone who can coach you. Tonya achieved a great insight when she wrote, *"I know that whatever happens will work out how it is supposed to, and my mind is at ease."* For you, once you have completed this process, and when the time is right, make a decision, and then don't look back. Even if things don't work out, you took the time to learn and grow. No one can do better than that. The next time you choose a relationship, you will be starting out far ahead, and with a much greater probability of success.

You Matter:

Tonya worked her process through by herself and later shared it with her partner. However, James and Sarah worked theirs through together, with a very different but equally effective process.

James and Sarah had been in a committed relationship for three years, most of their college experience. They were getting close to graduation and were faced with some difficult decisions. James had received a great job offer in San Francisco, but Sarah had planned on moving back to Seattle. They had to deal with two issues: whether Sarah would move to San Francisco with James and, if so, they then had to deal with the issue of living together before getting married. The following is the process they went through.

First, they developed their relationship and commitment vision.

James and Sarah – Our Relationship Vision:

*We accept each other for who we are and complete
each other's opposite qualities.
We make each other laugh.
We work together as a team to clarify life.
We learn from each other and challenge one another.
We express how we feel and say, "I love you."
We are each other's best friend.
We settle our differences peacefully and are ready to forgive.
We are passionate about life and our careers.
We are proud of each other.
We trust each other completely.
We have fun traveling and exploring new adventures together.
We are faithful to each other.
We communicate openly.
We are thoughtful of each others needs.
We make time for each other.
We help each other and take care of each other.
We surprise each other.
We respect each other's families and spend time with them.
We are confidant in ourselves and in each other.
We enjoy simple time together.
We are affectionate.*

Second, they each did individual journaling of what they were feeling about the situation, plus what they thought the other was feeling about it.

Understanding how each of us feels about moving to San Francisco –Sarah's feelings:

"I love James and I am so proud of him and excited that his hard work has paid off in such an amazing job opportunity. I have always imagined we would live in the Seattle area because it is a place that I love so much, and I thought James did too. San Francisco was sort of a shock to me. As I get used to the idea of moving there, I realize it is the next best thing to Seattle. It is not a super-long way from home, we have friends there, and there are a lot of career opportunities for me there. It could be fun. My main concern is that my parents will be sad, and I will miss out on special occasions. Also, I want to get married at home, and that will be hard from California. I need time to get used to the idea, and to know I have my parent's support. I don't want James to think I don't want to be with him, because I do. It is just a big step for me, but I am going to take it, hoping he will give me as much support as he can."

Sarah's view of what James feels:

"I got the best job ever. It is my chance to get out of here and show everyone that a kid from my hometown can really make it. I loved San Francisco when I visited because it is a new city to explore and there is a lot to do. My job is awesome. I want Sarah to come with me because I know she will end up loving it, and we can buy a Victorian house and be really happy. This is the best opportunity I have ever had, and I am so excited. There is no reason not to go."

James' feelings:

"I am so excited to move to a new place and start my career and life. I really don't feel bad about leaving my family because this is what I worked for. I am confident

I will enjoy and succeed at my new job. I am excited to learn all about San Francisco and what the city is like as a resident. I have been waiting so long to be free from WSU and relieved to know that I have the best opportunity for a good career given to me by this job. I am ready to learn from the best, and perhaps it will help me to be able to someday develop my own resort. I know I will be financially secure, and I want Sarah to come with me. I want her to be just as excited as I am, and I know she could find a job that she would love in San Francisco. I hope she wants to come with me because it will make it easier to adjust, and I would love to discover all the fun things in the area with her. I just want her to be as happy as me, no matter what may happen.

James view of what Sarah feels:

"I am ready to leave college, but I want to stay close to my family. I want to find a job that uses my best qualities and one I am passionate about. I want to help James and be with him, too. I think I will like San Francisco, but I will miss my family. I know I have been away from my parents for long periods of time before, and I have been okay with it. I may be unsure of what job I would like, but I know James will take care of me. He loves me and wants me to do whatever makes me happiest.

Sarah's parents were very important to both Sarah and James, and they both wanted to think of the parents in the process. They then shared all of this with each other, decided what they wanted to do and what it would take, and developed their plan.

James and Sarah did decide to move together to San Francisco, and Sarah immediately started her job search. As soon as they could, and before they moved, they met with Sarah's parents and shared their decision and the process they went through, and asked for her parent's approval and support, which they received. Sarah found a great job opportunity, and immediately after graduation they moved. James and Sarah are now married, and are very happy.

Should We Get Married?

To marry or not to marry is a huge decision. It is not my intention here to provide a process for making this decision. The process that Tonya used can help, but there is much more. One of the best books available on marriage is *The Seven Principles for Making Marriage Work*, by John Gottman and Nan Silver. Dr. Gottman has spent many years studying married couples and makes the very bold statement that he can predict with 91% accuracy whether a marriage will succeed or fail after watching a couple interact for five minutes. His seven principles involve much of what you have been reading: fondness, admiration and gratitude for each other, shared meaning and purpose in your relationship, supporting each other in becoming the best you can be, and dealing with conflict and solving problems. I think John Gottman's book should be required reading *before* a couple marries.

In the meantime, if you are considering marriage, it is important to know that the most common contributors to marriage breakups are money, sex, children, and dealing with conflict. So before you go any further in your process of decision-making, or even if you have already decided to get married, ask each other, and talk about, the following eight questions.

The Most Important Questions to Ask Before Marriage

1. I think my parents are great (or not), what do you think of them?

2. Do we agree about having or not having children, and who will be the primary caregiver?

3. Do we agree on how we will manage money?

4. Have we fully disclosed to each other who we are?

5. Can we comfortably and openly discuss our sex needs and desires?

6. Are we able to argue and fight fairly, and without doing harm?

7. Is my partner helping me to become the best me I can be?

8.   Does each of us feel fully confident in the *commitment* of the *other* to marriage?

(Source unknown)

Don't Forget To Have Fun!

It must seem like all of the work in this chapter is so serious. Well it is, but is not intended to take away from the fact that one of the most important things for you to do is to have fun together. Spend as much time as you can enjoying each other's company and learning about what makes each of you laugh. Play games, go hiking, watch the sunset, read stories to each other, be able to laugh at yourself, and find joy in being in life together. Build on all the things you did when you first met and were attracted to each other. Also, try some new experiences together, things neither of you has done before. Make your lives an adventure and, of greatest importance, never stop telling your partner how much he or she is loved.

It's important to remember that a serious relationship needs to be fun, joyful, and a balance of meeting the needs of both of you. Look out world, here you come.

Key Takeaways from Making Your Relationship Work

➤ It will take work, paying attention, and action to make the relationship successful.

➤ One of the biggest mistakes you can make is to meet someone and "fall in love" too quickly.

➤ You have the ability to attract the person who is right for you.

➤ Most people go into a relationship thinking that their partner has the same beliefs and expectations, and desires. The only way to know is to check these out together.

➤ Focusing on and expressing what is right, rather than what is wrong, has a wonderful effect on the body, on the mind and on the emotions.

> ➤ The highest level of trust in and respect for each other is essential to your happiness and to the health of the relationship.

Important References and Resources:

The Heart of the Five Love Languages, Gary Chapman, 2007, Chicago: Northfield Publishing.

The Seven Principles for Making Marriage Work, John Gottman and Nan Silver, 2004, London: Orion.

How to Create a Magical Relationship: The 3 Simple Ideas that Will Instantaneously Transform Your Love Life, Ariel and Shya Kane, 2008, New York: McGraw-Hill.

Getting the Love You Want: A Guide for Couples (20th Anniversary Edition), Harville Hendrix, New York: Holt Paperbacks.

How to Love Your Marriage: Making Your Closest Relationship Work, M.A. Eve Eschner Hogan and Jack Canfield, 2006, Alameda, California: Hunter House, Inc.

The Seven Levels of Intimacy: The Art of Loving and the Joy of Being Loved, Mathew Kelly, 2007, New York: Fireside (Simon & Schuster)

The Law of Attraction: The Science of Attracting More of What You Want and Less of What You Don't, Michael Losier, 2010, New York: Wellness Central (Hachette Book Group).

The Mastery of Love: A Practical Guide to the Art of Relationship, a Toltec Wisdom Book, Don Miguel Ruiz, 2002, San Rafael, California: Amber-Allen.

CHAPTER 6

WHEN BAD THINGS HAPPEN:
Accidental Injury, Serious Illness, Near Death, Death of Loved One/Friend, Depression and Suicide

"When there is a mistake, don't look back at it long.
Take the reason for the thing into your mind
and then look forward. Mistakes are lessons in wisdom."
(unknown)

You can overcome difficult challenges and setbacks, and/or be there to help others in need.

As difficult as some of these stories might be to read, there is a common and important theme. All of these young people learned how to recover from the experience and how to move on and live the life they wanted. Included here are actual stories about the suicide of a friend or relative, serious injury accidents, serious illness, near death experience, the death of a loved one or friend, and depression. There are two reasons for including these tragic events. First, none of us will go through life without either experiencing some of these things personally or having something similar happen to someone we care about. Second, when these traumatic events came up in class, a number of students did have a personal experience or friend/family experiences, but many had no experience with any of these traumatic events. Everyone was surprised at how much they learned from these stories, especially those with no personal experience, and how appreciative they were for the insight and knowledge. The point here is that even if you have never had one of these experiences, you will learn a lot from reading this chapter.

Suicide

It is a sad statement to make, but by our early adult years almost everyone knows someone who has committed suicide. I am no different. There were several suicides when I worked in the school district, but the one that hit me the hardest was a sixteen-year-old boy whose family were very close friends of mine. Mark, his younger sister, and his parents went on a ski weekend with my two daughters and me. We had a great weekend! Mark was a fun, happy, smart, outgoing, athletic, and compassionate fellow. I enjoyed the person he was and loved him like a son.

As you read, write your thoughts and feelings in the margin.

We all left the ski area Sunday, as Monday was a school day for the kids. On Tuesday evening Mark's neighbor, a close family friend, called me. He was distraught. He told me that he had heard what sounded like a gunshot next door. Mark's parents weren't home yet so he went over to see. He found Mark lying on the floor, dead, with a revolver next to him. It wasn't an accident, as Mark had put the revolver together and had loaded it. There was no note. This was one of the most horrible calls I have ever received. What had gone wrong?

We never found out. No one at school had noticed anything out of the ordinary with Mark, nor had his friends. I found myself feeling guilty because I had worked with kids for many years and was good at picking up problems, yet all I had seen was a happy kid two days earlier.

While I could only imagine the shock for his family, it was an incredibly painful experience for all of us, compounded by the fact that we never got to understand why it had happened. I flew over to be with Mark's parents and sister, the neighbor couple, and other close friends, and we all talked and cried and shared stories. This was the first time in my life that I realized how important it is to grieve and not hold the pain inside, to realize healing cannot be done in isolation. We all needed each other. I still think of Mark with love, but my pain has subsided with the passing years.

In class there were examples of students who had friends or family members who had committed suicide. Most often there would be no one who saw it coming or could understand why, and the pain ran deep. Trying to make sense of it, or to understand the reason why rarely helps. In fact, it is likely that you will never know.

As you will find in the Self Search Experience in the Appendix on page 246, journaling about your feelings and experience can help you through the shock and the pain. In fact, grieving and talking to people you trust is far better than holding the pain inside. Many have found that writing your deceased friend a goodbye letter and expressing love can bring a sense of peace and some closure (as you saw with Karlo in the Introduction). Though I had never done this before, I did write a letter to Mark, and the process helped a great deal. I hope you hear me saying: it is just not healthy to hold all those feelings inside.

Accidental Serious Injury

As you read the following stories, notice the attitude and resiliency of the injured individuals. Equally important was the insight each gained into his own life and how each used that knowledge to better his own life. Instead of focusing on the tragedy, they chose to recognize the new opportunities and made new choices. While the experiences are difficult, I think you will enjoy the outcomes of these two stories.

Dan—"I knew I was very close to my death."

Probably the event that changed my life the most happened the summer after my junior year. My dad owned a concrete plant, and I worked for my dad every summer since I was fourteen. I was the loader operator. I filled the bins with material so my dad could load the material to make concrete. It was in my last week of work when I had a bad accident.

The sand that the trucks were bringing in was wet, so sometimes I would have to go bang on the bottom of the hopper to make the sand go up the conveyor belt. It was a real pain in the ass. One time the sand was stuck, and I got lazy and I jumped into the hopper to try and kick the sand down. The sand had made kind of a land bridge, and I fell into the middle of the hopper. I really didn't know how much trouble I was in, but I quickly realized I screwed up big time. I was in the middle of the hopper and sand was all around me. It was higher than my head and, if the sand fell, I was going to suffocate to death. My feet were starting to go through the bottom of the hopper. My boots were

In traumatic situations it is important to talk to someone.

dragging on the conveyor belt and the force was slowly pulling me through the bottom of the hopper. I started to yell, but with the noise of the conveyor belt there was just no way anyone could hear me. I started throwing sand out of the hopper hoping someone would see it. I was really in a bad spot.

After about a half hour, the bottom edge of the hopper had worn through my leather boot and the metal was digging into my ankle. After my boots made it through, my knees were now on the conveyor belt. I had sand all around me, and I couldn't move anywhere. My knees were starting to get ground on the conveyor. I tried to wiggle my legs out, but there was no way in hell. It would just give me more pain going against the conveyor belt. I remember thinking that I did not want to die. I also thought about my two grandpas and thought I would probably see them in heaven. I just kept praying to God. I also thought how awful it would be for my parents to find their son buried alive.

It was tough to keep my head through all this. After another hour of my knees being ground on the conveyor belt, my dad looked in the hopper. I yelled, "Shut off the belt, shut off the belt" He ran down to the switch and turned it off. The bookkeeper called the fire department and they were on their way.

The first thing the fire department did was put a barrel over my head so the sand wouldn't fall around me. It was a different kind of rescue than they were used to, so they just made it up as they went along. After about another hour they got all the sand out. Next they put a brace on my back in case I had a serious back injury. I think it was about three and half hours after I had fallen into the hopper.

It was about a week and a half before I finally got to go home. I had casts all the way up both my legs. It was good to get home, but I still had a long way to go. I remember the first time I saw my injuries. The doctor removed the casts, and I almost started to cry. I had no idea how bad my injuries were until then. I had stitches and staples all over my legs. It was just shocking to see my injuries for the first time.

I think the accident has affected me in many ways. I know I am not as confident to overcome adversity. as I once was. I don't wear shorts out in public very often because my legs are scarred up pretty bad. It's a continuing process that I have to deal with the rest of my life. I have gotten better about it after time has gone by. I also know that I can handle adversity. I can overcome this, so I can do just about anything. The accident has shaped who I am as person more than any other event in my life.

Chris—"The day I was run over by a car changed my life."

The day I got run over was one of the defining moments of my life. I was partying at a campsite when it all happened. A man, who was probably drunk, was towing his boat back to the campsite. Well, I managed to fall and get run over by the wheel of the trailer, which completely crushed my leg. I now realize the dramatic effect this event had on my life.

Getting run over that day is what ended up being me hitting the bottom. This was the beginning of the end: the end of all the guilt, all the fear, all the paranoia, all the sleepless nights, and all the negative thoughts. I had a problem, and it took something this traumatic to make me realize it. The events that led up to this defining moment were a matter of being young, lost, and completely irresponsible.

At a very young age, I had my first drink. I was about fourteen years old. My friend Brian (who is now a recovering cocaine addict) had convinced me to try drinking. This was the day that set me up for a long five years of partying and getting into trouble. When I took my first shot, I thought I would feel the effects instantaneously. I didn't, so

I took another and another until I basically dropped to the floor. When you're in eighth grade and you do something like this, it doesn't just stay a secret. I was a partier, a druggie, and later in my teenage life, an alcoholic. It is really hard for me to be writing all of this right now because it is something that has caused so much pain in my life. I have disappointed so many people and have caused so much pain. In fact, I'm beginning to tear up right now and I don't remember the last time I've done that. I just can't understand why I put myself through all that pain.

Attending treatment, having two DUIs, getting into fights, parents not trusting me, doing stupid things at parties, and sleeping with random people had all been too much for me. I couldn't live with myself anymore. I knew what I was doing was wrong and that it needed to stop, but for some reason I couldn't. I began thinking terrible things about myself, about how I was worthless and had no self-control. Drinking helped me shut out my bad feelings. After a while I couldn't even sleep at night. I felt such an immense guilt about what I was doing. There were so many negative things going through my head I became seriously depressed. All the while I prayed and prayed and prayed.

The day I got run over was the day God finally answered my prayers. My guess is that he had tried before but I wasn't listening. The day I got run over changed who I am. Lying in bed for eight days unable to walk, allowed me to consider my life decisions. What was I doing to myself? How did I get myself in this period of excruciating pain? For more than a year, I had been living with so much guilt and fear that it had completely overwhelmed me. I made a decision to live a different life and no longer be afraid. I realized it was me causing the guilt, the humiliation, and the bad reputation. It was me who could change this, and only me.

Today I understand that I am no longer an alcoholic. I am not a partier or a trouble maker. I was young and irresponsible. I didn't know how to deal with my emotions and I didn't know how to deal with the real world. I lived a lie, thinking that getting drunk would solve my problems. I lived a lie, thinking that getting drunk is fun. After being sober for eighteen months, I realize now how to really have fun and how to enjoy life.

Writing this has helped me to understand how far I have come and how great a thing I have done on my own. I picked myself up, and I couldn't be more proud of it. I look at life in a completely different light today. I have become the responsible one in my group of friends, and they all look up to me. Almost everyday someone tells me how much I inspire them because of the way I live my life today. I've helped so many of my friends get out of the same rut I was in. There is so much more to life than trying to find a good time. Life is a good time in itself.

This quote really hit home for me, and I will always remember it. "We either make ourselves miserable, or we make ourselves strong. The amount of work is the same." (Carlos Castaneda) Looking back it's apparent that it took so much energy to make myself feel that bad inside. I could have stopped it at any time, but I didn't. It took just as much work to reverse those feelings and live life as happy as I do today, but it is so much better to live life happy. It feels so much better.

Dan and Chris each came away with some great life insights. Instead of self-pity or blaming others they accepted what had happened, learned from it and focused on having a better life. Dan came away knowing that he was a stronger person and could "overcome any adversity." Chris had been on a very destructive path, and he really got that. He was able to change his life so much that he then wanted to help others. He became an inspiration to his friends. His takeaway— "It is much better to have a happy life"—is one of the keys to putting one's life on course.

You Matter:

Through the Self Search Experiences in the Appendix on Page 225, you can experience the same processes that Dan and Chris worked through.

Serious Illness

It is so easy to take our health and our everyday lives for granted. They almost seem to run on automatic, until something like the occurrence of a sudden illness intrudes. Next is an example of the occurrence of sudden illness and its impact. There is much we can learn from the experiences of others in how they deal with what happens and the choices they make. Some simply give up. Some choose anxiety, grief, and even denial. Others, like Stephanie, choose to face the challenge and all of its fears and discomforts, and put their energy into their fight!

> **Stephanie—"At nineteen I was diagnosed with cervical cancer."**
>
> *"Live today as if there is no tomorrow." Faith is a concept that has guided my life. Re-gaining my passion for living has been a personal struggle. Here is what happened.*
>
> *I am a freshman! I love Washington State University and all the excitement surrounding school and my social life. As an eighteen year old, my life certainly has changed. In the last four months I have graduated high school, moved away from home and now I am in college. This is such an exciting time in my life.*
>
> *In the middle of this month, I went to the on-campus medical center to get a regular check-up. My gynecologist is a wonderful and lively woman who is very compassionate. I appreciate her compassion since she is between my legs and that is a bit awkward for me. One week later, I receive a phone call. My gynecologist tells me that there is something up with my pap and she wants me to come in for a repeat. I start to ask her if everything is okay and she just thinks that the test got messed up and this happens all the time.*

I have an appointment for my biopsy at Family Medicine. I am nervous. This check-up is going to tell me if I am okay or not. Earlier this year, my aunt had breast cancer, doctors removed both breasts, and now she is in radiation. Her daughter, my cousin, has ovarian cancer and has a ninety-five percent chance of never having children. This all makes me nervous. I have not told my parents anything yet, nor any of my friends, nor my boyfriend.

I am in my apartment and the phone rings. I have been expecting this phone call for a while now, as it has been two solid weeks since I had my biopsy done. After answering the phone, the woman on the other line tells me that I need to come in immediately. Freaked out, I ask her, "What is the problem?"

"You have low grade cancer."

I make an appointment and rush down there. The doctor is already waiting. I am in a dimly lit room, a little children's room. I am alone. I have never felt this alone in my entire life.

The doctor enters and just gives me this huge hug. What is going on? I am confused and mad at this point. We sit down and she explains everything and I have no idea what she is saying. All I am hearing is there is something wrong with me, and yet I feel completely fine.

Surgery or no surgery. That was my choice. If I have surgery, then I eliminate the problem, but there is a possibility that my body would take care of the situation on its own. I also have not told anyone. If I have surgery, that requires me to call home. If I choose to not have surgery, I could risk later having to do chemo and radiation and the possibility of never having children. I am scared and alone.

This time, it was different. They had given me this sedative that made me loopy. I am back in that same chair, but this time, there are about seven people in the room and all this extra equipment and television screens. I lie back and I am feeling sleepy. The nurse had made me sign this form that states if I die during this surgery, I would not sue. After I signed that form, she gave me a local, so I feel nothing from my bellybutton down. Relaxed and spread wide-eagle in this contraption, I feel this sharp pain. I sit up, not realizing that the doctor is still inside me and I start to freak out. I want to leave. I am done. I hate the doctor's office, I hate this chair, I hate this medicine that I am on, I hate the bright lights and more, I hate the seven faces that are telling me to calm down.

Finally, the phone call that changed my life. "You are cancer-free."

YES! I am fine and I knew I was going to be fine!

Even in a situation like this, happiness has come out of it. The most surprising side affect was my dad. My dad and I are close, and I am still in shock. When I found out I had cancer, his life changed also. He no longer works long hours, is not as up-tight, and takes the time to "smell the roses." Dad is now in yoga and he runs daily. His relationship with my mom is renewed, and their love is back. I am amazed, and I love him more than ever for taking care of himself after years of taking care of us.

Life is precious. Passion in my life has been reawakened. By writing about this experience and taking in every moment and living like there is not going to be a tomorrow, I have my passion back. I have overcome so many obstacles in my life, and I understand the importance of taking care of myself. Meditating, practicing yoga, and taking some time out have made me healthier. Since last January, I have lost twenty-eight pounds. There is so much in this life that I want to accomplish, and I have a good work ethic to back me. My short-term goal is to graduate, and then I am not sure. I know I will be successful in whichever field opens its door to me, as long as I have my passion.

Sometimes it takes a shock, like a potentially fatal illness or a near death experience to cause our reawakening to how precious life is. Stephanie's story is inspirational, and is even more so when we see the effect she had on her father. She reawakened her passion for life and his passion as well, and she created a life plan with goals and a deep intent to live to her fullest.

Near Death Experience

This story was one of the most inspiring in terms of courage and determination. Imagine: Andrea was suddenly and totally incapacitated at the age of nineteen.

Andrea—"The next thing I knew it was three weeks later, and I was in a hospital."

This is a story I do not share with many people, and so when I tell my story to the class, it will become another part of my stretch as I relive those horrible days in the hospital and the misery I went through. I am brought back to a horrific experience that has changed me, and my life forever.

I was a normal, happy, giddy, always smiling girl. I lived a good life. I was friends with many people and had a lot of adventures and was always trying something new and challenging. My passion was and still is skiing.

There were no symptoms. No one had any idea. It was just a regular day. I went to class, went home, changed, and drove up to Stevens Pass to ski. Three weeks later I woke up in a blue room. There were many tubes coming out of me. My whole left side was numb and immobile. I couldn't move any of it. I was exhausted so I closed my eyes thinking that I was dreaming. When I woke up later, I was still in the same position and blue room that I had been in earlier. Still, I thought I was dreaming. This couldn't be true. What had happened? I had no idea.

Turns out, I had a blood vessel rupture which has very similar symptoms and outcomes as a brain aneurism. I was born with this defect. The veins in my head were tangled, and neither I, nor anyone in my family had known of this. As I grew, the veins became tighter and tighter. The day that I had gone skiing was the day the veins decided to rupture. From the mountain, I was driven straight to the hospital and then flown to Harborview Hospital in Seattle, Washington.

I spent my first week of being conscious just trying to wake up. Then I spent four weeks in intensive therapy. The surgery had affected my short-term memory and my left side was without function. All the muscle memory had been lost, so I had to do therapy to regain the muscle movement. I did it all: occupational, speech, and lots and lots of physical therapy. Unless you have gone through it, you will never know of the internal suffering that goes on inside those rooms. I would have never known had it not been for my own experience. It's a depressing place to be.

What can you learn from Andrea's story about dealing with bad things in your life?

I shocked myself by how much will I had in me. I worked hard, harder than any time in my life. I had a determination in me that I never knew existed. I did extra exercises when I was not in therapy, not only for my body but for my mind as well. I had to learn how to do everything again. That was the hardest part of the whole recovery. I had to start back at square one. It felt like knowing what square ten was like but having no ability and starting back at one. I knew how to do everything, but I just couldn't do it.

By the time I went home I was more focused on regaining my personality and my soul. I was not myself. I can't even say that I was a mind in someone else's body or that I was a body without the right mind. I had seemed to lose both mind and body. Everything was foreign to me. I didn't know who I was or where I was going. My friends tried to help me but that only frustrated me. My struggle became a mental challenge.

The first glimpse of my happiness came on a day that a friend took me skiing! Go figure. Doing something that I had once done and had always loved gave me the glimpse of my old self. There was some happiness deep down inside that shell of a body somewhere! One of my problems had been that I was still living in the past. I would remember what it used to be like for me and how I used to interact with my friends. I kept questioning, "Why? Why did it happen to me?" What I did not know then but know now is that in life there is always change. That is just life. I needed to start focusing on the now and the future. I just felt sorry for myself, and instead of seeing the positive, I was focused on the negativity of my situation. I had a completely wrong way of thinking about myself. Instead of being grateful that it did happen to me, because I was lucky enough to have so much support from my family, friends, community, and even from people who didn't know me, I was being selfish and seeing it as a something against me. It wasn't until the realization that I was the only one who could fix me that I started working on myself. I needed to change my perspective and my future. I was slowly regaining my happiness.

I can now be happy. I can now look back at that experience as a good one. It has changed me and made me the person I am today, who I like by the way!

Look at the choices Andrea made once she regained consciousness and realized the state in which she found herself. Prior to this situation she had not seen herself as a particularly driven or determined young woman. Considering that she had lost her short-term memory and her ability to talk or walk, she could easily have given up or dropped into any myriad of negative emotions. One of the most common responses is to focus on the question: "Why did this happen to me?" Many get stuck here and move into self-pity. Instead, Andrea dwelled on it for a little while and then was able to move to "start focusing on the future." I am convinced this is what helped her turn the corner and regain her health.

Death of a Loved One Or Friend

It is surprising how many young people have had experiences with the death of family members or close friends. Very few of us have been taught much, if anything, about how to deal with death and dying, whether the death is sudden and a surprise, or is the result of a long-term illness. So few have any understanding of the process and the importance of grieving, of talking through their experience, and of working though the pain. Remember, everyone at one time or another will experience the loss of someone they love. How we choose to deal with this situation will determine how deeply it will affect us and how long we will carry the pain. Here are some very important things to know about dealing with death and dying.

1. Feelings of loss and grief are real and normal. Letting yourself experience the feelings and not trying to hold back or repress them is important to both your physical and emotional health.

2. Expressing your feelings and talking about the person, even if it is hard, is healing and a healthy thing to do.

3. Not dealing with the feelings, carrying the loss, pain, and/or guilt for a long period of time can be very harmful to you.

4. The "stages" or reactions to death and dying happen to survivors as well as to victims of terminal illness. These stages are commonly described as denial, anger, bargaining, depression, and finally, acceptance.

There were many stories from students about losing their mothers, fathers, grandparents, brothers and sisters, best friend, and boy friends and girl friends. All were sad to read. Yet our focus was on getting through this and moving on with their lives. An understanding of the above four points was helpful, but there is one thing that was most consistently of greatest help to those still in pain. As odd as this might seem, what was most helpful was having them write a letter to the one they had lost.

The following are the points from their letters that seemed to have the greatest positive impact.

• Remember the fun, the love and all the good things you experienced together.

• Express your regret, pain, and sense of loss.

154

- Bring closure by allowing yourself to let go and move on, always carrying the love forward.

- Don't wait. Let the people now in your life who you care about know how much you care about them while they are still here.

The following are three examples of letters that are touching and insightful, and were freeing experiences for the writers.

Jake – "My best friend died in an auto accident."

Dear Brian,

What the hell happened? One moment you were raising hell, like always, and the next you were gone. I didn't even get to say goodbye. I miss you so much. I guess I needed a reminder of what a loss your death has left all of us feeling. Yah see, I think I have been so preoccupied with trying to heal that I just have been kidding myself. I've just been trying to hide the hurt away. Well, damn-it, I gotta deal with it now. I thought we were supposed to rule the world. Although we weren't sure how we were going to do it, but damnit we were gonna do it. We were going to get out of school, save our money, and figure it out as we went along. You really had me convinced. Who knows, I think we would have pulled it off.

You were my best friend. I just wish we had been able to spend more time together the last few months. I was doing my own thing and you were doing your thing.

The reason I'm writing this is because I need to thank you. Thank you for being the loyal friend you were. Thank you for helping me with everything. Thank you for helping me see the big picture instead of being caught up with "the now." Thank you for not shaving my eyebrows on all of those perfect opportunities. Thank you for finally making me realize that friendship isn't something to take for granted. One good thing that came from this experience is I do value my friendships more now.

I just wish I could have given you this letter nine months ago instead of waiting until now. I miss you, friend. You'll never know how much you touched our lives, especially mine. You're a part of all of us and you live on through all of us.

Peace, Your best friend, Jake

Once Jake started writing, he was able to shift from anger and anguish to remembering the humor and fun they had together, and how much their friendship had meant. He was then able to focus on the future and the importance of his current friendships, and to never again take his relationships for granted.

Jenny—"My sister Mary died from cancer."

Dear Mary,

I don't know where to begin telling you all of the things that have been in my head and my heart since you died. I love you so much, and I feel like my life fell apart the day you passed away. There is a song by Sarah McLachlan called, "I Love You," and this is the song that perfectly describes my feelings about you and your death. The chorus includes these lyrics:

"I forgot to tell you I love you, and life's too long and cold here without you. I grieve in my condition, for I cannot find the words to say I need you so."

I did forget to tell you that I love you, and my life seems so strange now that you are not around. And I have been completely unable to express any of these feelings without breaking into tears for the past few months, because how can you tell someone that has been a part of your life and whole being for so long that they meant the whole world to you? This letter is my best attempt right now to at least tell you a fraction of how much I miss you.

I never knew how much I cared for you or how important you were to me, until it was too late. I miss you, and I wish that I could turn back the clock and save you, or at least tell you what a special person you were to me and to everyone else who knew you even a little bit.

I feel like a hypocrite for missing you so much, when I never took the time to show this much emotion towards you when you were alive. But just know that you made a difference in my life, and I will never forget your smile, your laugh, or your intelligence for the rest of my life.

It is hard for someone to honestly know how many lives they have touched, but I hope that you are watching over all of us now, and can see that you played a part in so many people's lives.

Thank you for being the beautiful, kind, unique person that you were, and for being my childhood best friend and my lifelong sister. I will hold you in my heart always, and think of you with every breath I take. People always say that when someone dies your grief subsides and you begin to forget the person a little each day. With me, however, I miss you more and more every day, and remember just one more thing about you and about our friendship.

It just seems so bittersweet that while I am getting ready to graduate from college, and begin my life as an adult, you never even got the chance to decide what you wanted to do with your life. So when I accept my diploma, say "I do" to my future husband, or see my child for the first time, please know that these accomplishments are both of ours, not just mine.

I love you and I miss you, Mary, and I can only hope that one day we will meet again and I will be able to say all of these things to your face, and you will be able to laugh at me for being so mushy. From all that is within me, I will never let your memory fade, or allow you to slip out of my life.

Your sister and best friend,
Jenny

Of course there were many more 1etters and many more who noticed that once they started writing, the pages flew by. This last one is different. It was written by Sue after she had written a story of the death of her boyfriend. She followed the story with a letter of farewell. Here is what she wrote as a reflection of what she had learned through this process.

Sue – "What I learned from dealing with the death of my boyfriend."

Life is Good.

It's so weird. I haven't cried over David in such a long time. I didn't even know that I had all these feelings left in me. I thought that I was truly happy. And I was, to a certain extent. David's life is not something that I want to forget.

But I've changed since writing my letter. The longer term effects I don't know, but right now it feels ... right. I feel right in my heart. I could always improve in life but right now, in this moment, it's perfect.

I feel empty but not hollow. It's a good emptiness. Clarity. That's what it is. I can feel clearer. Fresh. Like I just came out of a waterfall. Relieved. I'm still me, still here.

I'm so grateful. I know why I am here on this earth. My purpose is clear. And that is to love. Without this experience my love was shallow. But through David and all the other people and events that have happened, my love is complex; deep might be a better word.

This love I want to share. Sometimes I'm baffled by my own happiness. Is this real? Can I, should I, really be THIS happy? Do I deserve all this?

Well, whether I deserve it or not, I have it. And I want to keep it. So I will.

Depression Is More Common Than You Think

How much has your life changed in the last three to four years? How many of the following changes have you experienced: left home, moved to a new city, living with new people, not enough money, working a new job, taking new classes, having to achieve in academics, starting a new relationship, breaking up, making new friends, and on and on? The amount of change you go through can have a direct affect on the amount of stress you experience. The shorter the time frame, the more stressful things can become. Handling stress is about knowing yourself, paying attention to what is happening to you, and learning how to manage the impact of all this on you.

When you (or anyone you know) reach your level of stress intolerance and the stress continues or even increases, it can cause a significant negative impact on your body, your emotions, and your thought processes. Here are some examples of experiences with depression.

Christopher—"Stress over grades, finances, and being alone caused my depression."

One of the first things I really shared in my papers was the depression I felt this past summer. I referred to it in my paper as "being engulfed in my emotional life," as the word depression made me feel that I was. I was not willing to admit at that point the feeling of being weak. The root of my depression was stress over grades and finances, as well as the feeling of being alone. I seemed to cry on a daily basis, which was not normal for me, as I am a person who rarely, if ever, cries. I tried engulfing myself in school and work, even picking up a second job in order to occupy my time so that I would not be at home thinking about how lonely I was. Eventually this depression passed, but I realized how easily someone could slip into depression. It is not the sign of weakness that I had once thought it was, but rather it was a cry for help in dealing with all of the feelings I was experiencing.

You Matter:

Perry—"I even thought about suicide a few times."

I know quite a bit about depression. I suffered from depression for a long time. I used to have a really hard time dealing with things. I used to have a really low self-esteem, and I would get down on myself all the time. I didn't really realize that I was depressed. I just thought I was crap. I even thought about suicide a few times my freshman year. I used to go on weekends and drink a lot. I would drink until I couldn't remember what happened. I would drink to feel better but it would just make me feel worse after I sobered up. During my freshman year, when I was at my worst, I had a knife and I would use it to carve on my arm. Not really bad but just till it started to bleed. I knew what I was doing was really bad but I don't remember exactly what I was feeling. I just didn't realize how crazy and stupid what I was doing was. One night I was starting to drink and I gave the knife to a friend of mine and I told her to take it and not give it back. The next day when I stumbled home she was waiting for me and she made me talk to her. She also made me promise to go to counseling or she would call the cops on me. I ended up going to counseling and they put me on an antidepressant for a while. I don't know if it was the antidepressant or the counselor, or just the fact that she cared so much for me. But it got me kicked in the ass and headed in the right direction for recovery. Now I understand that I am a good person, and the help just made me a really better person.

Be Aware Of Serious Depression

Serious depression is treatable.

It's important to pay attention to what is happening to you. It is very easy to move into a mindset that minimizes your feelings so that you keep adapting as things slowly continue a downward spiral. As you adapt, it leaves you feeling "good enough," even though things have gotten worse. For Kerry, depression developed over a three-year period. She kept trying so hard to hold her head above water as she became increasingly over stressed and slipped into depression. This is what she wrote, describing her thoughts and feelings as she was getting to a bad place.

Kerry—"I wonder if anyone else feels worried all the time."

I feel like I'm trying to swim against a strong current that is not only pushing me back, but is pulling me under. I have not been able to get help because I have been too scared. I have been scared that I will be turned away again by my professors and that my friends would think differently about me. That would make me feel more alone than I already do.

I wonder if people can imagine what it feels like to be in a room full of friends and feel like nobody is there. I wonder if anyone can imagine sitting through a class and just wanting to cry because it is impossible to concentrate. I wonder if anyone notices when I really do cry. I wonder if anyone else knows what it's like to just want to go sit in a room in the dark and be sad, because sometimes that is all you can think of to do. I wonder if anyone else can't eat. I wonder if anyone else can't sleep and can go for weeks with less than four hours of sleep a night. I wonder if anyone else feels worried all the time. I wonder if anyone else feels like dying might not be so bad.

I haven't really had thoughts of suicide. For that I am grateful. I have, however, felt like it wouldn't be too terrible if I died. Every time I fly, I imagine the plane crashing and everyone else surviving but me. I could never wish anything terrible on anyone else and I could never do anything to harm myself.

Last Sunday night I lay awake and thought about how sad I am now. All of a sudden it occurred to me that this is the one thing in my life that I haven't been honest with myself about. I have been trying hard to convince myself that I don't have a problem. It has gone on too long.

Depression can happen to anyone. Have you ever had any of these feelings but tried to hold them down or hide them?

It can be hard to ask for help.

You Matter:

I decided on Monday that it was time to go talk to a doctor. I called three times to make an appointment and hung up the first two times a receptionist answered. The third time I cried on the phone when I told her that I wanted to see a doctor about the possibility of depression. I went to see the doctor on Tuesday afternoon. I was so scared. I was shaking and started crying immediately when he came into the room. He asked me how long this has been going on. When I told him, he didn't even ask me why it took so long to come in. I think he knew how hard it was.

This was the biggest challenge I have ever faced. I have always been a very independent person, and it was hard to admit that I couldn't fix this problem on my own.

Most don't want anyone to know something is wrong.

Here's the thing. High stress is directly related to harmful physical and emotional health. What is overwhelming to you may not be a big deal to your friend. And what your friend finds way too difficult, you may view as easy. We all have our intolerance points and when your stress is over the top, especially over a period of time, it creates anxiety, affects your self-esteem, weakens your immune system, and can move you toward depression, whether mild or severe. Much of the time, things lighten up as the stress and anxiety diminish. All of this is interconnected as it affects you. So what can you do?

Many are in denial that anything is wrong.

When it comes to dealing with anxiety and depression, most people pretend it doesn't exist, or at least deny the heavy impact it is having on them. In all of the examples above, they didn't admit to themselves that there was a problem, and instead they pretended that nothing unusual was happening. Most don't tell their friends or family because they think it's a sign of weakness as a person, or think that they are supposed to deal with life issues by themselves. Many are embarrassed or ashamed to even consider seeking help. Picture the levels of depression as on a continuum. It is not a matter of either being healthy or depressed. Instead it ranges from stressed and unhappy to some bouts of depression, to actually being depressed, and eventually to severe depression. This is something that we can all experience at some time as a normal reaction to grieving, like in a relationship breakup. It can come on suddenly and be paralyzing, or it can develop over a period of years. No one, no matter how strong, mature, or aware, is immune to depression.

What You Can Do

Serious depression doesn't usually go away by itself. The smartest and best thing to do is get some help. Counselors see depression all the time and are really good at helping people through it. In conjunction with counseling and to help you figure out the level of your depressed feelings and their causes, there are some important things that you can do.

- Write out what you're going through. It really does help to let it out on paper. It will help you gain a new perspective. You may see new ways of dealing with things and gain new insights, and will have a great starting point for a counselor.

- Talk to someone who can help you. This can't be emphasized enough. Share with this person what you have written. **To ask for help is not a sign of weakness, it is an indicator of wisdom, strength and courage.** It needs to be someone who cares about you yet does not try to solve your issues, not a rescuer.

- Develop your plan for addressing those causes of your anxiety and stress over which you have some control. Identify those things you can do something about and those you cannot do anything about because they are outside of your control.

- Pay attention to your health, and take even better care during these times. Consciously choose to get enough sleep, eat foods good for you, and exercise regularly. These are the areas most neglected when experiencing some depression and yet are most helpful in the process of lifting out of depression.

The beauty of all this is that, though it can take a period of time to reach this depressed state, it can take very little time to turn it around, and regain your happiness!

You Matter:

It is so important to be alert when challenges appear and to see them as an opportunity to learn and grow. This will also help you to be more prepared for the challenges that will come as your life progresses. No human being can go through life without challenges and personal stretches. At some point you will be able to look back on the challenges that were presented to you and, with hindsight, will either feel good about yourself because of how you moved through a hard time, or wish you had done things differently. All of the people whose stories are included can be proud of themselves because they had the courage to face their life challenges.

How was it that in almost every situation, they were able to get through the traumatic experience, learn from it, and refocus their lives in healthy directions? In the Appendix you will find the **Self Search Experiences: Overcoming Bad Experiences** (Page 246).

Key Takeaways from When Bad Things Happen

> ➤ No one goes through life without some significant challenges.

> ➤ When someone close to you dies, it is important to grieve, find support, and not hold the pain inside.

> ➤ Suicide and accidental injury happen more often to men. Alcohol is frequently a factor.

> ➤ Writing your deceased friend a goodbye letter and expressing love can bring a sense of peace and some closure.

> ➤ Instead of focusing on the tragedy, you can choose to recognize there will be new opportunities.

> ➤ No one is immune to depression.

> ➤ Serious depression doesn't usually go away by itself. The smartest and best thing to do is to go get some help.

> ➤ Counseling can greatly help in understanding what happened, in regaining confidence and in moving on with life.

Important References and Resources

Dealing with the aftermath of **suicide** and dealing with the **death** of a loved one:
www.thelightbeyond.com. This is an excellent resource.

The Healing Book: Facing the Death, and Celebrating the Life of Someone You Love, Ellen Sabin ,2006, New York: Watering Can

Dealing with **depression** and **traumatic experiences:**
www.helpguide.org/mental/depression_tips.htm

The Mindful Way through Depression: Freeing Yourself from Chronic Unhappiness, Mark Williams, John Teasdale, Zindel Segal, and Jon Kabat-Zinn, 2007, New York: Guilford Press

Healing from Trauma: A Survivor's Guide to Understanding Your Symptoms and Reclaiming Your Life, Jasmin Lee Cori and Robert Scaer, 2008, Cambridge, MA: Da Capo Press

Healing Your Emotional Self: A Powerful Program to Help You Raise Your-Self-Esteem, Quiet Your Inner Critic, and Overcome Your Shame, Beverly Engel, 2007, New York: Wiley

CHAPTER 7

OTHER BAD THINGS HAPPEN: SEXUAL ABUSE

*"You gain strength, courage, and confidence
by every experience in which you really stop to
look fear in the face. You are able to say to yourself,
"I have lived through this horror. I can
take the next thing that comes along."
You must do the thing you think you cannot do."
Eleanor Roosevelt*

If it happened to you, you can live beyond this horror. For the rest of us, true compassion comes from understanding what others have experienced.

In life, bad things do sometimes happen to good people. These difficult experiences, some would call tragedies, and would re-shape how you think, how you feel, and the choices you make. This is why I refer to them as "life shaping experiences." You can learn from the bad experiences others have lived through and if something should ever happen to you, having seen their choices may help you through your situation. Even if you don't know anyone who has experienced sexual abuse, by reading this chapter you will have greater compassion when you do hear about it, and a better opportunity to help.

Sadly, in many situations victims often blame themselves. The emphasis here is on facing and addressing these difficult experiences and when necessary, seeking help. There are counselors who are familiar with and know how to work with the common reactions to a traumatic experience: avoidance, shame, repression, and/or pretending it didn't happen. Good counselors have a solid foundation of knowledge and experience to help you more quickly through the process of recovery. It is important to know that there are people who understand and will help you *if you let them*.

Author's Note:

I had a personal connection with each of the students who wrote about their experiences, and I saw first hand the range of their initial emotions from pain and bewilderment to anger and rage. I watched as they worked through their challenges and saw with my own eyes the emergence of their strength, their courage and their self confidence as they chose not to let the experience take them down, but instead to use what they learned to propel them forward with their lives. I have separated the "bad things" that happen into two chapters. This chapter is about a variety of sexual abuse examples,

This chapter may be difficult to read. But do take the time to read the stories. They each offer an exposure to an understanding of what can happen, and the knowledge that individuals can come through to the other side of a traumatic experience healthy, wiser, and with more compassion. Reading this chapter can also provide you with knowledge that could help you avoid a difficult situation, or you may have an opportunity to support someone who may need your understanding.

As you read, see the tragedy, yes, but then also see how they got to the other side; were able to ask for and accept help; and, how they summoned their courage, armed with new knowledge of their own capabilities and resourcefulness; and how these individuals were able to move on with their lives.

Sexual Abuse and Rape

Author's Note:

Although I am well aware that sexual abuse and rape happens to boys, all of the examples here had happened to girls and young women. Therefore, I have used the feminine pronoun throughout this chapter. I think it is vitally important, however, that men also read this section as these are experiences that could happen or may have happened to a girl friend, a sister, a mother, a future wife, a close friend, or even someday, a daughter. You may have an opportunity to help someone you care about or you may even have an opportunity to prevent something like this from happening to someone. Perhaps one of the most important factors here is that we can all learn from each other, we can express our compassion, and we can help support each other through difficult, even traumatic times.

The reports of sexual abuse and rape fell into three categories:

- Childhood abuse

- Date rape

- Manipulation and control

It is pretty much impossible for the average person to understand what goes on in the minds of those who commit these acts. The intent here, however, is to gain an understanding of what happens to the victims and to see how they have been able to overcome the trauma they have experienced.

Childhood Abuse

Jamie—"When I was six years old, it was a stranger at a park."

My negative experience came from a man I don't even know. He was a stranger who molested me in a public bathroom when I was six or seven years old. He took my innocence away at such a young age. I can't even remember why I was alone. My siblings were there and my dad and his wife were there, but the stranger must have gotten to me when I was running back and forth from the park to the track. This man told me he saw spiders crawling in my pants, and that he could get them out for me. Being a little kid, terrified of spiders, I put my trust in him to get them out. He ruined my trust at a young age. He told me not to tell my parents, and I didn't. I didn't tell my mom until I was seventeen and she was the only one I told. There were times when I felt like it was just a dream or a nightmare, but no little kid could dream of something horrific and real as that. I was lucky though, he didn't take me with him and he didn't kill me. As bad as that was, it could have been a whole lot worse, and I am grateful for that.

As part of her Self-Search Experience, Jamie wrote a letter to her molester, not with the intention of sending it, but instead with the intent of clearing her fear and pain and letting go. She wanted to learn to trust again and not have her bad experience interfere with her life. Surprisingly the letter also became one of forgiveness, and remarkably the forgiveness was really for herself. This resulted in helping her let go and move on with her life. It is important to see how Jamie moved from the innocence of a child, through loss of trust, then coming to terms, expressing her anger, and then setting herself free. Here is what she wrote.

Dear Asshole,

Forgive sounds good. Forget I will not. As much as I want to forget it will always be with me. You took my innocence at a young age. You took my trust at six. You did something to a little girl that no little girl should ever, ever, have to go through. I was that little girl you molested in the public bathroom. I was that little girl you told had spiders down her pants and that you could get them out. I was that little girl who trusted you. I was that little girl who was changed at six. I was that little girl who never told a soul until I was seventeen. You will never know the affect it had on me, and you will never know that I turned out to be a strong person.

What kind of sick person would do that? What man made from God would take a little girl into a public bathroom at a park and touch her, saying that the spider laid eggs and you Mr. Almighty kind man would get them all out. I cannot fathom what you were thinking when you were touching me. I want to puke when I think of you. I want to scream at the top of my lungs showing my disgust for you. If this were my daughter I would cut your hands off the most painful way possible. I would cut your genitals off so that you could never experience pleasure again. How could you look at me with my little hands, my little body, my blonde hair and blue eyes and lie to me so you could just touch me? How could you do that when you saw the scared and confused look in my eyes? What unbelievable sickness did you have to touch me when there was a chance of other men coming into the bathroom? You bastard, you asshole, you are the scum of the earth. How I wish that you would just rot in your own guilt. How I wish that you could feel this pain that I kept in me for fifteen years. I would give anything to look you in the face and show my absolute disgust. I would give anything to just hit you so hard for everything you took away from me, and everything that I have kept buried deep inside. I believed you, and when you told me not to tell anyone I didn't, not until I was seventeen.

I thought it was me, I thought it was my fault. I know that it's not my fault. It's you. It's your fault! At twenty-one I have found my voice. I am not going to sit here anymore and let the memory of you torment me. I am going to tell my story and hope one day you will pay for what you did. I pray and hope that I was the only little child you touched. I would give anything, absolutely anything to be the only one you did this to. I would not want another child to feel the way I did. I think to myself that it could have been so much worse; you could have made me do things to you; you could have raped me; you could have kidnapped me; and you could have killed me. As much as what you did to me was horrible, I was being protected from anything worse.

Today I am a twenty-year-old college student. I am a strong young woman. I don't have much anger, and I don't have much worry. I do have a lot of walls and trust issues, but that is nothing to complain about. I don't hate you. I don't wish death upon you, and most of all I forgive you. That day in the park will always be with me, but it will never haunt me anymore. I am letting go of it, and I am letting go of you. I hope you find your way before it's too late. What you did was unimaginable, disgusting, absolutely heart wrenching, but I want you know if you have changed and you are sorry, I will forgive you. I don't want you to forget it, but I want you live in peace, which is where I am now.

Why do you think writing this letter helped Jamie?

I have finally spoken. I can finally fly. I can finally breathe. I can finally start trusting again. No child should ever go through what I went through. I will make it my goal to get sick men away from innocent children. I will make it my goal to help others who have had this done to them to speak out and not hold it in deep within. I will let them know it's okay to speak out. I am a strong confident woman who is no longer afraid; I am no longer going to hide you deep within. I am finally free.

Perhaps the most important part for Jamie was in her third paragraph, where she forgave herself. (There will be more about the importance of self-forgiveness later in the book.) The Self-Search Experience Jamie went through can be found in the Appendix, page 250.

This next story points out how unique we all are and how uniquely we handle situations in our lives. Note how Tammi went to shame rather than anger and carried it as a fear of being labeled, so she never told anyone and remained "stuck." How sad that she carried the weight of it all for so long.

Tammi—"It was my daycare provider's daughter."

When I look back at my childhood there is only one thing that stands out as something that has "damaged" me, something that I am ashamed of. When I was six years old, I was molested by my daycare provider's daughter. I remember it like it was yesterday and still shudder when I think about it. I remember the first time and how I told her that I did not like what she was doing. She told me that it was supposed to feel good and that I should like it because she did. I remember crying and telling her that I wanted to go home. She looked at me and told me that I could not tell anyone what had happened, that it had to stay our little secret. She told me that our parents would be mad and that I would be the one to get punished. I was ashamed so I never told anyone, not even my parents.

I think about the fact that I never told my parents about what was going on, and still have not to this day, and I wonder why. I now realize that this is because I don't want to be labeled as "damaged" or someone with "issues."

Over the last two weeks I have come to forgive the girl for what she did to me. I have been working on forgiveness for a long time and this class has finally given me the strength to let go of my anger towards her. She was around the same age as me so I know that she had to have learned it from someone else. I somehow feel deep down that she had to have been experiencing something far worse than anything she ever did to me. I feel her pain, especially considering what she must have been going through. I can only imagine the pain that this has caused her.

I also now realize that this fear of being labeled has led me to never dealing with the problem. I have thought about seeing a counselor about this in the past but I always told myself that I don't need a counselor. I can't be that messed up about it. I know that what happened was not my fault, but never dealing with it was. It is time to deal with the pain.

As soon as Tammi finished writing this she made the decision to get help. She is now free of her fears, has forgiven herself and has been able to move on in her life with confidence.

In the next story, it took Sherry several years, but she was able to work through a very traumatic experience.

Sherry—"When I was eight it was my seventeen year old neighbor."

I had a traumatic experience when I was about eight years old. Usually my neighbor, Susie, came over to babysit me while my parents went to a meeting. But this time Susie was unavailable, so her older brother Jim came over. He was probably about seventeen or eighteen years old. We were playing cards and talking and he asked me, "Do you know the difference between boys and girls?" I thought he was telling me a joke so I said no. Then he told me he was going to show me. He took me downstairs to a room with no windows and sexually abused me. I knew what he was doing was wrong, but I remember feeling like it was my fault because I misunderstood it as a joke. I tried everything I knew how to do to get out of the situation, but nothing worked, and he was a much bigger person than I was. When it was finally over, he told me "You better not tell your mom or dad what happened or you will get in a lot of trouble." Being the little girl who wanted nothing more than the love, affection and most of all approval of her parents, I took this deeply to heart. I didn't tell a soul what had happened that day until ten years later when I told my father.

I had completely blocked this part out of my memory for ten years. When the incident finally resurfaced, and I told my father, he did not have much of a reaction. I later found out that my father was so shocked and upset that he couldn't even show a reaction. We have since talked about it, and I know that he does care, and that he was upset. But still to this day, any of those topics are absolutely off limits to me, and when they are brought up, I can feel my entire body shutting down, and the sounds around me muting.

This pattern is similar in almost all sexual abuse situations. The child:

- -is frightened and told not to tell,

- -is made to feel that it is her fault,

- -tries to repress it; it seems to be a bad dream,

- -avoids telling anyone or seeking counseling for fear of being labeled as damaged.

This is so sad because the victims often carry this pain and fear inside for years keeping them from being fully connected in their relationships. Counseling is a very wise choice. Working with a trained professional who has helped people with experiences similar to your own can be a freeing experience. Just imagine how healthy it is to be able to let the bad experience go and live the life you want!

Date Rape

At first it was quite surprising to me to find how many young women had experienced date rape. There is a pattern here as well. The two were on a date or met somewhere and left together; a car, his place or her place. Often alcohol was involved. It is usually not a premeditated event. Obviously there are male-female differences in thinking about sex. This is a generalizing, but guys tend to want sex anytime, anywhere, and if alcohol is involved, with anyone. A slight sign of receptivity can be very encouraging to him, so he may get more assertive and sometimes more controlling. The problem is that in each of the situations she is the one who gets deeply hurt and often carries the pain for a long time. The experience for a young woman is similar to what happens to a child. She is made to feel that it is her fault and then carries the guilt. She is afraid to tell anyone, even a counselor and fears she will be negatively labeled as a "slut" or worse. She tries to repress what happened, and she often has great difficulty trusting men in future relationships. Here are two examples.

Renae—"I was raped by my college classmate."

To some extent everyone experiences some form of trauma in his or her life. Some people's situation may be worse than others, but the pain and sorrow is there and real. It is up to each individual to determine how they handle life's trials and decide whether they will see it as a hindrance or a stepping stone in their life.

I am brought back to the time when I was raped last year. I have yet to deal with these issues, and even as I sit here writing I feel my heart beating faster and my mind starting to run. I feel like I am at a point where I should begin sharing while it is still a tender subject and while I haven't completely tried to forget or discount my experience.

I was raped by a classmate, not really a close friend, but someone I was getting to know. We were assigned to the same group in our class. Our groups lasted the entire semester. The rape happened the week before finals when the two of us got together to finish up a paper. Because I knew the guy, it was difficult for me to see what happened as an actual rape. We only had a couple of drinks. My perceptions of rape involved some guy jumping out of the bushes - a stranger.

After it happened, I sat in the rain for hours replaying the whole event and vowing to myself that I would tell no one. I was trying to convince myself that the rape never happened. I went home and crawled in bed, because it was the only thing I could do to be away from everyone. After hours of lying on my bed I realized I had to face life. But how?

Through a past conversation with my roommate, I found out that she too had been raped before, so she would be a safe person for me to talk to. My roommate helped me figure out my options and took me to the hospital where I spoke with several doctors, counselors, police, and had a complete rape exam done.

It has been just over a year now and I am still going through stages of denial, guilt, blame, what if's, and replaying the event in my mind. I try to deny the situation to lessen the pain of dealing with the memories. I feel guilty and want to blame myself for my naïveté and not being more forceful. I experienced the freeze mode where while I was being raped, I laid there crying and biting my hands to lessen the pain. Why didn't I scream??? Why didn't I run out of the room screaming rape??? And why did I sit and finish the paper? Shock, I guess. Terrified. He was a big guy around 230 pounds and 6'4". What could I do against his size? I was in his fraternity surrounded by guys I didn't know. I guess I did what I could, but in my mind it wasn't good enough. The memories don't come as often as they used to, but now that I am writing they are strong.

The biggest help for me is telling my story. At first I told myself not a soul would find out, but I find a certain release by sharing this with others. It helps me to process, and this is why I share it in my writing. I am currently seeing a counselor but we've yet to really focus on the rape. It is time to.

I am afraid. Afraid of what? The pain of healing? Although I cannot change what happened I do have control over how I deal with my thoughts and feelings that are resulting from the rape. I have control of what happens in my life going forward.

Renae is a strong and courageous young woman. Having the strength to reach out to her roommate and to seek professional help took courage. It also gave her the strength to deal with her fears and pain and to take "control of what happens in my life going forward.

Annette's story is also difficult.

Annette—"I was raped by my sports team classmate."

It was my junior year in high school and life was great. I had a lot of friends and I was successful in school and sports. When the time came around to celebrate my seventeenth birthday, my friends and I decided to have a party in the boathouse of my rowing club. Since I mostly rowed with guys, I also invited a few girlfriends from school to make it a little more interesting. The night started out great; we had a lot of fun. A few guys played the guitar, and we shared a lot of stories, laughter, and a few drinks. We were dancing.... having fun.

There was one rower there who I had always had a crush on and basically everybody knew about it. Throughout the night we danced together and talked. At some point as we were sitting on the sofa, our hands found each others and he whispered in my ear to meet him in the men's locker room in a few minutes and then he left. My heart started racing. Could it be? Is he interested in me? That was what I have been waiting for, for so long. So I waited a few minutes and went upstairs. Everybody was having a lot of fun; nobody noticed when the two of us disappeared.

Once I came into the locker room, he locked the door so that nobody would walk in on us and took the key. I did not question that at the time, it seemed pretty reasonable to me not to want anybody to walk in. He looked at me with these hungry eyes and walked over. He grabbed me and started to undress me. I stepped away a little, trying to look in his eyes, but he wasn't present. I tried to walk away but he held on to me. I knew something was wrong when he would not kiss me. He just wanted to get me undressed as fast as he could. I tried to get out of his arms but he was so much stronger. I tried to call for help, but nobody could hear me, they were having fun, the music was loud... I tried. When he finally wrestled me down he had a really hard time penetrating. I was not ready. Not ready for the first time I would ever have sex. He spread my legs even further and finally got in. It hurt and it hurt him too. After a while he just got up, cursed something about me wanting it all along and left me there. I wiped off the blood and tears, tried to put myself together and went back down there. After all, I was celebrating my birthday. A few of my friends asked me what was wrong with me. I just said that I wasn't feeling good, that I probably had too much alcohol. That day I did not just lose my virginity, I lost a part of my soul. I didn't tell anybody. I was blaming myself. It wasn't till about three years later when I started dating a guy that I realized that I wasn't okay. I didn't want to have anything to do with him; I did not want to be naked.

I have waited for almost six years to face my fears. I finally began meeting with a counselor. At first it was a little awkward to speak to someone about my past, especially since it is so personal. However, as we got more accustomed to each other, I was glad to be there, because I could talk to her and she seemed very understanding of what happened and her past experience suggests that she has heard similar stories before so she knows what the people are experiencing. At first talking about the past was very emotional for me and I had to have her read what I wrote about that day because I couldn't speak. But later on when the emotions subsided a little we could talk about

*some things and I had a little easier time expressing how
I felt.*

If anything like this ever happens to you, begin the healing with "it was not my fault." You may have made some poor choices, but that does not give anyone the right to abuse or take advantage of you. Annette made a very healthy choice to work with a counselor who helped her sort through what happened, and deal with how wounded she felt. Renae was actually relieved to know that she no longer had to deal with it by herself. She very soon was able to move on and live the life she wanted to live.

Manipulation and Control

Through the eyes of others it is difficult to understand why someone would remain in a manipulative, controlling relationship in which she/he completely loses self- esteem. It doesn't start out that way. If it did, most would immediately run away. The relationship often begins in the normal way; a mutual attraction, feeling connected, having sex, and making comments and even promises about the future. Then slowly and consistently self-esteem is stripped away and one becomes dependent on the controlling person. Sonja's story is a typical example.

Manipulation and control develops slowly.

Sonja—"For three years I let him use me."

The person who has changed me the most is Chris. He was big and moody and never smiled. Strangely enough, I found his darkness a kind of attractive quality. After my college freshman year he began to come around and talk to me, but I didn't think much of it. Soon into my sophomore year he began to pursue me. The next thing I knew we had been sleeping together and I had become very attached to him.

But it was weird because he called me during breaks to tell me how much he missed me, but when we were in public he was completely different. It was almost like he didn't want anyone to think that we were anything more than just friends. He continuously manipulated me through this ridiculous game and was constantly playing with my mind and emotions. I would ask him how he felt about me, and I see now that he was just saying enough to keep me around. He would tell me how much he liked me and thought about me, but that he just didn't have enough time to really have a girlfriend. If I tried to pull away and tried to stand up for myself he would find a way to get me to change my mind.

Before Chris I was a happy person who knew who she was, and had passion and drive for everything she did. But after Chris I dramatically changed. I became insecure, depressed, and felt unworthy of anyone or anything. After a year, and a big fall out I began to hear a lot less from him. But still, frustrating enough, I was occasionally spending the night with him. One day, I found out he had been dating someone else for three months. It crushed me and sent me into a spiral of hurt and the feeling of inadequacy. I found myself asking, "Why not me?" "What's wrong with me?"

Unfortunately, this horrible controlling game between Chris and I continued for three years while he was still committed to someone else. I was never happy or proud of myself and always had this emptiness. But I had created this addiction and dependency to his control and I had this need to always have approval from him. I had lost what it felt to live my life and love myself. This horrible cycle with Chris made me, in a sick way, feel wanted and good about myself and worth something for that quick moment I was with him. But ultimately, it didn't close the hole in my heart and it didn't make me happier or fulfilled. I constantly wanted to hide in my room and not be around a lot of people, and I began to be desperately depressed. It finally got so bad that I had to tell my parents everything.

Not blaming oneself is immensely important for healing.

I began to see a counselor and became more open with my feelings of desperation and confusion. I didn't' hold back and I told my story. Throughout this past year I have released a little bit of shame and guilt and have tried to forgive myself in order to rebuild my strength and believe in myself again. It is very hard to do but each day gets easier and easier. In some messed up way Chris has changed my life and the person I am today for the better. I know that I don't want to experience that kind of life again. On the other hand, the whole situation has made it very difficult to trust a man's intentions.

Through the fog I lost sight of what and who is really important in my life. As the fog settles I have seen that my family and friends have never stopped caring about me or loving me even though at times I felt like I didn't deserve their support. I have become more thankful for the people who are in my life.

Understandably it took a while for Sonja to see what was happening. By the time she realized it, she was in too deep to climb out by herself. Can you see where the shifts in her process occurred? Isn't it interesting that her depression actually turned out to be a gift because it drove her to share her story and seek help.

The stories continue with Nan. Today Nan is a bright, confident, attractive twenty-two year old who appears to really know who she is. Six years ago however, she had an experience that continues to affect her ability to develop a meaningful relationship. It is still very difficult for her to trust a man. Here is her story.

Nan—"I found that I had given up my pride, friends, and myself."

His name was Daniel. I was freshman at a new high school while he was a senior. He was my first boyfriend and my first love. The first few months were filled with conversations until three o'clock in the morning under the covers, thirty-minute goodbyes, and sweet butterfly kisses. I was happy because I loved and was loved in return. He showered me with gifts, chocolates, and roses of all colors. He reminded me every day of how beautiful he thought I was. I never looked in the mirror and thought I was beautiful until he came into my life. He made me happy and made me, a former tomboy, want to be pretty for the first time. I was made into something beautiful.

Control frequently becomes physical abuse.

Little did I know, the next several months, seven to be exact, was me giving up my pride, friends and on top of that, myself. Don't get me wrong, Daniel loved me more like completely infatuated with me. He was irrefutably crazy about me and held onto me so tight it was as if he was squeezing the life out of me. He developed rules, which I had to abide by in order to not anger him. He forbid me to get a driver's license, only to ensure that he knows exactly where I am and whom I would be with. He threw temper tantrums when I did not answer his phone calls and disapproved of me of attending church. Before I knew it, he was crowding my life and was present at all times. My friends and family inevitably became second on my priority list, only in hopes to not anger him. It was my absence that not only angered my friends and family, but developed worry and animosity within them and they began to ask questions. My answers to those questions were that I was fine because in essence, he was a good boyfriend. He took care of me, loved me, and gave me the attention any girl would have wanted. I thought that maybe I had been the cause of his temper tantrums. Perhaps I should have ran to the phone faster, or have expressed my feelings more effectively, or maybe even had too many friends.

Our once thirty minute goodbyes soon turned into a thirty-minute scream session of how horrible I was, followed up with an apologetic voice-mail from him in tears. Arguments became more frequent and those apologetic voice-mails more constant until I lost all desire to work out the issues at hand. I remember moments where he would stand over me shouting while I, having lost all hope in trying, stood inanimate and helpless. During those times, I had no friends to talk to about these issues because I had literally pushed them out of my life. I was too prideful to have to admit that my fairy tale love story had been a fake. I held onto him because he was all I had left. Without him, I felt I would be alone and a complete failure. I wanted to be loved and I didn't think I deserved anything better than him and more importantly, hated not feeling beautiful. My focus for the following months was to tiptoe around his feelings and repair the relationship we had in the beginning. I desired happiness and thought I could achieve it through changing who I was into something he wanted me to be. This became a vicious cycle of abuse for me, both emotionally and physically.

It wasn't long before he had started to aggressively shake me and push me around. These three sentences repeatedly rang within the walls of my head: I angered him, I am not good enough, I deserve this. Sadly, it didn't stop there. He even tried to force himself on me, time after time. Refusing to give myself to him, I had to constantly fight him off of me. There was a time when we were at his house watching a movie when he attempted once again, this time with insolent force. I remember screaming and begging him to stop, over and over again. If it wasn't for his little brother walking into the house at that moment in time, I do not know what would have happened. His little brother heard my cries from upstairs and ran over to restrain his brother from me. It was at that moment I knew that I could no longer go any further. It dawned on me that I had failed. I was petrified, my limbs were shaking, and I even lacked the energy to release the heart wrenching cries exploding within my chest. I laid there for hours, half naked and half exposed. I never went back to that house after that, never even drove past it. That night, I spoke to my mother about everything. She sat and held me in tears until I fell asleep

After overcoming my abusive relationship with my first boyfriend, it has been hard for me to fully trust a man. It's almost as if I keep one foot on the ground when it comes to love. I hope to become more open and accepting of what may come, but despite the many years that followed Daniel, I have yet to fully let go. One thing I am sure about is that I am confident being who I am. I don't regret going through what I had gone through in the past because I wouldn't be the person I am today if I had not. They are lessons that I take to heart, teaching me to identify a good person while teaching me to grow as well. As a woman, I believe I need to protect and guard my heart and especially my body. I made a promise to God and myself to wait for the one I will love and admire forever in my heart and soul. I want to offer my whole self to that special person. I want to be able to say that I have been waiting for him all my life. All this I can do because I know in my heart that on that day, whether I look like an obese edition of a Troll doll or not, I will feel beautiful evermore.

Feeling insecure, helpless, and unworthy sets up the dependency and makes it very difficult to leave a terribly unhealthy relationship. Because the relationship begins with the feeling of being loved and because the changes take place so slowly, the individual adapts to the abusive dominant behavior and that new behavior becomes acceptable as normal. It's not seen as domineering, possessive, or jealous. As dysfunctional as it may sound, many individuals have no awareness of the developmental steps of the dysfunction within the relationship. They usually stay in the relationship working harder on themselves, trying to please the other partner at great costs to their personality, behaviors, and self-identity, even though the relationship is doomed. Manipulation and control by women does happen to men, but not nearly as often as men playing out the dominant roles of control and manipulation.

If a friend becomes aware of changes in their close friend's behavior, due to suspected manipulation, control, domination, and/or abuse, supporting that person by talking about shifts in behavior, even at the risk of losing their relationship, is vital. Unless a person can see that something is wrong, they don't have a chance to change it.

Counseling can be a vital option for someone just coming out of a very abusive relationship. This can help that person identify the underlying reasons why she allowed another person to treat her with disregard and disrespect in the first place.

In the Appendix on page 250 you will find a Self-Search Experience for dealing with a sexual abuse experience and an example of its use. If you know someone, share this with them. It can really help.

Key Takeaways from Other Bad Things That Happen: Sexual Abuse

- ➢ Sexual abuse often follows this pattern: she is made to feel that it is her fault; she is afraid to tell anyone for fear she will be negatively labeled; she tries to repress what happened; she has difficulty trusting men in future relationships.

- ➢ Sexual abuse mostly happens to women.

- ➢ Alcohol is frequently a factor.

- ➢ It was not your fault.

- ➢ Get professional help as soon as possible. You do not need to carry this with you.

Important References and Resources:

Love without Hurt: Turn Your Resentful, Angry, or Emotionally Abusive Relationship into a Compassionate, Loving One, by Steven Stosny, Reed Business Information (2005).

Reach for the Rainbow: Advanced Healing for Survivors of Sexual Abuse, by Lynne Finney, Perigee Trade (February 24, 1992).

The Sexual Healing Journey: A Guide for Survivors of Sexual Abuse, by Wendy Maltz, Harper Paperbacks; Revised edition (February 20, 2001).

Why Me? Help for Victims of child Sexual Abuse (Even if they are adults now), by Lynn Daugherty Cleanan Press, Inc.; 4th edition (February 1, 2007).

Excellent Websites:

Liz Claiborne website on teen abuse: loveisnotabuse.com/index.html Topics include signs of abuse, prevention of abuse and where to get help.

www.compassionpower.com   Expert Advice on Surviving Abuse, Stephen Stosny, PhD. Topics include: You Are Not the Cause of His Anger or Abuse, No One Escapes the Effects of Abuse, How to Get Your Angry or Abusive Man to Change, How You Can Know That He's Willing to Change, How Victims Recover and What They Can Expect, How To Know if He Has Truly Changed and Tips for Husbands to Reconnect.

Women Empowered Against Violence (WEAVE). This organization works closely with adult and teen survivors of relationship violence and abuse, providing an innovative range of legal counseling, economic and educational services.

Contact Information:
Women Empowered Against Violence
Lydia Watts, Executive Director
1111 16th St., Ste.410
Washington DC 20036
PH 202-452-9550
Email: info@ccssd.org
Emergency toll free crisis line: 888-272-1767
Email: helpline@ccssd.org

Further resources can be found through Google's search engine: "help for sexual abuse."

CHAPTER 8

TAKING CHARGE OF YOUR LIFE

*It's not so much that we're afraid of change or
so in love with the old ways, but it's that place in
between that we fear. ... It's like being between trapezes.
There's nothing to hold on to.*
Marilyn Ferguson

How to create your own future, and navigate your journey.

How Do You Want to Live Your Life?

When students would come see me about doing their "personal stretch" project, they were often a bit confused and not sure what to do. I started by asking, "How do you want to live your life?" This of course would cause them to be even more perplexed. It seems that most of us have grown up thinking that we just deal with life as we go along. Few were taught that they could, in fact, have a very powerful impact on creating and designing their lives in a very meaningful way. Now here's the question: how do you want to live your life? You don't have to figure this all out right now. Simply plant the thought in your mind, in case you haven't given this some thought before.

Jot your thoughts down as you go along.

You Choose Your Future

You are heading in some direction, and you are going to accomplish things. You are in the process of creating your future, even as you are reading this. Your future is being created by the thoughts you have and the choices you make and the feelings you have about yourself and about each situation you experience. Each situation creates new possibilities, which lead to new choices, and more new possibilities. Even when a bad thing happens, you choose how you are going to deal with it. You can make things worse by focusing on the all negatives, or make it better by making the decision to not get stuck in that crap. To navigate your future you have to be conscious of your life.

There are areas and times in our lives where we are walking through the days without being conscious of the thoughts we are having or the choices we are making. We see much more that is wrong and complain about it using *can't, not, don't and won't* in continuous streams of negative thoughts that go through our minds and out our mouths. Others go through their lives impulsively doing whatever they see in the moment, without thought to potential consequences or impact. They, too, are in control of their destinies, but are doing it without conscious awareness. You can consciously take charge of your life, or you can be unconscious and let life dictate your next moves. One is proactive: making and acting on conscious choices. The other is reactive: living life in reaction to life situations.

Serena wrote one of the most powerful life-changing statements that I've seen. Though she was successful in her classes, her life had been spinning way out of balance. She had become a very unhappy young woman and wanted to change her life. Here is what wrote, and then began to live.

Serena – "Making My Life Mine"

My Present State:

I have realized in the past few weeks that I am the one in control of where my life is going and how it will turn out. I do not regret where I have come from or what situations that I have gotten myself into, but I do want to change how I react to these kinds of situations in the future. I want to focus not on the negatives of my past, but on just how positive I can make my life become in the near future. I will not forget my past by any means, but I want to be able to use my past to motivate myself to better myself, to make better choices and live the life I really do feel I deserve. I do not want to let how others treat me control my life. I do not want to use any medicine or drugs to try and be happy again (i.e., antidepressants, alcohol, etc.) but instead through my writing and exercise.

For a really long time, I have just not been happy with my life. I need to stop wishing that it will change, and take the initiative to make positive things happen. The realization of my issues was the first step. Now, I need to make seri-

ous changes in my life. Without this action, I will continue a downward spiral into my depression and poor choices.

What I have learned:

-Acknowledging a problem/issue really is the first step to making a recovery and moving on from a past situation

-Depression: After denying and hiding the fact that I have been diagnosed as clinically depressed, I have come to terms with it. Everyone has problems, and I do not need a drug to fix me. If I care about myself and really focus on making my life better, it will be better. There is nothing wrong with me, unless I let there be. I no longer want to avoid treating it because I need to love myself before others can love me.

-Abuse: I have a history of growing attached to men who are abusive, whether it be emotionally, physical, or sexually. I trust easily, and I need to learn to not put myself into bad situations with men who I never should have trusted to begin with. I must learn to be strong on my own before I can stay strong in a relationship with another person. There is nothing wrong with me, unless I keep repeating the same mistakes over and over again. I no longer want to avoid being stuck in this same situation.

-Relationships: To go along the same lines as abuse, I need to focus on trust. I am a lovable person. I am a good person. I need to focus not only on not trusting those who do not deserve my trust, but on allowing myself to trust the people who do care about me and do want what is best for me. My friends and family do love me and want to be there for me during the good times and the bad. There is nothing wrong with me, unless I shut out the ones who truly love me and want to better my life. I no longer want to be alone in my thoughts and life when others want to be a part also.

You Matter:

-Drugs/Alcohol: I have been abusing substances, thinking they will better/help/ease situations in my life. I have grown dependent on these things, and I do not like who I am becoming. I want to be in control of my own life, and that means not succumbing to what I see is the "easy way out." I am afraid, but I need to learn who I am and how to be myself. For the longest time I have tried to know myself, but I cannot when there are drugs tainting my own vision of myself. There is nothing wrong with me, unless I let substances control my life and use them as my motivation. I no longer want to rely on substance to allow me to be happy when I can I do it on my own.

Where I want to be:

"Any change, any loss, does not make us victims. Others can shake you, surprise you, disappoint you, but they can't prevent you from acting, from taking the situation you're presented with and moving on. No matter where you are in life, no matter what your situation, you can always do something. You always have a choice and the choice can be power."

-Blaine Lee

I will learn to love myself. I am a great person. I am smart, kind, and beautiful. I am a best friend, a daughter, a sister, and a student. I play hard, and I work harder. I will enjoy the little things in life, and I will know that I am never alone. I will appreciate all of the world's beauty, and will not be evil towards anything or anyone. By loving myself, I will love everything around me, and vice versa. I will write consistently. I will use my writing not only to vent, but to appreciate the people I love, the people who love me, the joy and life this world has to offer me. When I am lost and confused, I will turn to my faith in myself and in others. I will always remember that this life is beautiful and worth fighting for.

I am strong. I do not deserve to be hurt, and I do not deserve to have my dreams crushed. I am not at fault when another tries to hurt me. It is their fault. I will not let myself become a victim again. Those who try to tear me down only win if I let them. I will stop looking for men to fall in love with who I know are going to be harmful. I will stop putting my faith into men who I know will never change their ways. I will always remember who I am and where I'm going and those who are not helping me are hindering me. I am independent and extraordinary, and I do not need to be treated like I am worthless and not deserving of true love.

I will stop being afraid of loving those who love me. I will open up to those who care about me, because they really do want me in their lives. I will stop being afraid of being hurt, because those that love me only want what's best for me. I will work more on breaking down the walls that I, and others, have put up instead of putting them up. Everybody deserves to love and be loved. I am no different, and I must always remember that. By being a good friend to others, I will be a good friend to myself. I do not need alcohol or drugs to make my life complete. I will stop using drugs to try and better my life or to shut out how I feel. Using substances in this way will only make my life worse. I do not need them to be happy. What I do need in my life are my friends, my family, and the activities I am passionate about. I cannot replace these things with a bottle of booze. I will not use alcohol or drugs as a crutch anymore. I am a fun, exciting person without substances, and these substances change who I am and who I want to be when I use them negatively.

When I feel lost or confused, I will remember that I always have things I can turn to, whether it be my friends, family, writing, or exercise. I have healthy options and those are the only options I need.

My future:

I must never lose sight of what is important to me. I have always known that I was born to be a mother. Though

You Matter:

I do not know for sure yet, I believe there is no greater joy than holding a beautiful, innocent life in your hands, and knowing that you are in complete control of how they turn out. I experience pure joy watching my plants grow from seeds, so I can only imagine how happy a child will make me. I truly believe children are a gift from a higher power, and just thinking about raising my own future kids brings tears to my eyes. I want to stop doing things that could in any way negatively impact my future children, and in order to do that, I need to quit old habits and form new, positive ones.

I have always known that I will raise my beautiful kids with the man that I fal1 madly in love with. I have not met him yet, but I know he is out there somewhere. In order for me to fall in love, I need to open myself up to the thought of being in love again. I will not let past experiences with relationships and men deter me from trusting a man with every piece of my heart. I will be bold and I will take chances in love, because I realize this is what I need to do to be truly happy in my life. I will never let a man hit me or hurt me ever again, and I will not be afraid to stand up for myself anymore. I want to make a good life for myself, but an even better life for those around me. I do not wish to have a huge home or a fancy car. I only wish for a loving husband and a healthy family. I will continue to be a great friend to those who deserve it, and I will be a great friend to those who aren't always so grateful. I know that my life is as I make it, and in order to be happy myself, I must make everyone around me happy as well. I will continue to work on friendships that may ultimately fail, because I know that some of my best friends tried so hard with me. I will continue to believe that everyone is ultimately good and has a kind soul. I will always work to better the world around me.

Yes, I will make my life mine.

It All Begins with Awareness

You can't change something if you're not aware that it's happening so, yes, it all begins with awareness. For example, if you are in a relationship and you are doing something that is very annoying to your partner, unless you are aware of this you can't change it. We all develop patterns of behavior that we continuously repeat. They become behavior habit patterns. A habit pattern means you behave in some way without even thinking about it. Habits are tendencies that you consistently repeat. Driving a car can be a habitual unconscious pattern. (Of course, if you make a mistake, you can become very conscious very quickly!) People develop these patterns of thoughts, continuously thinking and seeing things in the same way. Patterns result in repeated unconscious choices. These patterns are normal and not a problem, unless they result in your life not working the way you want. Then these behavior patterns can become a big problem, often leading in the direction of unhappy and unhealthy consequences.

Going back to the previous example, let's say your partner now tells you that you are very annoying. That's a pretty general statement and could cause concern confusion and tension. "Am I always annoying? Am I an annoying person? Are you angry with me?" Or, "What am I doing that you find annoying?"

"Well," she says, "here goes. You talk constantly. It seems like you never stop. I don't feel like you ever listen to me."

- "How come you never told me this before?"

- "I was afraid you would get mad at me."

- "How can I change it if I don't know?"

Once you are aware of something that is causing tension in others or causing you to be dissatisfied or unhappy, only then can change occur, if you so choose. It looks like this:

Once you are aware, you then have choices. You now get to make a decision about what you're going to do. Your choices give you control over your life in many situations and provide opportunities for new outcomes. In the example described about being annoying, now that you are aware, you can choose to change the behavior. Or you can choose not to change the behavior. After all, in this example the continuous talking is likely an old and unconscious pattern. One choice and outcome could make the relationship stronger. Another choice and outcome could cause an end to the relationship. Once you decide to take charge of your life, you will determine many new outcomes.

Or you might say, "I don't know how to change. I'm used to the way I am. I am more comfortable this way." Every response will determine an outcome. Which outcomes are you striving to achieve, and will this decision lead you to your desired outcome?

Sometimes choosing to take charge of your life will force you to move out of your comfort zone.

What are examples of staying in your comfort zone.

How To Make Life Changes

The way you do things becomes what you are used to doing: your *comfort zone*. Your comfort zone contains the patterns of behavior that are continuously and often unconsciously repeated. It is always easier to continue doing these things than it is to change what you are doing, or trying something different. The persistent thoughts may be "This is the way I am. This is the way things are."

Take a moment and do the following little exercise. Fold your arms across your chest (something we all do frequently). Notice which hand is on top of your upper arm and which is on the underside. Now re-cross your arms so your hands are reversed. How does that feel? Awkward? Uncomfortable? How long will you leave your arms like this before uncrossing and reverting back to your old way of doing things? This is obviously just a simple behavior. Think of all the complex behaviors that are repeated for the same reason, every day. They become the way you do things, your comfort zone.

Repeated Patterns Become Comfort Zones

Like crossing your arms, you will continue doing things the same way because this is what is "normal" for you. Unfortunately, people will stay with these patterns even when they no longer work, and even when they are counterproductive. For instance, you probably know someone who has stayed in a bad relationship, even an abusive one, instead of getting out of it. For these people it is far more difficult to leave the known and familiar, even when the known and familiar is painful, than it is to remain in the old comfort zone.

Breaking Out of Old Comfort Zones

A *comfort zone* is both efficient and powerful. It is efficient because you know what you are doing. Everything is familiar, routine, and comfortable. It is the area of the known. It is safe. A comfort zone is not necessarily stress free, but there is far less stress staying there than leaving it. A comfort zone exerts tremendous force for staying there, and it can take a great deal of energy to break out of an existing comfort zone. It provides a sense of security, and we all tend to hold on to what makes us feel secure.

The following is a simple illustration of the *comfort zone* phenomenon. It will help explain why change is difficult, and how to initiate a successful change process. Begin with the concept of three concentric circles. These represent different levels of comfort or discomfort you experience from one situation to another.

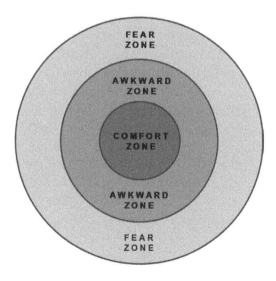

What are examples of being in your Awkward Zone?

The inner circle is your *comfort zone*. This is the place where everything is known, familiar, and relatively safe. You know your job. You know the environment and the people around you. Some may be difficult at times, but they are known variables. People like to operate within their comfort zones because it is far less stressful. You have developed the ability to cope with some of the undesirable parts, tolerate others, and be basically secure that things will remain the same. It is your safe place, and you can be both effective and efficient. *However, you will not learn anything new in your comfort zone. You* already know it.

The second largest circle represents the *awkward zone*. This is also the *learning zone*, because this is where learning and change take place. People can feel awkward and vulnerable when they get out of their comfort zones, and the farther out, the more awkward they may feel. Most people don't like feeling awkward. It brings up feelings and fears of failure, insecurity, or of humiliation. Sometimes you feel dumb or confused and don't like that either. You worry about what others will think of you or will say to you. You don't want your boss to know, or your significant other, that you might not be able to do something well. You are afraid you won't be able to please them or that they will be disappointed in you. The farther out you go, the greater the fear and tension can be. When you reach your *edge*, powerful forces can drive you back, usually all the way back into the old comfort zone. These forces are primarily from two sources: *1)* your own internal fears of failure, not being good enough, and of embarrassment or humiliation and, *2)* intense pressure from those close to you and peers who do not want you to change, or be different from them, nor want you to push them out of their comfort zones. However, moving out of your comfort zone is where learning will place, and change will happen.

The third and largest circle is the *fear zone*. Once you pass your "edge" of the awkward zone, the intensity of fear and resistance to the change increase dramatically. The fears, which began to surface as you near your edge, now become real. One common sign that you have reached your edge is when you begin to perform poorly, or are unable to perform at all, frozen in your fear zone. The strongest tendency is to avoid the fear zone, and if you get too close, to head back to your comfort zone.

Here is an easy illustration of a situation in which different people will experience the three different zones. Let's say that you are a participant in a class or workshop called *Leading and Living*. On the first day of class the instructor addresses participants saying, "To check out comfort zones and fear zones in this room, I'm going to randomly select three people to come to the front of the room. I would like the three of you selected to speak to the class for a couple of minutes on your beliefs about the meaning and purpose of life." As the instructor gazes around the room seemingly to identify those to come forth, many of the participants now avoid eye contact, while some pretend to be taking notes. Yet others appear relaxed and confident.

The instructor then asks for a show of hands. "How many would be quite comfortable doing this?" "How many *really* would not want to be to be called on? How many were praying, 'Dear God don't let him call on me?' How many were thinking, 'if he calls on me I'm out of here.'" There will always be a lot of nods, laughs and insights about the differences between individuals in their comfort and fear zones.

Remember this: What you experience as your comfort zone could easily be the fear zone of someone with whom you are in a relationship. In the change process you will need to make use of the awkward/learning zone concept. The majority of your life knowledge and skills have been learned when you were willing to risk feeling a bit uncomfortable and experience something new. This is the range that good teachers and coaches use to stretch your awkward zone, careful to not stretch you too far, throwing you directly into your fear zone. In teaching a child to swim, you would not just throw the child into deep water. If that child did learn to swim, he or she would not be doing it for the love of swimming, but rather because of the fear of drowning. *Everyone has their fear zones. In normal people, there is no such thing as "no fear."* Basically it comes down to this: You will have to get out of your comfort zone if you are going to learn new life skills, or make any significant change in your life.

What zone would this experience put you in?

Mastering the Art of Change

The following is a very profound principle of change:

You Matter:

If what you're doing isn't working, you will have to change what you're doing before anything will change!

Instead of using this simple formula, most will simply do more of the same, and with greater intensity. We will think more, worry more, talk about it more, drink more, argue more, and continue trying to make whatever it is work. The tendency is to increase the intensity of our attitude and actions, expecting a different outcome. Part of the difficulty stems from the fact that we usually don't realize we are doing the same thing, and with greater intensity. We do things the only way we know how, and we unconsciously repeat the same patterns. Ask yourself, is what I'm doing in this situation working? If not, you will have to change something significant before anything changes.

The farther any change pushes you out of your comfort zone, or the more you feel you have at stake—position, power, influence—or the greater the threat to your self-esteem—fear of failure, humiliation—the more fiercely you are likely to hang onto your old ways. This is one of the reasons why change can be so difficult.

Focus on Your Future, Not on Your Past

If you want to make changes in some part of your life, here is what will help you. Focus on where you're going, not on where you've been, on what you are going to do, not on what you have done. Focus on what you want, not on what you don't want, on what is good in your life, not on what is bad, on who you want to be, not on who you have been. Focus on today and looking forward; on what you want to do or who you want to be to accomplish your goals.

This concept is fundamental to the Law of Attraction and is one of the most important relative to creating what you want in your life. Whatever you focus your attention on, positive or negative, is where your energy goes. It becomes what you think about and what you talk about. These become habit patterns of thought, and are often unconscious. This is why these patterns are so difficult to change. Remember the professor who gave the assignment to not complain for twenty-four hours? The people in his classes and seminars couldn't do it. Why was it so difficult for them to change just one significant habit pattern?

Could you? Are your complaints conscious or unconscious (not aware that you are complaining)?

Do you mostly focus on the past or on the future?

Some people constantly have negative thoughts and always talk about everything that is wrong. Where does this form of thinking come from? Many have been told since childhood that what they want to become or accomplish is not possible. They have been discouraged instead of encouraged. Many children are told that they aren't good enough and that nothing they do is good enough. Do you know anyone who got all *As* and one *B*, and the parent says, "Why did you get a *B*"? This level of focus on the negative has a negative impact emotionally and physically, in addition to being deeply dispiriting. Those who focus on the positive create positive energy for themselves, and this too affects the emotions and body, but in a positive way. This is not to say that you should never have a negative thought. Of course you will. Just don't dwell on it. Acknowledge the thought and then move on. You absolutely can control your thoughts and emotions and their effects on your body, but you must first have awareness and a positive desire to change things. Here is one way you can take charge of your life.

Transition and Change

A transition refers to the process you go through in changing from one state of being to a new state of being. Here is what it can look like and also how it works.

A Transition Model and Process

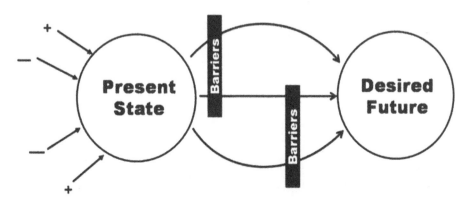

You Matter:

Where do you want to spend your time and focus? Most people get stuck, either in their past or in their present. There are many little arrows extending from your past that have contributed to your present state. Many are fun, inspiring, positive experiences, such as your parents, friends, accomplishments, and different people who have had a positive impact and helped shape who you are today. Some are negative things that have happened, like bad people, accident, or illness, or bad choices you have made that had negative consequences.

Traps That Prevent Change

The most common traps that prevent transition and change are: first, „getting stuck in the past, and second, being stuck in the dissatisfaction of the present state and unable to get out. Being stuck in either state indicates a focus on either the past negatives that contributed to the situation, or a focus on those negatives that exist in this situation now. Ironically, this focus on the negatives most frequently results in four behaviors that actually keep us stuck. We:

- Complain and Blame—"This wouldn't have happened if my dad wasn't such a …"

- Justify—"If I had enough money, I would be able to do what I want to do."

- Defend—"If it hadn't been for you and what you said, I would not have …."

- Rationalize—"Maybe someday I'll be able to make that happen, but it's just not my fault."

Trap #1– Stuck in the past

All four of these thought patterns, Complain and Blame, Justify, Defend, and Rationalize, can keep you stuck in the role of "victim" and render you helpless to change.

There is nothing you can do to change anything that happened or choices you made in the past. When you're stuck the fault will always appear to be "out there"—out of your control—things others have done to you. However, there are two things you can do to keep from getting stuck, or to get unstuck.

- Learn from your past, let go, and move on with your life. Catch any negative thoughts and redirect them into a thought about something you are grateful for or that you appreciate.
- Focus your thoughts and energy on your Desired Future. How do you want to live your life?

Trap #2 – Stuck in the present

The multiple arrows moving from Your Present State to Your Desired Future indicate that there will be a number of different pathways that can take you there. This is important to know because most people have been taught or have come to believe that there is "one way" to get where you want to go. In most situations this is simply not true. If you are willing to look, you will find that there are many perspectives and possibilities.

The rectangles across the arrows mean that there will always be some perceived *barrier* to where you want to go and how you want to get there. *Change your path and the barrier changes.*

How to Manage Your Life Transitions

If there is someone (your relationship) or something (your job, career path, finances, etc.) that isn't working for you, that is causing you stress or anxiety, then you can change it. You can make a transition from where you are to something better. Here is how.

One of the best books in this area is *Managing Transition: Making the Most of Change*, by William Bridges and Susan Bridges.* The Bridges point out that a transition takes place in three phases that you must go through in order to make a change: 1) Ending and Letting Go, 2) Neutral Zone with/Disorder and, 3) New Beginnings. These phases are directly related to the Transition Model on Page ….

You Matter:

Phases of Transition

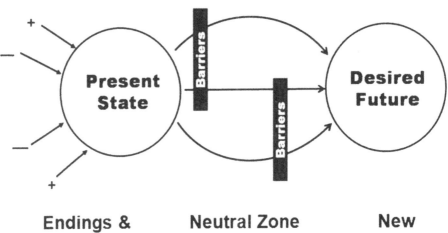

**Endings &
Letting Go**   **Neutral Zone
Disorder/Chaos**   **New
Beginnings**

Phase 1 – Endings and Letting Go

This is an ending to what you have been doing or experiencing. It begins with you deciding you want to change something in your Present State. This requires Letting Go of the old way(s) and your old identity. It is choosing to cause an Ending.

Ask yourself: "What should I change that would be for my greater good?"

Think of any change you have been through, such as a relationship breakup, leaving home the first time, leaving a job, or moving into a new one. Each change started with a decision, an ending and letting go. No decision, no change. No letting go and no ending, no change. You may have had to let go of a relationship you really wanted, leave for a new job, and you may have to let go of your old peer group and/or friends. The more important or significant the thing you are ending, the more difficult letting go can be. This is why so many will "blame, justify, defend, and rationalize" and fail to let go.

Phase 2 – The Neutral Zone

This may not feel like a neutral zone. In fact, you may experience it as a time of disorder, somewhat chaotic. This is the psychological dissonance between an old reality and a new one that often occurs, especially if it is a significant transition. There can be great uncertainty. "

202

Am I doing the right thing?" "What if it doesn't work out?" Uncertainty creates fear. When you learn to accept uncertainty as part of the process, the fear dissolves. You may want to rush through or even bypass the neutral zone, which is a common mistake. As you move through this phase, you may even experience grief, anger, anxiety, bargaining, sadness, confusion, even depression. The most important thing is to acknowledge whatever you are experiencing and know that it is normal. "This is really difficult right now, but I will come out of it in a much better place. There are new beginnings for me!"

2. If I make this change, what might I need to let go of?

According to the Bridges, "It is the chaos into which the old form dissolves and from which the new form emerges."

Phase 3 –New Beginnings

This phase begins when you decide you want some change in your Present State, or when you focus on your Desired Future and then you realize that there is something you must change in order to get there. As represented by the arrows in the Neutral Zone, once you begin to get clear on what you want in your life (Desired Future), many new opportunities will appear to you and a number of ways to get there will present themselves.

How to Create Your Future

Following are three real-life scenarios using the Transition and Change Model and Process. Each has proven to be an effective approach for creating a focus on the future or for creating change in your life. They are: 1) Changing a Negative Pattern, 2) A Vision Statement for Living and, 3) Getting Over an Addiction: Smoking.

Changing a Negative Behavior Pattern

Kevin came to the realization that he was carrying a lot of past negative patterns into new relationships, and he was concerned that this was keeping him from being able to form a lasting relationship. Here is how he addressed the issue.

Kevin—"I need to change if I'm going to be in a lasting relationship."

How do I perceive myself now? (Present State)

You Matter:

I currently feel that I'm overly critical of myself. I can see a great many positive things about myself, I just have trouble really believing them and taking them to heart. I'm easily stressed out with a tendency to jump to negative conclusions. I portray a positive attitude to everyone around me, even if I don't quite believe it myself. I feel that in past relationships I've had to put on a face or act like someone other than myself. I've met people to whom I wasn't really attracted and had to sell myself on the idea of being interested in them. I don't jump on every opportunity that comes my way for fear of leaving my comfort zone, and I then regret my decisions and wonder what could have been. I don't appreciate everything that I know and bring to the table. I have difficulty letting go of past situations that only seem to bring me down.

Who will I be in the future? (Desired State)

The following is a present-tense description of how I want to see myself two to four years from today. I wrote this with the idea I was writing a letter to myself, now describing how I see my life at this later point in time.

When I look at myself I know that I'm much more confident than I used to be. I know that I'm tall, fit, funny, and very charming. My friends and the people around me are very happy to call me their friend. They know that I bring a different perspective to things and will do whatever possible to make them laugh and enjoy themselves. I've been able to meet some really smart, attractive, and interesting women recently. I feel confident in what I have to offer, and I know they appreciate my eclectic interests. I know I don't have to put on a face or act like someone other than myself.

How do I get from here to there? (My Goals)

* *Learn to relax, stay focused, and let go.*

- *In an effort to help my mind and body to relax I plan to make a one-month commitment to practice yoga and meditation.*

- *Stay financially sound.*

- *In an effort to save money for the things that are important to me,*

- *I'll create a budget and take better control of finances.*

- *I will balance my checkbook on a regular basis and write down my expenses and understand where my money goes.*

  - *I will stop spending so much money at the bar and on eating out.*

  - *I will save money for important things, and avoid spending everything that I earn.*

- *Never stop learning and growing.*

  - *I will avoid getting sucked into TV and other passive activities.*

  - *I will continue to read as much as I can, whatever it may be: books, magazines, newspapers, and so on.*

  - *I will take every opportunity I can to grow and learn something new and interesting.*

- *Stay socially active.*

  - *I will avoid spending time alone when I could be out meeting new people and being socially active.*

  - *I will join a club or an organization that allows me to meet people with common interests.*

  - *I won't let myself think that other people don't like me or are judging me.*

  - *I will be confident and outgoing when talking to women.*

- *Find new challenges and ways to push myself.*

- *I will seek out new experiences and push myself out of my comfort zone.*

- *I will quit making excuses and get out and do things.*

- *I will enjoy my life.*

How do I make it stick?

To hold myself accountable, I'll make reminders of my goals, focus on how I achieved success in the past, and how I can translate it to the future. I'll inform important people I trust and ask them to hold me accountable, and give me a kick in the ass when necessary. I'll stop at certain points to evaluate my progress and make necessary changes to insure my success. I will set small goals to set a path to my larger goals. I'll stick with it and continue on the path that I've set out for myself.

Here are the steps Kevin took:

1. Describe the present situation. (Current State)

2. How do you want it to be? (Desired Future)

3. What will you do to get there? (Goals)

4. How will you make it stick? (Accountability)

Creating a Vision for Your Future

Sasha simply wanted to create a vision of what happiness means to her. This was her first experience of doing this work.

Sasha – "A Vision Statement for Living My Life"

- *I live each and every day of my life with balance and with love.*

- *I always look to the future; I plan, I dream, I accomplish.*

- *I enjoy the time I spend with my family, and I look forward to the day when I have my own family to enjoy.*

- *I want to have healthy, happy children that know how much they are loved and supported.*

- *I want to be "in love" with my husband forever.*

- *I value the people I work with, and I strive to bring something special to each new relationship.*

- *I will travel. I will experience the world, its people, and their cultures.*

- *I will learn new things.*

- *I smile, I think positive, and I am an optimist.*

- *I know that I am successful, and I want to help others achieve their successes.*

- *I will be influential, and I will make a difference.*

- *I believe in equality, honesty, and respect.*

- *I believe that by giving a piece of your soul, you can and do make the world a better place to live.*

Sasha was quite proud of and excited about her vision. She wanted to know what to do next. My response was, of course: "What would you like to see happen with it?" I suggested she decide on which areas she would like to focus first, and develop a plan to go after just a couple at a time. It was a very successful experience for Sasha.

Getting Over an Addiction

Michelle—"I'm making a big change: quitting smoking."

The idea of facing something that you need to face, but haven't, is a scary thought. Especially if that something is also tied to a physical addiction you may have. I have recently decided to quit smoking and have been forced to deal with my physical and mental attachment to cigarettes. Throughout this process, I will be trying to figure out why I have been having such a hard time letting go of something I did not even want in my life originally, along with how I will go about doing so.

My goal:

The main reason I wanted to quit is because I knew smoking was a habit that was not going to get me anywhere in life other than the hospital and cosmetics counter. I needed to know that I could get anywhere I wanted to in my future, and be healthy at the same time. The problem I am facing now is the fact I still want that cigarette, which brings me to my goal of finding out why and determining how to move on with my life smoke-free.

Why I became addicted:

After actually sitting down and thinking about specific situations in which I smoked, it became very apparent why this has been such a problem for me. When it comes to why I originally started and continued to smoke alone, there is a definite pattern. I found that most of the time, it was because I needed to get away from a particular situation I was in. I found that being able to take time for a cigarette was when I could just sit back and let my mind relax and not think so much about what was going on in my life.

How might you apply these steps in your life?

Why I want to quit:

The main reason I want to stop smoking is for my health. Not being able to walk to class without becoming short of breath was and still is something I find very annoying, but on a physiological level, I got to the point where I was no longer relaxed when I smoked. My mind was still going around in circles about all kinds of things— one being that I had became more physically addicted to cigarettes than I thought I would ever let myself be. I also felt inner turmoil about how I needed to quit before I found myself at the age of forty old, sick, and wrinkly.

The next step:

I need to pinpoint the specific situations where I end up thinking about wanting a smoke. By doing this I will be able to avoid them, or find a solution for each that will help me until I am able to no longer think about wanting to smoke:

The bar: *This one will not be as big a problem as it could have been. With the new No Smoking law in effect, I will not be around the smoke. The only problem here is the fact that when I drink, I want to smoke. This is where I will need a little help, but by having friends who support what I'm doing, I will be able to steer clear of the temptation.*

When I'm bored: *This one is easy! With all the things that have been filling up my schedule, I know there will not be a time where I will think of wanting a smoke instead of finishing something on my to-do list.*

When I'm stressed out: *I need to find a way to make myself relax besides smoking. Actually, just finding a hobby or something that I enjoy doing would be a great replacement for smoking. I have a few things like this: reading, cooking, knitting, and talking on the phone to friends and family back at home.*

The results: *By just writing out the what, why, and how of my problem, I have realized that there is really no more problem. Yes, I know I will be dealing with the physical withdrawal for a little while longer, but that does not mean that rest of the situation has not been solved. In the process of resolving some issues with my roommate, finding out what are the triggers and how to avoid them, and then doing some personal research about what tobacco really does to you, I can honestly say that I no longer want to be associated with smoking. I have been able to let go of the fear I had of never being able to get over my addiction. By working out the undefined situation, I was able to find a person inside myself of who I am proud. All together, I have now been able to stop smoking. I am coming out of this situation with much more than I thought I would. I am*

Do you have any addictions or inhibiting habits you want to address?

*now more confident in my ability to do anything I put my
mind to, and I'm doing so smoke-free!*

As you can see, Michelle used a similar process to that of Kevin but focused primarily on the "what, why, and how." Sometimes it is really important to understand "why" the pattern exists, in order to change it.

You Get to Be in Charge

Here are perhaps the most important takeaways from all of this: How you live your life is not pre-determined. You have the ability to create your own future. You will be presented with situations, and you can make choices. The choices you make will, in most situations, determine the outcomes. You really are, can be, in charge of your life. You can choose how you want to live.

There will always be obstacles, barriers, and setbacks. It's all part of the process of learning and becoming. Some of these will seem like defeats. Some will seem to happen for no reason at all. At times you may want to just give it up. Then why is it so important to find your path if it can be so difficult? Because once you have overcome the setbacks and defeats—and you will—you will be filled with a greater sense of confidence, enthusiasm, even euphoria, and these are the ingredients of happiness.

You Create Your Happiness – In Conclusion

First, know that happiness is a result of what you think about, what you do, and how you feel about what is going on in your life. Happiness or sadness—both are emotional states you believe you are experiencing. You will often let your "happiness" be determined by others: your love interest, parents, friends who you want to impress, your boss, and so on. The reality is, you can choose to be happy, or not.

Since happiness is an emotional state, you can learn to increase it whenever you want or need to. Here is how to check on the state of your emotions. How are you feeling right now, both in this moment and with where you are in your life? You don't want to be too quick with this, so give it some thought. Are you loved, that is, do you let people love you? Do you have love for others *and* let them know this? Are you pleased with the person you are and the person you are becoming? What kind of friends are you choosing? Do they contribute to or take away from your feeling good about yourself? Have you made successful choices in your love relationships? Do you have a passion for your work, or are you doing just enough to get by? How happy (or not) are you feeling with your life right now?

Next, look at the following example of an Emotional Scale. Start at the bottom and move up until you find the emotional descriptors that come closest to describing some of your predominant feelings. Put a mark on the arrow at this point.

Levels of Happiness and Joy

Joy, Passion, Gratitude

Love, Reason, Freedom

Empathy, Compassion, Delight

Enthusiasm, Optimism, Hopefulness

Positive Expectation, Belief, Trust

Courage, Affirmation, Empowerment

Pessimism, Irritation, Impatience

Anger, Revenge, Cynical

Judgmental, Fear, Worry

Jealousy, Competition, Sadness

Insecurity, Unworthiness, Hatred,

Levels of Sadness and Pain

Powerless, Hopelessness, Loneliness

Now write down the five most important and wonderful things that have happened to you so far in your life then the names of the five people who have most significantly touched your heart and positively affected your life, and what they did for you.

Keep these experiences and thoughts in mind while you refer back to the Emotional Scale once more. Where would you place your mark now, relative to the emotional descriptors and what you are experiencing in this moment?

In this present moment experience, did you find that you moved up the Emotional Scale? So what does this tell you? The scale is based on concepts from the Law of Attraction and its impact on our lives. What you think about and focus on is where your energy goes, and this affects what you see and how you feel. When you focus on the good experiences and the good people, do you find yourself moving up the scale? Where on this scale would you like to spend the majority of your time? How might you do this?

It is absolutely true that in your life you will experience good people and bad people, good things and bad things. What you think about and how you deal with the people and events in your life will determine the choices you make. You can't change what has happened in the past, but you definitely can choose how you think about it and what you do going forward. Look again at the top three levels of the Emotional Scale: Empathy, Compassion, Delight; Love, Reason, Freedom; and then Joy, Passion, Gratitude. These evoke feelings of "happiness," and they are within your reach.

The Ending and the New Beginning

I was thinking about how to end this chapter and, all of sudden, two things popped into my mind. (I love synchronicity.) First, I had been looking out the window at an eagle's nest that is about fifty feet in front of me. An eaglet, about three months old, was sitting on a limb exercising its wings in preparation for its first flight, which will probably happen in the next few days. I have seen it before. The eaglet sits on the branch most of the day, stretching and flapping its wings up and down, building strength and confidence, but it will not let go of the branch. Then one day, it lets go and soars off into the air. In the beginning, it's not a very pretty site. The eaglet is awkward and obviously in totally new territory. Once I saw it flying along, and it suddenly flipped upside down and went into a dive. It recovered and headed back to the tree, landing awkwardly on a branch. The first branch landing is not always successful.

This made me think of you at this point in your life. What an exciting time. The first flight is always scary. You can end up way out of your comfort zone. You are likely to flip upside down as you move along, but you will right yourself. Landings can be really scary, especially if the wind is blowing. Yet, to make it back to the nest, you have to land on a tree branch. Then one day the parent eagles say it is time for you to go: no more food, no more security; but they know, and you know, that you are ready. Now for another new beginning.

The second thing that popped into my mind was a memory. It was about a book I read to my daughters when they were young. I have also used it in many workshops I've conducted on change. This great wisdom came from Dr. Seuss.

> Congratulations!
> Today is your day.
> You're off to Great Places!
> You're off and away!
>
> You have brains in your head.
> You have feet in your shoes.
> You can steer yourself
> any direction you choose.
>
> You're on your own, and you know what you know.
> And YOU are the one who'll decide where to go.
>
> Oh, The Places You'll Go!

HAVE A WONDERFUL JOURNEY!!

Bill

Key Takeaways from Taking Charge of Your life

- ➢ Your future is not predetermined. You get to determine your future. If you are aware, you can change. If you are unaware, you can't.

- ➢ If what you're doing isn't working, you have to change what you are doing.

- ➢ To make significant change or to learn anything new, you must get out of your comfort zone.

- ➢ Focus on your future, not on your past.

You Matter:

> ➤ Focusing on the negatives that happened will keep you stuck in the past.

> ➤ There is nothing you can do to change anything that happened in the past.

> ➤ Learn, Let Go, and Move On – Take Charge of Your Life.

In the Chapter 8 Appendix, Pages 253 to 265, you will find Self Search Experience examples for: making major life decisions, overcoming a bad experience, determining how you want to live your life, and creating your personal mission and vision statements.

Important References and Resources

Change Your Mind and Your Life Will Follow: 12 Simple Principles, Karen Casey, 2008, San Francisco: Conari Press.

Managing Transition: Making the Most of Change, William Bridges and Susan Bridges, 2009, Cambridge, Massachusetts: Da Capo Press.

SHED Your Stuff, Change Your Life: A Four-Step Guide to Getting Unstuck, Julie Morgenstern, 2009, New York: Fireside (Simon & Schuster, Inc.)

The Alchemist, Paulo Coelho, 2006, New York: HarperCollins.

The Power to Transform, Chris Majer, 2009, Emmaus, Pennsylvania: Rodale, Inc.

Websites:

http://www.life-with-confidence.com/life-change.html
Life With Confidence – a positive way of thinking: Catherine Pratt

www.lawofattractiontrainingcenter.com
The Law of Attraction Training Center

APPENDIX

NAVIGATING THE JOURNEY OF YOUR LIFE

Wherever we are, it is but a stage on the way to somewhere else, and whatever we do, however well we do it, it is only preparation to do something else that is different.
Robert Louis Stevenson

YOUR SELF-SEARCH EXPERIENCES

Your Self-Search Experiences

All of the Self-Search Experiences mentioned throughout this book are contained in the Appendix for easy reference and accessibility. They are designed to take you to new places of insight as well as discovering solutions to challenging situations in your life. It is highly recommended that you do those in Chapter 1– Who Are You, Really? From there on just do those that interest you or are specific to your current needs. You will get the greatest benefit if you keep everything you do in a journal.

The following is a list, by chapter, of the Self-Search Experiences in this Appendix.

Contents

YOUR SELF-SEARCH EXPERIENCES

Chapter 1—Who Are You, Really?

Self-Search Experience: Who Am I? Part 1

Here is a process for your own self-development. As you complete this process it will provide you with what you need to know, where you want to go, and what you will need to do to get there.

This brings us back to some beginning questions. What do you really believe about yourself? How will these beliefs impact your relationship with others, especially a significant other? How will these beliefs impact your potential success and achievement in life? The good news is that you are now at a point where you can take control and determine how you want to live your life. If you want to change some part of it that is not working well for you, you can. If you want to strengthen a part that you like about yourself, you can; but first let's get a clear picture of where you stand today.

Begin your Self-Search experience with the answers you wrote to the questions in the book margins. This is not something you will want to hurry through. Take some time and go as deep as you can.

- Who am I, really?
- What do I love about myself?
- What do I not like?
- Who am I capable of becoming?
- What am I capable of doing?
- What is my potential? How do I know that I can ... or that I can't?

Now ask three friends: a) What are your three greatest strengths, and b) What it is you do that makes them think this? Do one more thing:

A Self-Esteem Assessment.

Answer these questions yes or no:

You Matter:

Are you happy most of the time? _____

Do you have one or more friends you know you can count on? _____

Do you deserve to feel loved and respected? _____

Are you okay with not being perfect? _____

Do you like who you are and who you are becoming? _____

Are you sad less than ten percent of the time? _____

Are you as happy now as you were three years ago? _____

Is the majority of your "self-talk" positive? _____

Are you able and willing to ask for help when you need it? _____

(These self esteem statements were compiled from a variety of self-esteem assessments.)

Add to your Self-Search paper any of these statements to which you answered NO. Keep your Self-Search Part 1 available, as it is a component of Part 2.

Self-Search Experience: Who Am I? Part 2

First, go back to your Who Am I, Part 1, and compare your list of strengths with those your friends listed about you. Any surprises? Incorporate your friends' perceptions into your own and into your self-talk. Reinforce your strengths. Most people focus on weaknesses. You get to be aware of your weaknesses, but *focus on your strengths*.

Second, if there are any Self-Esteem Assessment statements where you answered "no," then write that statement here. For example, if you answered "no" to the statement "The majority of my self-talk is positive," then include that statement. Except now write it as an affirmation such as, "from here on the majority of my self-talk is positive."

Affirmations are positive statements of the truth, or of the existence of something you want in your life. They often begin with "I am …," "I can …," "I will …."

For example:

I am competent.	I can lose weight.	I will feel good things about me today.
I am loveable.	I can be positive.	I will challenge myself to change today.
I am forgiving.	I can let go of fear.	I will lose weight each day.

Affirmations work in concert with the Law of Attraction. Writing affirmations and reading them each day is a powerful tool for creating a new way of being and living.

Third, look at what you wrote down about the four "self limiting beliefs" on Pages 39 to 45

1. Comparing yourself with others.

2. Negative "self-talk" and/or listening to negative "other's-talk."

3. Creating the wrong YOU.

4. Being too hard on yourself.

Pick one of these statements that you would like to change, and work it for twenty-eight days. This is how long it takes to make a lasting change in a habit pattern. Just know that each time you do make a change in one of these areas, it will get easier the next time. You can pick another later, after you have experienced success with the first one.

Chapter 2—Insights That Can Shape Your Life

Self-Search Experience: Synchronicity In Your Life:

1. Begin by focusing on where you are in your life right now: physical location, what you are doing, the path you are on in your life.

2.   Go back to your childhood and see whether you can identify events and experiences throughout your personal history that may not have seemed connected, but with twenty/twenty hindsight you now begin to see as a pattern. Some experiences may have been very negative or even traumatic but then drove you to do something positively different.

3.   What opportunities appeared? What consequences? What choices did you make that took you in a new direction? What new possibilities appeared—perhaps sooner, perhaps much later?

4.   Now focus on the future that you are creating for yourself in your Self-Search Experience. What do you want the future you create for yourself to look like?

5.   It is no coincidence that you are here now doing what you are doing— right or wrong, good or bad. Life will continuously provide you with new possibilities, and you will have new choices to make. You can choose to continue on the path you are on. You can choose to modify it. You can totally change the path. The choices are yours.

Self-Search Experience: Expressing Appreciation and Gratitude

Do one or more of the following (refer to your notes on Pages 61 to 65):

1.   Write down the top ten things for which you are grateful.

2.   Write a letter or email to your significant other, parent, or special friend saying how much you appreciate them and why.

3.   Write down the names of the people to whom you are most grateful, and those whom you most appreciate. In some form or another, let them know.

4.   Do something special for someone just because you want to.

5.   Call an old friend you haven't talked to in a long time.

6.   Write a thank you note to someone who has helped you.

7.   Write down how doing this made you feel, and how any of the responses you received made you feel.

Self-Search Experience: Forgiveness Is a Liberating Experience

First, here is a wonderful story from Stephanie that includes many of the elements presented in Chapter 2: love of self, forgiveness of self, forgiveness of a boyfriend who had "dumped" her, feeling at fault, being a victim, the Law of Attraction, and being freed up to move on with life. This story is followed by the Self-Search Experience and process.

Stephanie—"All I needed was to love myself."

Relationships are always difficult, whether the people are deeply in love or deeply unhappy. I have to admit I have dated quite a few people, but have had very few serious boyfriends. Most of the time I end up hurt and distraught, thinking the breakup was because of me, something I had done or said, or something I had not done or said. I usually could not see the breakup coming and instead it would hit me like a train. One such relationship was with a boy named Tyler. For my Self-Search Experience I wrote letters of forgiveness and letters of thanks to various people who are or have been in my life. One was to Tyler, and when reading the letter I realized that two of my first sentences perfectly summarized the beginning and ending of our relationship: "You effortlessly swept me off of my feet and I was soon in a whirlwind, completely wrapped up in you," and, " I never could have imagined you would be capable of hurting me the way you did." However, writing this letter has helped me more than I could have thought.

Through my letter, I was able to express all of the negative feelings I have had toward him over the past two years. By the end of the letter I had no anger left, and instead was thanking him for helping me become the person I am today. It is quite clear how desperately I had tried to hold onto him while simultaneously feeling completely betrayed. Here are a few excerpts from my letter:

"Being dumped as your girlfriend and then being dumped as your friend was a huge blow to my confidence and my trust. I didn't know why this was happening. I wanted

to know what was wrong with me to make you do that. I thought it must have been me. Afterward, I didn't see myself as lovable. It was not your fault I had problems loving myself; that had been established years before—but I can tell you this: You certainly didn't help. I am not seeking a relationship with you now, but instead I am looking to forgive you. I need to let this all go. I now know that I AM lovable. I now know that I DO love myself! I know that what you did has nothing to do with who I am as a person, and I need to stop blaming myself. I know that being angry with you does no good. So here it is. I am letting it all go. I am no longer mad at you; I am not holding a grudge. You served a purpose in my life and I wouldn't be who I am today if you had not walked into my life. I love my life, and I love who I am, so thank you."

All of this leads into an interesting turn of events, quite possibly something to do with the Law of Attraction since I have been thinking about Tyler more of late. Today, I was going about my normal business and walking through campus. I was running a little late and was paying little attention to the people around me. There is an elevator that I had to pass to get to my class, and ten feet away, I realized there was Tyler standing waiting for the elevator. I was completely surprised, because last I heard he was not even going to school. I cannot be sure that he saw me as I walked by, but I have a very strong feeling he did. I was in such shock, seeing him in the last place I would have expected, that I just walked past. As soon as I was inside the building, I instantly regretted my decision. This was something very unfamiliar to me, because I have spent the last year and a half dreading to run into him, or getting mad whenever I saw his car. In fact, if I ever had any sort of encounter with him, I would immediately text my best friend to tell her I had seen him and how uncomfortable it was. Instead, this time my reaction was extremely different. I wished I had stopped and just said hi, or at least have him see me acknowledge him. I texted my best friend Allison about seeing Tyler, and I think it was the last time. This is how my text read: " Finally, I was able to see him without getting mad at him and instantly feeling annoyed by the sight of him. I'm so relieved to be completely over that now. I think if I see him again, I'll go say hi and give him a hug."

My attitude toward Tyler has changed so much in the past week, and it is so wonderful! I never would have imagined something so "simple" as a forgiveness letter could be so effective. "Simple" in quotations because the concept is simple, but actually following through and writing that letter is anything but simple or easy! I felt like, at least for me, if I have been mad at someone for an extended period of time it is so much less effort to continue that attitude and never change it. It seems easier to stay mad at that person than to forgive them; but I now know how wrong I was! I think staying angry has taken far more energy than if I had just forgiven him!

I have spent my whole life trying to please other people, and not caring enough about myself. I have learned that in order to best serve others, I have to be selfish sometimes and just take care of myself. This is what I have done in my letter to Tyler. I took care of myself. I did not wait until he finally came around to say that he was sorry, which is something I had previously been doing. I was waiting for him to take that first step but I did not need him; all I needed was to love myself.

Forgiveness of Self and/or Another

This process is useful for ordinary situations of hurt and anger. Do not try to use this for acts of violence, abuse, rape, etc. These experiences are addressed in Chapter 6 – When Bad Things Happen.

Be in a quiet place, without interruption, and write the situation down. Write your thoughts as they come to you; don't edit or interrupt the flow of words. Don't be concerned about spelling or grammar or how you state something.

You Matter:

1. Express your feelings; don't hold back. Express anger, rage, hurt, pain, fear— whatever is there.

2. Wait a day or two, but not more.

3. If the experience was caused by someone else try looking at the other person's life through their eyes as best you can. Try to look without the fog of your emotions or judgment. What happened to them? Why are they the way they are? Why did they do what they did?

4. Make notes about the highlights of what came to you. (You don't need to write it all out.) Ask yourself, "Has this enabled me to see things differently?"

5. Accept responsibility for what you contributed to the situation, and forgive yourself. You might say, "I forgive *me* for putting myself in this situation. I have learned and I'm moving on."

6. There are lessons for us in almost every good and bad experience. What were the lessons for you in the experience you had with this person? What lessons in forgiving and letting go do you experience?

7. Let go and move on with your life. You can't change what happened and you can't change the other person, but you completely control what you think about and what you do going forward.

Key points to remember about Forgiveness

Forgiveness begins when you:

- Stop blaming others for the situation.
- Accept that you can't change the person who hurt you; you can only change yourself.
- Acknowledge your anger and hurt.
- Take responsibility for your life and your future happiness.

You stay stuck when you:

- Continue to complain and/or blame.
- Can't let go until you get an apology.

Bill Maynard

- Act from a place of anger, and need to seek retribution.
- You fantasize about revenge.
- Continue to focus on blame.

When you carry the anger and pain, you get trapped in your own prison. To think or say, "I will never forgive," means that the person who hurt you is still in control. And this person doesn't know and doesn't care.

Chapter 3—Raising Your Parents

Self-Search Experience: Changing a Difficult Relationship with A Parent

The following process works exceptionally well in dealing with issues and/or improving the relationship with your parents.

1. Journal the situation, expressing your thoughts and your feelings.

2. Identify what you would like to see change.

3. Write a letter to your parent(s), first expressing that for which you are grateful, then expressing what you would like to change.

4. Before sending it, read your letter and try to see what you wrote through the eyes of your parents. (You may be surprised by what you learn from doing this.)

5. Try not to create expectations in your mind about how you want your parents to respond. (This can lead to unnecessary disappointment.)

6. As soon as you can, get together with one or both, and have a conversation about your letter, and your thoughts about how to do things differently. Listen to them as well. (This might be awkward the first time, as some parents aren't used to having this kind of "adult-adult" conversation.)

Here are two real life examples of some very challenging situations that were addressed using this process.

Christopher began by journaling the situation he found himself in and how he felt about being used by both parents. He became very clear about what he wanted to see changed, then he wrote a single letter for both parents in order to ensure that they would both be reading the same information. After reading the letters "through the eyes of his parents," he felt certain that he needed to be very firm in how he wrote the letter. This was a totally new experience for him in dealing with his parents.

Christopher—"We all know that our family is dysfunctional."

Dear Mom and Dad,

I am writing both of you this letter in the interest of opening our communication. The purpose of this letter is to share my feelings, opinions, and views, and to explain what I need from both of you in my life. It is not meant as a personal attack of any kind, as I love both of you very much.

I am proud of who I am, who I'm becoming, and the direction I'm headed in life. I surround myself with great people and always look to stay as positive as possible, as I have found this has a great impact on my life. I am thankful for all the opportunities that I have been lucky enough to receive in my life. I appreciate everything both of you have done for me, as it has helped me become the person I am today. I am focusing on what I want, instead of what I don't want.

We all know that our family is dysfunctional. The tension has continually increased throughout the years, instead of becoming better, and has reached a point that is incredibly unhealthy. This is not good for anyone involved. There are certain things I need in my life in order to become the person I know I can be.

The hostility must stop between the two sides. It's a shit situation and we all know it. Continually talking <u>about</u> each other without ever talking <u>to</u> each other does *nothing to improve the situation—not to mention that it leaves both me and [my sister] in the middle trying to keep peace. The amount of stress this adds to both of our lives is unreal. It's been nearly two decades now. For you, it is time to accept that the past is the past and you can't change it. All you can do is work toward a better future full of happiness, laughter and good memories.*

If you continually focus on the past and what happened, whose fault it was, who's to blame, and how horrible the other is, it only compounds the tension we all experience. Understand this, the divorce was neither my fault nor my sister's fault.

We are all in this life together. If we don't change where we are going it is likely we will end up in an even worse place. The negative potential of where we could be is staggering.

Dad, I am not a moron, dumb ass, idiot, or screw-up. I am not a failure. I am proud of who I am and what I have accomplished. I cannot make you feel proud of me or what I have accomplished. I don't feel that I should have to convince you to come to my graduation, as I am the first person in our family to graduate from college. Let me say, this is huge for me. I hope that you would be here because you want to be, because you truly feel a sense of pride in what I have accomplished and come to revel in this incredible moment of my life. I want you to come and experience a snapshot of where I have been and where I'm going, the people I have in my life, and the things I have done, without judging, yet simply accepting who I am. This event is very significant to me and is a major turning point in my life.

Mom, I know that the years have been rough and times are even rougher now. I know you feel like you have missed out on a lot of my time, but the time we <u>have</u> had has been continually getting better. You need to find what makes you happy again and stop focusing on the past.

What's done is done, and no one has control over that. Every time we talk it seems like we cover all the things that went wrong over the past eighteen years, and fingers get pointed at someone. Every one of us is partially responsible for the overall current condition of the family, and the only way it is going to change is if we stop assuming that there is no way to change the situation. It will take effort from all of us to work toward a more positive future. I truly think it is possible and hope that one day we can all be there together.

There is a lot at stake for me in writing this letter, but the potential for gain is monumental. My intention is not to make personal attacks or tell either one of you how to live your life. It is more a call to action, toward the steps we can take and the potential that exists for all of us to have a truly fulfilled life. We are not going to get anywhere by pointing out flaws or placing blame. Changes in our actions, thoughts, and feelings now can and will have a massive effect on where we all end up, and the quality of life we have when we get there. I do love both of you sincerely, and hope that this letter is taken in the most positive way possible.

Sincerely and with Much Love,
Christopher

You can imagine the shock that Christopher's parents experienced when they received the letter. It was not a surprise to him that his mother wrote back within a few days, and his father wrote back a couple weeks later. When Christopher went home he had a conversation with his mother, and another with his father. He told them he loved them and asked for their help in making life better for him and his sister. They both agreed, and began working on it. Christopher is well aware that, under stress, people will often regress to some old behaviors, and he was prepared to deal with it in as positive way as possible. His dad did attend his graduation, as did his mother. They didn't sit together.

Curtis' mother and father went through a messy divorce when he was a high school senior. He had had no contact from his father since, and he realized, four years later, that he and his mother had never discussed the situation. Through the Self-Search process, he decided that he really wanted to have a conversation with her about it, so they both could get this past out of their way.

Curtis—"Mom, it's obvious to me that you carry a lot of guilt about the divorce."

Dear Mom,

I wanted to let you know that I love you. It is obvious to me that you carry a lot of guilt about the divorce, but I wanted to let you know that I do not resent you at all. In fact, you are the strongest-spirited person I know. You have a unique gift that enables you to love unconditionally. The dedication and commitment that you have for your kids does not go unnoticed. Your hard work and sacrifice is not appreciated enough at the office or at home.

In May of my senior year in high school, you and dad had decided to get divorced. Instead of running to get divorce papers right away, you wanted to wait. You wanted to wait until after I had gone to college and established myself. That meant more to me than anything in the world. You were unselfish to the point that you actually lived with dad and slept in the same bed as he did for seven months, just so I would continue my education. Ever since you told me that, it has been my main motivation for succeeding in college.

You had no choice but to move forward and better your situation. I do not blame you for this. If there has been one thing you've taught me, it is to be unselfish and take care of those closest to you. You were the victim in the situation, and you handled yourself with grace and confidence. You are the unshakable. You are my rock.

I think it's time for us to talk about all this and get it behind us. Would this be okay with you?

Love,
Curtis

They did get together and talk. Curtis said it was one of the best they had ever had, and that they committed to each other to continue on this path.

Self-Search Experience: Forgiveness of Self

If you had a really bad experience with a parent, it can be very difficult to let go and move on. If you feel any guilt, shame, remorse, have been hiding, pretending or repressing pain or hurt, then doing a "Forgiveness" experience for yourself can help you through this.

1. Choose a quiet place, without interruption and write the situation down. Write your thoughts as they come to you; don't edit or interrupt the flow of words. Don't be concerned about spelling or grammar.

2. Express your feelings; don't hold back. Express anger, rage, hurt, pain: whatever you're feeling.

3. Wait a day or more.

4. Write yourself a letter of forgiveness. What are you forgiving yourself for and why do you feel it is necessary? Read your letter whenever you feel yourself slipping backward or feeling fearful or uncertain.

5. Let go and move on with your life. You can't change what happened but you can control what you do and the choices you make going forward.

Self-Search Experience: Building a Good Relationship With Your Parents

1. Start with thinking about a parent or both parents. Think about how you feel and what you appreciate about them.

2.   How do you want the relationship to be? What would you like to do differently? What you would like them to do differently?

3.   Write a letter expressing your feelings, appreciation, and the kind of relationship you would like to have with them. For now, leave out any issues and concerns, knowing that there may be an appropriate time in the future.

4.   Get together and have a conversation and see where it goes. You may be in for a nice surprise about the letter and its impact.

Self-Search Experience: Expressing Gratitude

Many have found the joy of expressing gratitude to one or both parents and have been delighted with their parents' surprise and responses. It is just a simple act of writing a letter and expressing both *what* you are feeling and *why* you are writing to them. Those who have used this found that a letter followed by a conversation worked the best.

Here are two examples of letters written to parents. The second includes the parent response.

Castilia—"I want to tell my stepfather how much he means to me."

I thought it important to finally address the issue I have with my stepfather. The issue is that I have never truly told him how I feel about him and how much he means to me. I decided to write him a letter expressing those very thoughts and then to send it to him so he will be surprised when he receives it. Jack, my stepfather, doesn't have too many more years to live due to major heart complications.

Dear Jack,

You probably think it is odd that I am sending you this letter, but I am taking a class that has given me a chance to look at the important things in life and remind me that I need to let those individuals who are in my life know how important they are to me.

You Matter:

I actually wanted to write you this letter a lot of times, but of course got too busy in the hustle and bustle of every day life, and I keep saying that I will eventually get to it. Well, now I am taking the time to do just what I want. I'm realizing now that I don't want something to happen to one of us and not have taken that little bit of time to tell you how I feel.

You have always been my Father. You have been there for all my sports activities and extracurricular activities. You have always reminded me who I am, when I seemed to forget, and that I am capable of doing anything I want as long as I put my mind to it. Most of all, you have loved me for being me. I know that it wasn't easy coming into a family and having to try to gain the respect of the children. Well, I want you to know that you gained my respect right away and, to this day, I respect you more than you will ever know. You gave up things in your life that were important to you so that we could live a good life and be happy. You dedicated time to establish a relationship with the two of us, and you stood back when you thought it was necessary, so we could be with our Dad. I look back at how much I learned from you and, wow, it is amazing what an impact a person can have on your life. You have taught me honesty, hard work, respect for self, respect for others, how to be stubborn. These characteristics I have learned from you, help make me who I am today. Because of you I am a better person.

There is something that I think is important to share with you. Since you and Mom got married, I really wanted to call you Dad instead of Jack. The reason I didn't isn't that I didn't think of you as a father. It was because I was too afraid, too afraid I would hurt/offend Dad. You have been and are an awesome Dad. Thank you for being you and for loving me for being me! I couldn't ask for any better man to stand at the right hand of my Mother.

I Love and Adore you!!!!!!!!!!!!!!!!!!

Your proud and very honored daughter,
Castilia

Elizabeth—"I want to tell my parents how much I love them."

Mom and Dad,

If I die tomorrow, I must cherish today, and I must tell you—my two guardian angels who have led me through this life. You have held my hand and have carried me on your backs, but never as a burden. You have shown me the greatest gift of all, life. You taught me to stand on my own two feet, you taught me to speak my mind, and you taught me to be me. You have taught me what love is—to love without fear of being hurt, without boundaries—because that is how you have always loved me, and how I love you with all of my heart, my soul, and my very being. I love you so much.

You are such mentors to me, and being your child is what I am truly most proud of in my life. I am honored to be yours and to be made by two so very special people. I was created and brought into this world in love, and tomorrow I will leave you with a true understanding and wisdom of what love is—a wisdom you have given me. Though I've said it many times before: I love you, I love you, I love you. Thank you. Thank you for me. Thank you for life and, most of all, I thank you for you.

Love Always,
Lizzy

Here is the response of her parents.

Lizzy,

We have always feared that if anything happened to you, we could not say the things we needed to say to you.

You Matter:

We have always worried about if we did enough for you. If we gave you everything you needed.

Wow! We didn't know how good we are. We love you and always will. If you were to die we would miss you so much. You brought an innocence, a joy, and a likeness that no one else in our family could bring to us. You are so much more mature and responsible than we ever were. You have loved so many without asking anything in return and showed people what it means to live. Even if you were to die tomorrow, you would have lived a full life. You've done all good things in your life. You are blessed with friends and family because of your endless love.

You are the epitome of our lives. We love you so much.
Mom and Dad

Chapter 4—Being in Love and Breaking Up

Break-up Patterns in a Relationship

How many of the fourteen "signs that something is significantly wrong" are present in your relationship?

- The relationship started off wonderfully, but now your thoughts are about being out of the relationship, or you are thinking of someone else.

- She went through a breakup within three to six months prior to getting into a relationship with you.

- He wants to talk about the future and you do not, or you try to avoid this conversation.

- The two of you have significantly different values around religion, money, sex, marriage, or having a family, and are not addressing these differences.

- You have chosen a partner who is very similar to others in your past relationships. You maybe didn't see this until now.

- One or both of you have been unfaithful in one or more past relationships.

- There are trust issues that have not been addressed.

- You have different views on what commitment means.

- You find yourself giving up being you in order to be loved by your partner.

- You've been together for quite a while but still don't know who your partner really is.

- You seem to argue and fight all the time.

- It's a long-distance relationship. They are difficult to sustain because you don't know each other in day-to-day situations.

- Your partner insists that almost everything be done her/his way.

- If your parents are divorced, the probability of you going through a breakup or divorce increases.

The following are two different Self-Search processes that have been used successfully. Each can help you to learn from your experience, to let go of the hurt, and to help you get to where you want to be. Try these and see which style works best for you.

Self-Search Experience #1: Relationship Breakup Discovery

1.   Describe the situation.

2.   What was it like when our relationship was the best?

3.   What went wrong? Two parts: First, write out what you see that went wrong. Second, try seeing the situation through your partner's eyes and writing out what went wrong.

4.   What specifically could I have done better or differently.

5.   Write a letter of anger to him/her, BUT DO NOT SEND IT.

6.   What do I need in my next relationship to experience happiness?

7.   What will I do differently going forward?

Self Search Experience #2: Getting Closure and Moving On

One of the most important steps in getting over someone is to journal about what happened. Here is what has worked, what was good about our relationship (be sure to use the person's name). Here is what attracted me, what I liked about this person. Here is what didn't work, what went wrong. Then look for any patterns you might have. Is he/she like others I've been with? When and why did I lose interest? Did I jump into it too fast? Am I running away from the relationship and, if so, what specifically might I be running from? Did it turn out that we are different people with different values and expectations? Did we become intimate too quickly and sex became our main focus, so we didn't get to know the rest of each other?

The following are two examples from students who used this Self-Search process and made great breakthroughs in understanding their patterns and in knowing what to do differently in the future. As you read these, read with the intent of discovering a variety of insights about yourself and a better understanding of others rather than judging the writers. You will also see how this process works and how helpful it was for them, and can be for you.

Example #1 of learning and moving forward with clarity

Cara—"I changed my focus from what is wrong, to being happy together."

At this point in our relationship, things were cooling off and I was going out a lot with my friends and drinking too much and letting myself get worked up about little things, then coming home and crying to John. It was probably really annoying, and it was having a pretty negative effect on our relationship. So here goes.

- *I am addicted to the adrenaline I get from moving fast (emotionally) in relationships.*

- *I crave the excitement and the risk of "falling in love." And the whole love at first sight idea.*

- *The difference is that, before, it's always been with whatever nice guy happened to be around and interested in me at the time.*

With John it's different because I'm actually impressed with him, and I'm not sure I deserve him, and I usually choose guys who I don't really believe deserve me. I've never felt this way. I'm already pessimistic about long-term relationships because many of them that I see around me are very dramatic and don't stand the test of time.

Lately, things have slowed to a normal, healthy pace with John and me. I have been assuming that this means something is wrong or he is losing feelings for me or getting sick of me. This is usually the feeling I get a month or so before I get bored and move on because I'm craving "the feeling" again.

This time though, I don't want to break up and move on. I am actually in love with John, and I want to build something REAL with him. I want to experience a REAL feeling with trust and companionship and true feelings.

I'm hurting John by doubting us constantly and blaming him when I know that it's me. If I continue down this road I am going to F@#! up something that is more than perfect because it is actually real. I love John and he loves me. I am worth putting up with, but now I have to STOP pushing him. I need to regain my sense of excitement and become happy, fun, and carefree again.

I need to really apologize and then let it go. If I find that alcohol compels me to return to this path I WILL stop drinking so much. I am not going to kill what John and I have found. I'm not going to stunt our relationship by trying to force it to grow too quickly or by trying to control it. Control is not and never has been my forte, and forcing something is always a losing battle.

So here is my game plan:

1. *We need to relax and talk about positive things and have fun again. No expectations except that we will reassure each other like we used to. I know I have been lacking in this department, and John has been suffering for it.*
2. *Less drinking for me. Drinking seems to make me depressed, which makes me over-analyze, which either makes me too sappy and I try to force the "future thing" with him, or I begin to doubt … or both, depending on what I drink. This is drama that only I cause and only I can prevent by not drinking more than four beers or three mixed drinks at a time.*
3. *No more letting my worrying drive my emotions. I am a happy, lucky girl and, really, I have nothing to*

worry about in my life that is truly significant. This means I should be one step ahead because I am so blessed. It doesn't give me an excuse to get bored and go looking for things that are "wrong" in my life. My parents are divorced because they couldn't make it work with each other. Divorce is not hereditary unless you learn nothing from your parents.

Example #2 of learning and moving forward with clarity

Carter—"I keep falling in love and then falling out."

My first experience with an extended relationship was with this girl I met at the community college I attended. She grew up in the same home town as I did, but had a completely different school and family experience. Marlene was Dutch, and her family was five generations deep in the Christian Reformed Church. She was very sure of things in the world. She had the idea that everything was black and white. I was from a family which viewed religion as a journey and that individuals had to discover it for themselves. I was brought to Sunday school as a child, but when I was in my teens, I was allowed to make my own decision regarding whether or not to go to church. During the time that I was dating Marlene, I was in the stage of discovering myself for the first time, and what exactly my beliefs were regarding religion.

Marlene would tell me of papers that she would write for college, and would use facts out of the Bible to support her arguments. She did not understand why they were not accepted, as she was used to using her Bible as a reference from high school papers. I think I carried on in this relationship for so long because I liked the idea of a structured unit. I felt that if I worked hard enough at the relationship, it should work. I figured that it was part of my duty to help make all of the different aspects of the relationship work.

I would attend Marlene's church with her on most Sundays. The message was always traditional and rooted in fundamentalism. Instead of safe sexual practices, they spoke of abstinence. Therefore she was against the use of birth control or other measures to insure that she would not become pregnant. Looking back, I was very lucky, not to mention naïve. I could have changed my life because of decisions that I was making in that relationship.

The turning point of the relationship came when my grandmother was dying of cancer. When I would talk to Marlene about it, she would be emotionless. At first, I did not understand why, so I asked her. That is when she responded, "You know your grandmother is going to Hell, Right?" I did not know how to respond to this. I was in a sudden state of shock. At first I thought: How could Marlene say something like this? Then it all became very clear. My grandmother was Mormon, so in Marlene's mind, there is no possible way that a Mormon could make it into heaven. Marlene expressed this by showing no emotion during the passing of my grandmother. I can remember how much this hurt me at the time. I still felt that this did not justify ending the relationship.

It took me two weeks later to get up enough courage to finally break it off. I don't know why I couldn't do it. I think it was the need for structure or the fact that I needed to avoid confrontation at all costs.

My next experience in a relationship shook me up the most. This was the first time that I fell in love and really had my heart broken. I started to date Tina about two months after I had broken up with Marlene. Tina was like a dream come true for me. Tina was the first girl to make me feel really wanted. I remember her running into my room during the middle of the day and jumping onto my lap, and staring me in the eyes with so much intensity it felt as if I would melt. Tina was the polar opposite of Marlene. She was strong–willed and liberal. Tina had opinions that she loved to back up with fact. She was the first girl I really loved to hear speak, because every time she spoke I felt as if I was learning something. when I was with Tina, I felt as if I was on a foreign adventure.

During the time that I dated Tina, I was still trying to figure out what I wanted with my life. My friends would warn me that the choices I was making when I was with Tina were not who I really was. I was in denial at first, because all they did was party, and I figured any choice that I made other than to drink all night was superior to theirs. I later started to realize what they meant. One night, I found myself doing stitching next to Tina, instead of going out with the boys. I was never into knitting or stitching of any kind before this. That moment I started to realize that the decisions I was making were to please her before myself. I was in love with this girl, and I would do anything just to spend time with her.

Tina finally decided that it was time to end the relationship. She rationalized that she needed a change of environment, and she needed to explore other things. I was completely devastated. At the time she was the only thing I really cared about in my life.

Five years later, I can still feel the love and the pain this relationship caused. It took me a while to bounce back from this relationship, but it helped to shape me as an independent person. The relationship helped me to formulate what I really want in a partner. I began to realize that making decisions 1 really wanted was part of being honest about who I am to my partner. The few times I had talked to Tina since we ended our relationship, brought me to realize that our goals for the future were too different to coexist. This helped to bring me some closure.

I have learned so much from doing this work, and I know I won't make the same mistakes again.

You can see how apparent the patterns become as each began journaling their experiences. Not only did this process make it possible for them to break the patterns and change how they approach a new relationship, but it also provided significant healing for each of them.

Chapter 5—Making Your Relationship Work

Self-Search Experience: A Relationship Exploration

Step 1: Focus on your current relationship. From the stories in Chapter 5, and from the Key Takeaways, write down any thoughts you have, any words that jump out at you, any significant sentences. Also look at your margin notes in Chapter 5. Pay particular attention to anything that stirs emotions, a disturbing thought, a memory that is upsetting, or any patterns that begin to emerge.

Step 2: Identify any issues that occurred between you that you know need to be addressed.

Step 3: Journal your thoughts and feelings about the issue. Without judgment, write down anything that comes up for you.

Step 4: Write out how you want things to be in your relationship going forward.

Step 5: What do you and your partner need to do to get from where you are today to where you want to be?

Step 6: Ask your partner to do steps one to five as well.

Step 7: Exchange what each of you has written in Steps One through Five. Get together and begin talking.

Self-Search Experience: Solving a Recent Quarrel or Disagreement

1. Do a re-enactment of your most recent quarrel or disagreement. Each of you play the same role you did in that situation.

2. Now reverse roles and each of you "play" the other in a continuation of the disagreement. Each of you try to feel the point of view of the other while acting as the other.

3. Have a discussion about what you learned from this experience.

Self-Search Experience: Becoming a Very Healthy Couple

Step 1: Both of you see if you can go twenty-four hours without complaining. Write down any complaints that do come up and what or whom it was about. Are there any patterns?

Step 2: Make a list of all the things about your partner for which you are grateful.

Step 3: Sit together and share both of your lists with each other. Then talk about what each of you got from this experience. You likely will have some serious insights and some surprising laughs!

We-Search Experience: Our Level of Trust and Respect

Step 1: Have some quiet time together and read the information on respect and trust in Chapter 5, Pages 127-130.

Step 2: Each of you talk about where you are on the continuum in your level of respect. Why this level? Is this where we want to be? Does each of us feel respected, admired? Why? Going forward, what would we each like from the other?

Step 3: Each talk about where you are in your level of trust. Why this level? Is this where we want to be? What's working? How might we take our trust to a higher level? What do we need from each other?

We-Search Experience: How Are We Doing?

Respect and trust provide the foundation for your relationship. Now that you have taken a close look at respect and trust, it's time to take a good look at where you are and where you want to be in your relationship. This may well be one of the most important experiences you will have together at this point in your relationship. Doing this requires that you each separately journal your responses to the following points.

You Matter:

Part One

1. Here is what is working well for me in our relationship:

2. My fears are:

3. Here is what I would like to see us change or improve:

4. Answer The Most Important Questions to Ask Before Marriage, Page 137.

5. My "non-negotiables" are:

Then get together and read aloud your responses to each other, one point at a time. Talk about the reasons for your thoughts and ask questions when you're not sure what your partner specifically means. The non-negotiables can be a touchy area, but it is better to talk about them now than to leave them in hiding only to surface later. A non-negotiable is something that one of you is firmly committed to or opposed to—such as not smoking—and you are not willing to negotiate any change where smoking would be okay with you.

Part Two

Together, create "Our Relationship Vision." This is a statement of what you want your relationship to be. Build a scrapbook, or do it on a portable whiteboard. You can use words, pictures, drawings, whatever works for you. Get as clear as you can about what you want your life together to look like, and have some fun with this. Put the result where you can always see it. Then:

- Develop a statement of commitment to each other for the achievement of your vision.

- Together, develop your goals for achieving your relationship vision.

Doing these We-Search Experiences together really does work. You will learn so much about each other, and will appreciate each other even more. If for some reason the relationship isn't going to work, you will likely find an indication of this as well. Better now than later.

Here is what Heidi and her boyfriend experienced.

Heidi—"I have a whole new outlook on life."

Now everything I look at, I have a different perspective than I had before. The air smells sweeter, people seem nicer, and my love for life has flourished. My boyfriend and I were at dinner the other night. The way we were able to sit down for a couple hours and have a nice dinner and talk about our relationship was amazing. Since we worked on my personal project (which was our relationship) both of us have opened up to each other a significant amount. We both thought we knew each other very well, yet we found out that there was so much more to learn. He expressed to me that he used to think about our relationship and had answers in his head about how our relationship was going to turn out—and the outcomes were bleak. Yet after just a couple sessions with each other, he feels like the possibilities are now endless for our relationship and the outcomes. We are like a totally different couple who actually communicate and respect each other's feelings. I think we are millions of miles ahead of our friends in understanding how a relationship works, and we are both proud of that.

You Matter:

Chapter 6 – When Bad Things Happen: Suicide, Injury Accidents, Serious Illness, Near Death, Death of Loved One/Friend, Depression

Self-Search Experience: Overcoming Bad Experiences

These five steps made a big difference for many students.

1.   Remember and write down the details of what happened.

2.   Accept your feelings as real: anger, rage, fear, helplessness, etc.

3.   Take the time for grieving and/or mourning. Talk to friends and loved ones about it.

4.   Let go of the past. Forgiveness of self and/or the other is helpful in letting go of the past. Be gentle with yourself as your unique forgiveness process unfolds.

5.   Get counseling! This can help so much in letting go and moving on without baggage.

Self-Search Experience: Overcoming a Bad Experience

Kylee—"Overcoming an experience of abuse."

Past and Present Situation

Within the last three weeks, I have had a major wake-up call about who I thought I was, and my world has been turned upside down. I have stretched my mind, body, and spirit to discover the real me. I dug deep to see how my past choices and actions have influenced how I view myself. I rediscovered emotions and experiences I did not know existed or have been trying to ignore, and 1 finally faced my inward struggles. I spent hours recalling memories from my childhood. Many of them are great, and I also have a few which are not so great. These are the one's which spark the deepest feeling of pain, hurt, anger, sadness, loneliness, worry, anxiety, fear, frustration, and depression. Little did I know that by bottling up my negative emotions, I was creating a greater negativity, which was destroying me on the

246

inside. I decided to quit running and face one of my biggest secrets.

I finally acknowledge the memory of being molested as a child. For the past six to seven years, I had been avoiding the memory and the pain. Bottling up my feelings, memories, and thoughts are only causing harm. I needed to begin expressing how I felt about past experiences and deal with my feelings.

What I have learned:

Once I allowed myself to take a step back and acknowledge my problems, I could then begin the process of letting go.

- *Now, when a negative memory or emotion pops up, I think back to where it originated in order to understand why I feel this way.*

- *Once I understand and acknowledge my past experiences and emotions, I can take what I have learned and then let go of the crap in my life.*

- *To help myself let go of bottled-up emotions, I have begun sharing with my friends and writing about my emotions and experiences.*

- *I discovered the power of writing things down. Writing my thoughts, feelings, and experiences can be therapeutic and is one step I am using to help let go of things.*

The power is now in my hands, and I am ready to explore my potential and create the person I desire to be.

My Future:

Now I have an understanding of how my past has been affecting me, and I have the desire to change my self image.

You Matter:

Goal One

My first goal is to find a job which will allow me to continue in the process of discovering my dream job. I am looking for a job where I work with and interact with people all day, and not sit in an office. For my personal life, I want to wake up every morning and live my life with ambition, inspiration, and enthusiasm.

Goal Two

I want to live my life truly appreciating everything life has to offer. I also want my life to be filled with enthusiasm because life is worth celebrating, and enjoying the time I spend with friends and family. I plan on making the best out of what life throws my way.

Goal Three

My vision for my family and friends is to maintain close, healthy relationships. My friends are awesome people, and I'm very fortunate to have them in my life. I plan on remaining in touch with the friends I have made here. My friendships are important to me because my friends are there to laugh with me, cry with me, listen to me ramble on about my problems, try new things, and are there when I really need a hug.

Goal Four

I want to have a healthy lifestyle. I am currently working on getting back into shape. Once I reach my desired weight, I plan on maintaining my goal weight by exercising and eating a healthy, balanced diet. Diabetes runs strong in my family; therefore I am at risk of one day becoming a diabetic.

Writing about myself has not been easy, however I now have a better understanding of who I am and how I want to live my life. Before, I really didn't have a plan or vision for my future. I have finally been able to open up and be honest with myself. I have been able to rediscover my life. I will no longer allow myself to bottle up my emotions, but will face them and learn from my experiences. By finally acknowledging my past, I am ready for the future and to live the life I desire.

Chapter 7— Other Bad Things That Happen: Sexual Abuse

Self-Search Experience: For Dealing with a Sexual Abuse Experience

How was it that in almost every story in the chapter, the victims were able to get through the traumatic experience, learn from it, and refocus their lives in healthy directions? There are six steps that made the difference for many. Here they are.

1. Remember and write down the details of what happened. (This may be very difficult, and it may take some time.)

2. Write about and accept your feelings as real; anger, rage, fear, helplessness, etc.

3. Take time for grieving and/or mourning. Talk to friends and/or loved ones about it.

4. Write a letter (without the intent of mailing it) describing the rage you feel toward your abuser. Express all of your feelings. Unload! Also express who you are now and that you are excluding this person from you life forever. **

5. Forgive yourself. It wasn't your fault.

6. Focus on the future and on letting go of the past. Create the you that you want and the life that you want.

7. Talk with a counselor. Bring what you have written to the counselor, as it will greatly help you both in getting clarity more quickly.

(See "Some Important Things To Know About Forgiveness," Appendix Pages 224-225.)

** If you have been carrying around thoughts and feelings of intense anger, hatred, or rage, or if you have a sense that you have repressed these thoughts and hidden them away inside you, then Step 4 can be of great help. The mental/emotional act of writing combined with the physical activity of yelling, crying, tearing paper, and even striking a pillow with a wooden spoon can help immensely in freeing yourself from the pain and from the burden of carrying these thoughts and feelings inside you. If you experience a great sense of relief and the negative thoughts no longer return (and are not repressed again), then you have made significant strides. Counseling will still be of great help in moving forward more quickly. If you find that the thoughts and feelings keep coming into your mind, then it is definitely a sign to get some help. Remember that whatever you think about and focus on, positive or negative, becomes larger, and you tend to attract more. It is very important to get help in breaking this pattern. Know that the work you have already accomplished will help immensely in moving you through this and back on your way to the life you want.

Here is an example of the outcome of this process in a real situation.

Carmen—"I had to come to terms with being raped last year."

For my self-search project, I had to come to terms with being raped last year while studying abroad in Rome. It was an experience that I had chosen never to address. For me, it is easier to put on a face than deal with the problems I have in my life. I had chosen to lie and say my life was perfect. Now I've decided that I need to stop lying to myself and recognize that what happened to me was traumatizing. It is an experience no person should ever have to go through.

His name is Giovanni. He is Italian and lives in Rome. He was cute, charming, and probably way too drunk for me to even be talking to him. Anyway, one thing led to another, and things got out of hand.

While writing my letter, I went through a variety of emotions. I was actually trying to see things through his eyes. Then came the anger. I was pissed. I had tears running down my cheeks. I was hitting the paper and marking it up. I swore a lot at him, both in English and Italian, just to make sure he totally understood. I wrote about how I felt when I thought about it, how just sitting around by myself I was overcome with urges to cry. Then I thought about the good things in my life, the things he couldn't touch. I am in a better place now, and he is not welcome to be there. I have decided that he was not worth my tears; he had taken enough of them. Then I stopped writing. I had nothing left to say.

It's two days later and I feel great. My mood has improved so drastically. I have more energy and am excited to wake up in the morning. Finally dealing with my problem helped me come to terms with what had happened and that it was not my fault. I know that being raped is not just a problem that I can get over in one day. It has taken a lot of time to heal and I'm well on my way.

It took Carmen two weeks to work her way through the process, which is not long, considering she had been carrying the pain for over a year. She discovered that there were still some things she had not been able to resolve, so she decided to see a counselor. The work she had already done expedited her time with the counselor in working through the issues. Carmen is a much happier woman now.

Chapter 8—Taking Charge of Your Life

There are two different kinds of Self-Search Experiences here. The first is about focusing on your future. It uses the Transformation Model, and you are provided with examples of five different applications.

- Creating Your Future

- Making major life decisions.

- Creating a life vision

- Overcoming a bad experience

- Finding meaning and purpose

The second is called Has My Life Made Any Difference? and begins on Page 262.

The Transition Model and Process – Creating My Desired State

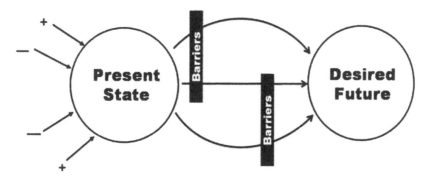

Self-Search Experience: Creating My Desired State

1.	Identify a present situation you would like to change OR, focus on your near-term future, such as your life over the next two to five years.

2.	Focus on your desired future. This is your "vision" for how you want it to be.

3.   The three arrows show you that there is no "one way" of getting there; life is not a linear experience. If you look, you will find many pathways, opportunities, and choices.

4.   There will also be "barriers," but they likely won't be the ones you see when you are sitting in your present state and without a vision for what you want.

5.   Focus on your desired future vision and begin developing a plan to get there. What will you need to do? Include accountability.

The following are four different examples of real life applications of the Transformation Model and process related to these situations. It can work successfully on a wide range of situations and applications.

A Self-Search Experience: Making Major Life Decisions

Erin was faced with making a number of serious decisions and was feeling overwhelmed. This made it even more difficult for her to set some priorities and begin to deal with the issues she faced. Here is how she was able to take control, get clear, and free herself up from the paralysis she was experiencing.

Erin—"Getting Past Overwhelm and Making Necessary Decisions."

Present State:

- *Consumed by responsibilities*

- *Feel pressures of others' expectations*

- *Feel that my personality has been smothered by my busy lifestyle*

- *Strong concern for mom's health*

- *Strong concern over how dad is dealing with his current state*

- *Feel like everything in life is spinning*

- *Having trouble understanding my own thoughts*

- *Cannot decide what the best choice is for me post-college; dozens of different possible paths*

- *Realizing that I need to make changes in order to be completely happy again*

- *Feeling a strong draw toward home*

- *Not sleeping well*

Prioritized list of decisions/burnings questions/things making me feel overwhelmed

1. *Is my mom going to be okay physically and mentally if I move away from home?*

2. *Is my dad going to be okay mentally if I move away from home?*

3. *These are hugely important to me due to all that my family has been challenged with over the past two years. A career will always be there and always be an option, but a life can be fleeting. I don't want to miss out on being with those who are most important to me, especially if it is very possible my mom may not be here even a year from now.*

4. *How much should I factor my boyfriend into my post-college choices?*

5. *Although he is my first boyfriend, I feel we have a very healthy relationship that need not have an abrupt end, unless I make a drastic decision for after I graduate. I do not want him to be a limiting factor with regard to my decision, but I also do not want to wonder what could have been if I make a choice that forces us to end the relationship.*

6. *Where do I want to be located after college?*

7. *This question is very important as it has a direct impact on the two questions above. If I am across*

the nation or even in another country, he and I would realistically need to come to an end, and I would be leaving my family at an unsteady phase of our lives.

8. *What do I want to be doing after college?*

9. *This question I ask myself frequently because I feel that, whatever decision I make, I will ultimately feel guilty, regardless of my choice. By not opting for one, I feel that I will always wonder if I am leading the life that is the most fulfilling for me.*

After using this process, Erin talked with her parents and with her boyfriend and then sat down and made her decisions. Here is what she wrote.

Results

- *Seek a job within driving distance of my parents. They are far too important to me and really need me now.*

- *Stay in and continue to develop my relationship with my boyfriend. It's really going well right now, and I think it has great potential, but neither of us is sure at this point.*

- *I will use these tools to keep from allowing myself to be overwhelmed again. In fact, I will use them now in making the decision on job choice.*

Here is how Erin modified the process for **Decision Making**:

1. Get clear on the decision(s) you want to address.

2. What are the vital factors of the Present State?

3. Prioritize the issues relative to your needs. Address only the most important issues.

4. What are your desired results? (Desired State)

5. What are your best choices/decisions?

Using this process, Erin was able to release the knot of anxiety and with confidence make one decision after another toward her goals.

Self-Search Experience: Creating a Life Vision

Jeff—"How I Want To Live My Life: Regaining Who I Am and Who I Can Be."

Step 1—THE REASON (present state)

I have come to a very eye-opening realization that made me want to change my life. Before I was diagnosed with diabetes in the sixth grade, I was a lot more outgoing and had a better personality. I had many more friends and a lot of confidence in my ability to do things. After being diagnosed with this disease, my outlook has never quite been the same. I have since become more introverted and reserved. My self-esteem has never been as high, and I have a hard time believing in myself.

I want to focus on a way that I can get back to being the person I was before being diagnosed with diabetes. I have created a list of changes, and I want to create a vision for what I want my life to be like and a one-year plan for how I will go about making this vision a reality.

Step 2—CHANGES

Things that I want to change about myself (in rank order):

- *My self-esteem*
- *My confidence*
- *Being introverted*
- *Being afraid of new things*
- *Setting unrealistic goals and expectations for myself*
- *Being afraid of regret*

Step Three—MY VISION STATEMENT

I embrace life by not being afraid of the unknown. I am able to welcome new things and challenges in my life with open arms. I have confidence in myself because I know I can accomplish anything I set my mind to. I surround myself with people I care about and who care about me. I am out-going and live life in the present rather than in the past or future. I live my life with compassion, integrity, and honesty. I have accomplished this by never taking things for granted, always making choices that I can live with, and by always being true to myself.

Step Four—MY PLAN

I will put this vision to work by setting goals and expec-tations for myself. I have devised a one-year strategy that will help me pursue these changes I want to make. The plan is laid out in steps and over the next year I will become the person I want to be.

Month One

- *Don't compare myself with other people. I won't focus on what other people do, only on what I do.*

- *Focus on my strengths. I will give myself credit for the things that I do well and not focus on what I did badly.*

- *Believe in myself. I can do anything I set my mind to if I remain positive. Embrace new challenges and experiences with open-mindedness. Tell myself that everything will work out fine.*

Three Months

Read VISON STATEMENT to myself.

- *I will do things that make me feel good about myself. Exercise always makes me feel great.*

- *Stay in touch with people I care about. I will let them know I appreciate them and that I want them in my life.*

- *Continue to live life for myself and not for others. I am able to do what makes me happy.*

- *Do something that I normally wouldn't do. I will continue to stretch my comfort zone.*

- *Talk about my feelings with other people. I can let them know that I am working hard make positive changes in my life.*

One Year

- *Revisit all of the things that I said I wanted to change and see whether I made those changes happen.*

- *Give myself credit for the changes I have made.*

- *Tell people who supported me and helped me make these changes, THANKS!*

- *Make sure my life is where I want it, and that I am doing what truly makes me happy.*

- *Make a plan for the next year. My life is a constant work-in-progress.*

I believe that if I follow this plan and really make an effort, I will become the person I want to be. It will take a lot of work, but if I am committed to making changes, then I have to do it. Every time I read the vision statement I wrote, it really gives me a feeling of determination. I think I have already made a ton of progress toward these changes. This has been one of the most beneficial experiences of my life. I can't say enough about how much I have learned. I am feeling really good about myself right now, and I want this feeling to last. I know that I can do this by following the plan I laid out for myself. If you had asked me a month ago to create a vision statement for myself, I wouldn't have even known where to begin. This has shown me that I have all of the tools necessary to live the life I want. I just needed to be pointed in the right direction.

Self-Search Experience: Finding Life Meaning and Purpose

Dan decided to approach his life through writing his own mini-biography and obituary. This then became his life vision.

Dan—"A Life Well Lived: My Obituary/Biography."

Preface

The purpose of this personal project was to stretch us, to get us out of our comfort zones, to boldly go where we have never been before. I believe that I have accomplished this task with the following paper. It has forced me to take a look at where I've been, where I am now, and where I want to see my life going. Will my life turn out how I wrote it? Maybe. I have always lived by the belief that our thoughts control our lives. If we have a good vision of how we want our lives to be, and we take steps day by day that support that vision, then there is nothing that can get in our way.

My hope is that this paper will be a road map for the rest of my life. It encompasses the hopes, dreams, and values that 1 hold dear. In the process of writing this paper I have discovered that I don't want to live the typical life. I want to make a difference, not just draw a paycheck.

Personal Philosophy

I can't deny that deep down I, too, desire some of the better things in life. However, I have come to realize that being rich isn't everything, nor is being well known or holding a political office. The things that truly matter in life, like family, close friends, and faith should take precedence. If you set your goals on attaining material possessions or personal wealth, you will never be satisfied and will find yourself always wanting more. There will always be a fancy car or high tech gizmo that you must have, and while you are working to afford it, life is passing you by.

Yet by the time these people retire, they have health problems from all of the stress and they can't enjoy it. I am looking for a job that uses all of my talents and skills. I enjoy working with people in a friendly atmosphere. I want to work at a place that has a good company culture, where employees actually look forward to doing their jobs, and money isn't always the bottom line. I want to travel and see the world, meet new people, and continue to learn. I believe that it is my calling to serve others.

A Life Well Lived (my obituary)

"The future belongs to those who believe in the beauty of their dreams," reads a quote that the late Dan M. kept in his wallet on a tattered piece of paper since he was a young man. Taking this advice to heart, Dan attempted to live the life he had always imagined. Although he was never a man of great wealth or fame, his years on this earth were full of people, experiences, and memories that provided the type of riches that can't be taken away.

As a young boy, Dan was always fascinated with learning. This quest for knowledge continued into his early adult years. His thoughts now began to focus on the eternal life questions like, "Why am I here?" What is my purpose?" and "What is the meaning of life?" The answers to these questions proved to be much more difficult for Dan to answer. One day while reading a magazine, he was struck by a simple phrase in one of the articles, "The meaning of life is to give life meaning." He came to the realization that life is a gift; you have the choice to make it ordinary or extraordinary. With this new insight, Dan began to formulate his own personal philosophy on how he would choose to live his.

You Matter:

Dan Morris is survived by his wife of forty-six years, three children, ten grandchildren, and many others he has touched along the way. Dan's life and legacy are true testaments to the fact that one man can make a difference. When asked once why he dedicated his life to serving others, Dan smiled and said, "Have you ever had a dream that you never wanted to wake up from?... This is mine.

Dan then presented his immediate goals for moving toward the life he wanted to create and his plan for achieving them. The best part involved how excited he was about the work he had done and his belief that he had a great deal of control over his destiny.

A Second Self-Search Experience for Finding Life Meaning and Purpose

Alison was seeking meaning in her life and really hadn't felt that she had made much of a difference in the lives of those she cared about. She sent an e-mail to her family and several friends asking them what they would say about her if she had died. She was quite overwhelmed with the responses she received. Here is what she did, and the response from her father is included.

Alison—"Has my life made a difference?"

THE E-MAIL I SENT OUT TO MY FRIENDS AND FAMILY***

Hi, all.

I know this is going to sound a bit unusual to some of you but I am doing a personal stretch project for one of my classes, so I'm hoping you might be able to help me. My topic is the meaning of my life. Now, to do this thoroughly, I am trying to see the meaning and impact I have had on my family and friends, and I will use this to help me see what I have done to better other people's lives.

Hypothetically:

If I were to die today, what would you say about me at my funeral: memories, feelings, emotions, thoughts, etc. Please be honest. What would you say in my obituary?

- *What do I mean to you as a friend or loved one?*

- *MOM and DAD: How and when did you decide to conceive me?*

- *How have I influenced you?*

- *How have I changed?*

- *Have I done anything you will never forget and will always remember?*

I hope this makes sense to you all, and I thank you for your help! I will let you know the results once the project is done.

My Father's Response:

Alison was born on August 31, a day that will live in my heart for many reasons. Alison was conceived during a single night of passion in Cincinnati between two business trips from California to New York. I was really undecided about another child, after Richard; however, Marie felt strongly about a second child and, of course, 1 was very willing to participate in the process.

I struggled with Marie's pregnancy early on and was really torn about another child, even to the point of suggesting an abortion. Thanks to the grace of God and my wife's strong will, the pregnancy went well and, nine months later, my life changed forever with the birth of my lovely daughter Alison. Even though she was the bluest baby, with the chubbiest body, she was adorable and had a smile for her dad thirty seconds into her beautiful life. She has managed to bring that special touch of femininity to our lives that only a loving daughter can.

For me, she makes the day worth waking for, the air worth breathing, and the sun shine all the time, regardless of the weather outside. She is always smiling and alive with life, from the day she was born, and infuses that to all around her. I have tried to be mad at her when she deserved it, but she made it very difficult, as she always had a way of making the really bad things not so bad through a smile or a hug, or even an "I'm sorry" at times.

She has managed to bring many things into focus for me when my "A-type" personality was in overdrive or things were not just right and I needed a lift. She has done this for all of us, including her mother and friends when they needed it, too. It is amazing that one who is so driven can help others to find the calm and peace they need, and that she can control her own "A-type" personality.

Alison influenced me by being Alison, a caring and loving person who could never be replaced in my heart. Perhaps the sun will shine again some day but it will never be as bright as it used to be. I am so proud to be her father.

What did I learn from this?

I now believe that our feelings need to be expressed, no matter what. If you tell people you love them, also tell them why. The <u>why</u> is the most important part, and the least often expressed. I would have never thought that I meant so much to so many people. Most of the things that were expressed by my loved ones are things I do unconsciously and do not even realize that I am doing them. I do them because it is who I am and what I am about.

I also think the biggest learning experience is that you do not really know how people feel about you unless you ask them, and the only way to get a truthful response (without you interrupting) is to ask them to write it down.

Summary: Keys To Making Life Change

1. Beware of the "traps of the past" that will keep you stuck:

   - Complain and/or Blame

   - Justify

   - Defend

   - Rationalize

2. Develop a vision of what you want, and focus on what you want. Focus on where you're going, not where you've been. Attract all possibilities.

3. Address your "endings," and "let go."

4. In the "Neutral Zone" there is disorder and chaos. It is important that you:

5. Uncover and dissolve your self-judgments.

6. Stop playing the victim.

7. Accept uncertainty and fear dissolves.

8. With a new vision ("New Beginnings") there will also be the likelihood of new barriers and setbacks that you will be able to overcome.

9. You don't need to do this alone, and there is no shame in asking for help from your friends, relatives or from a coach. You will greatly benefit.

10. Try several of the Self-Search Experiences and see what works for you. They will take you on some new pathways, and you will create new opportunities for yourself. After all, what have you got to lose?

Index of Stories

You Matter: